'One of the most engaging, pov[...]s
I've ever rea[...] [...],
the location [...] Scotti[...]

'This is em[...]s
war-ravaged[...].c
scrutiny, sh[...] l service
personnel o[...]

'Unsentimental and unsparing, *The Last Tour of Archie Forbes* does for
PTSD what *Slaughterhouse-Five* did for survivor's guilt.' ROBERT MORACE,
Professor of English at Daemen College, New York

'Highly recommended. This depiction of PTSD avoids the clichés and
embraces not only the complexity of the post-war experience, but
also the absurdity of it all … Don't be afraid to laugh as well as cry.'
RODGE GLASS, author of *Dougie's War*

'A novel for our time in which a yawning austerity culture threatens to
swallow u[...] even the brave. From front line to food bank … a journey
through [...] reality of Bedroom-tax Britain.' REV DR ROBIN HILL,
former ed[...]or of *Life and Work* magazine

'As Victo[...] Hendry so ably demonstrates in this riveting novel, some
of the w[...]nds suffered by soldiers in modern conflict are those that
are uns[...], out of sight but never out of mind. Her compassionate
understa[...]ing for the condition known as post-traumatic stress disorder
marks I[...]ut not just as an exceptional writer but also as a sympathetic
observe[...]' the human condition.' TREVOR ROYLE, military historian
and for[...] Trustee, Combat Stress

**Praise f[...] *A Capital Union***
SHORTL[...]ED for the Historical Writers' Association Debut Crown
BOOK O[...] HE YEAR SELECTION, Alan Warner, *Scotsman*
'A rema[...]able debut, with explosive moments of real poetry and
narrativ[...]ower. This is an excellent novel, very dramatic and engaging,
with a B[...]chan thrills quality.' ALAN WARNER

'Startlin[...]ly accomplished … [this] impressive debut novel wastes no
words.[...] the story gathers momentum so does Hendry's prose, raising
itself to[...]oetry.' JULIE DAVIDSON, *SUNDAY HERALD*

'Shows [...]he terrible strain that … conflict can place on individuals
beyond [...]he battlefield itself.' *EDINBURGH REVIEW*

ALSO BY VICTORIA HENDRY

*A Capital Union*

# THE
# LAST TOUR
# OF ARCHIE
# FORBES

## VICTORIA HENDRY

Saraband

Published by Saraband
Suite 202, 98 Woodlands Road
Glasgow, G3 6HB, Scotland
www.saraband.net

ISBN: 9781910192085
ebook: 9781910192092

Editor: Alison Moore

Printed in the EU on sustainably sourced paper.

1   3   5   7   9   10   8   6   4   2

*All characters and organisations in this novel should be understood to be entirely fictional, with the exception of historical or public figures, whose names have been kept. Geographical place names have not been changed. The news events included here were reported in a variety of news media from September 2013 to February 2014, but were not critically examined by the author. The opinions expressed by the characters in the novel should not necessarily be considered to be those of the author.*

*He who eats alone, chokes alone.*

ARAB PROVERB

# 1

ARCHIE COUNTED HIS STEPS from the park to the bank: 460 – a third of a kilometre. The numbers filled his mind, kept his focus in the present, and on the childhood savings passbook growing sticky in his hand. If he was lucky, enough interest might have accrued in the intervening years to buy him a hot meal.

As he reached the bank, his reflection followed him along the tinted glass window to the door and he pushed it open. Archie didn't smile because there was something wrong with his smile. People flinched when he bared his teeth. His lips turned up alright, but when their gaze raised itself to his eyes on the smiling cue, what they read there frightened them, and he usually apologised and turned away. He couldn't spot what scared them when he peered at his face in the mirror, leaning forward as he cleaned his teeth, or if he glanced at himself in a passing shop window. He looked like anyone else, but the sleepless nights written in the lines at the side of his eyes, the small, staring pupils – black dots zoomed in on far-distant memories of war – were unsettling. People looked down the wrong end of the telescope into the horror that played over his soul, hiding inside, barely held in by the muscles of his face – an almighty scream, a continuous roar of anguish. There was no place for it in this bank, this ordinary place with beige carpet tiles, sponged wallpaper and the company logo inlaid on the surface of the counter. So neat, so tidy, so well fitted together.

The teller was wearing a hijab. Not one of those black numbers he remembered from Afghanistan, but a flowery scarf wrapped round her heavy hair.

'That's your copy, sir,' the girl said, passing him a sheet of paper. 'Just sign at the bottom to confirm you wish to close your account.'

It was dated the 12th of September, 2013. She passed him £3.14, which had lain there untouched for years.

'Oh,' he said, looking up. 'I thought it was September the eleventh. Like 9/11.' Even as he said it, he knew he had made a mistake. Her mouth became a thin line. More than the Twin Towers had collapsed that day. Something about trust had gone too. Something about President Bush's holy war had filled the gap – a war on terror – and Archie had become one of its foot soldiers. The fine dust of Afghanistan seemed to pour from his clothes. It sat in his pores, turning him a grey-pink. He saw the teller flick a glance at the security guard. What was it the brigade adviser had said? Use cultural empathy to build strong relationships. 'Look. I've been in theatre,' Archie said. 'I get it.'

'Which theatre? What do you get?' she asked.

'That 9/11 is nothing to do with you. I just thought it was the eleventh.' He leaned on the counter. Talking like this was tiring. He'd been walking since 6 am when the church night shelter had turned them out. Early morning was the longest, coldest part of the day. 'All friends together, eh?' His face was close to hers. She turned her face away. He wondered if he smelled and sniffed under his armpits. She pushed her chair back. There was no glass barrier in this new world of free communication with the customer, just cameras, pointing their lenses like sights on rifles. Eyes everywhere; closeted in basements, watching; watching for cracks as they appeared in the happy picture; ready to send in agents to paper over them, to restore that happy normality that made money, filled bellies, fuelled cars and marriages.

The guard who had been hovering near him ever since he came in walked over. Archie held out his hands. 'Sorry,' he said. 'I'm not being funny. Genuine mistake.' He turned to the girl, 'Sorry,' he said, and smiled his killer smile.

The guard took his arm. Archie shrugged him off. 'Let me take the three quid,' he said. The guard nodded, and Archie scraped it off the counter with his too-big hand and slipped it into his pocket. 'I'm leaving,' he said. 'No need to see me out.' He laughed into the silence.

The guard watched him go. The old lady seated near the door kept her eyes on the carpet, as if wondering how all those tiles fitted together. Her husband looked up, saw Archie reach for the silver handle and spot the 'Press to Exit' pad only after he had pulled the door twice. Outside, the traffic stopped at the lights, and pedestrians began to cross with the jolt that signalled the start of movement after the moment when, just for a second, everything stood still.

Pausing at the junction, he decided to walk to Leith, to the Homeless Writers' Group. The tea was free. Crossing the Meadows, he passed from Princes Street, with its department stores and women window shopping, onto Leith Walk. The Walk was a huge downward hill, a long slope to a port that had once been great. It was lined with shops: second-hand furniture emporiums; quiet doors offering discreet advice to pregnant, single mothers who wanted to keep their babies; pawn shops dressed as bargain stores where, for enough cash to buy that week's food – if you were careful – you could pawn your guitar, or your mobile phone, and hope that somehow, next month, it might be different. It was a place where you could allow yourself to believe that it might not be worse, because somehow, something always turned up, didn't it? He looked into the window of the Polish delicatessen, past the peeling, white, vinyl letters that said 'Polski Sklep', and over the jars of pickles and sausage. It looked like a museum to another world, a sepia memory of a distant culture, trying to survive here on a concrete road, with crumbling gutters and bus fumes sticking in grey particles to the window. He drew a love heart on the glass, and then a cross through the middle of it. It was a gun-sight. A gun-sight, for fuck's sake. He began to shake. A gun-sight. He leaned against the glass, his handprint obscuring the mark. The man inside the shop looked over and shook his head. He waved him on, and his lips moved to form words, the shape ugly, or polite, or indifferent, impossible to say. Perhaps he wasn't even speaking to him; perhaps it was to the customer. Perhaps it was about the ignorance of the locals; this uncouth land that wasn't home. Archie walked a few steps and bent over, feeling sick. A woman pushed her pram round him, looked at him as if he might be drunk. He walked on. Did he reach the door to the group five minutes later? Was it an hour? They were slow to answer the buzzer. A small metallic voice asked him to repeat what he had said. 'I'm here for the writers' group. The writers' group,' he said, and the door swung open on a room filled with computers.

'Nice to see you ...' the group leader glanced down at her notebook, 'Archie. Nice to see you, Archie,' she repeated. Word perfect now. She waved him over to a seat pulled up at a central table with six men seated round it and two female volunteers, unmistakably better fed than the men, one bespectacled, one American. Specs and Peanut he called them in his head: a refugee from a lonely retirement and a gap-year student, here to launch their magazine into the e-zine forest on the internet. 'Some kind soul, who wishes to remain anonymous,' the organiser smiled at Mike, who called himself Archie's new, best mate, 'has donated a lemon meringue pie, or am ah' wrang?' she said.

The group failed to laugh at the old joke. Specs passed him a cup of tea and a silver tin of sugar, with coffee-coloured lumps riding high on the white snow field within. 'No sugar, thanks,' he said.

'Let me guess, you're sweet enough,' said Specs, and he imagined her head exploding like a watermelon hit by a practice shot. She stood up and mumbled something about putting the kettle on again. 'Go, Suki,' he said.

The group leader looked over.

'Suki put the kettle on,' he muttered.

'I'd like to remind the group of a few ground rules,' she said, not looking at him. 'The group operates on the principle of mutual respect – of kindness – of supportiveness.' A passer-by paused to light a fag outside the window. She looked across at Archie, and her smile was pointed, dazzling. 'So if we're all on the same page? We're going to discuss the contents of the next issue.' Her head swivelled away. 'I think you said you wanted to include something about the bedroom tax, Mike?'

Archie looked down at his pie, steaming from the microwave.

'Sorry we don't have any forks,' said Specs, standing at arm's length. 'Can you make do with a teaspoon?'

He nodded. There was cat hair on her sleeve. Mike was reading a draft of his article about the bedroom tax in a sonorous voice – a poet, a prophet. 'This unjust, unworkable tax penalises the most vulnerable in society, docking their benefit payments for a second room, even a box room.' He paused. 'I have cited an article in the local paper about the so-called help-line staff saying to that disabled man who phoned up to ask where his son could stay when he came to visit, "Ever heard of an inflatable bed?" An inflatable bed? That really got my goat. They expect him to go into a one-bedroom flat, only there aren't any available. I'm going to have to move too. I can't afford my second room. It's going to cost me £14.95 extra per week. That will put me into debt.' He looked round the room. 'My article should get them rattled. That gives me some satisfaction.'

Archie looked down at the table. 'Why have you all gone quiet?' demanded Mike.

Them. Who was Them? The word sank into Archie's stomach, reassembled itself with the pie into a picture-perfect world: mum's home cooking, the crust just so; the army that looked after you, the country you served that loved you; that cheered you on parade on the High Street, marching from the Castle to Holyrood Palace, another long slippery slope, but lined with flags and bunting. The world he used to inhabit. The one where his wife waved in the crowd with his tiny son in her arms. The boy who was his spit. His spitting image. All watched over, kept safe, by the great, invisible Them.

'John Swinney announced that the Scottish Government has earmarked several million to make sure that there are no evictions, Mike,' said the organiser. Was she called Clare? 'Something will work out.'

'Something. Something will work out,' Archie repeated.

'That's right, Archie,' said Clare. 'Something will work out.'

This pie-in-the-sky compassion was killing him. 'You're killing me,' he said.

# 2

THAT NIGHT IN THE HOSTEL, Archie lifted up the end of the bed and put his shoes under the legs to keep them safe. It looked like a cartoon bed, or his granny's legs – wooden sticks fitted into shoes that gaped like someone sailing in a boat standing up, a gondolier, a Charon on the Styx. If this pair walked like his last ones, then there would be hell to pay. The bastard had taken his phone too. These shoes were a Paul Smith designer bargain found in the charity shop in Stockbridge near where he used to live. The old neighbour behind the till hadn't recognised him, or had pretended not to. He was getting used to it, choosing not to challenge them with a wry grimace, or a joke, and see the fear they tried to hide as his new face refused to morph into their memory of the man they had known: the financial lawyer; the lovely family man; the army reservist.

He settled himself under the sheet and closed his eyes. Time stretched in a blank elastic as he moved across the bridge towards sleep, which was always one step ahead of him. He was returned to consciousness by the sound of sobbing. He could doze through the coughing and snoring, even the shouting, but the drip, drip, drip of this quiet exhalation in the dark, this seeping of misery from a would-be sleeper, denied his release into a dream world where there were no problems to solve, and food was abundant, and women were young and sizzling hot in short, short skirts … this crying pulled him even closer to the surface where he tried to float in the night, afraid to fall too deep into sleep; to where his memories roamed, hungry for the energy of his mind, ready to feed again on his mashed brain. It tripped his ears, which still rang with the rat-a-tat-tat of his gun jerking in his hands. The mindless chatter of death. He swam across the room to the weeping man and whispered, 'Are you alright, pal?' before reaching out to touch his shoulder. He stank.

'Fuck off, ya' poof,' he said, and spat. 'Ah'm no yer pal.'

Archie's hand tightened into a fist and he punched him hard. The guy sat up. 'For fuck's sake,' he shouted. 'Ya bam. Ya fucking nut.'

Archie backed away, looking down at his fist, wondering at the reflex that made it ball, the shout that triggered it, and he felt like a dangerous weapon: a cocked gun, the hammer just one press from driving the bullet into the chamber. The girl from the front desk appeared. 'I know,' he said. 'I'm going.' He lifted his bed off his shoes.

'Come and speak to me next shift,' she said. 'Try to calm down.'

He nodded. They both knew he wouldn't come back. His shouting was the loudest in the night. No one would miss him. 'I mean it,' she said, 'don't disappear.'

'Too late,' he said. 'I'm Captain Invisible. King of the worst fucking nightmares you could dream up. The Kid of the not-Okay Corral.' The light was beginning to show behind the faded blind, the faint dots of flies visible where they had been rolled flat in the morning.

'At least it's not cold out,' she said. 'You'll get breakfast at St Philomena's from seven.'

'Yum, yum,' he said.

She pressed the door release and he braced himself for the buzz. Mechanical sounds were the worst. This world was never going to be silent.

Outside, the sun was rising, its lemon light stretching between the trees on the Meadows, casting long shadows. His stick-man figure rippled over the grass and he sat down on the first bench he came to. He zipped his jacket up to his chin and relaxed his shoulders as he breathed out. A jogger went past fiddling with his iPhone, jogging on the spot in front of his bench before taking up the rhythm of his run, disappearing along the narrow track worn in the grass between the trees. A cyclist sped past in the opposite direction, padded Lycra bum raised off the seat to avoid the roots that snaked under the tarmac path, his briefcase strapped to his bike with bungee cord. Archie remembered those days. Days so busy with meetings that gym membership never paid for itself, and he had cancelled the direct debit and begun to cycle to work to keep fit. How was it that every second mattered then? There was no time to write those reports, far less read them; the synopsis was king, and coffee the fuel; days so fast that they melted together, and project deadlines and blue-sky thinking, and pushing the envelope were a new language that everyone spoke, confident in their jargon in the land of jargonese. Conquerors of the digital age. All friends in a huddle. There was none of that here for him in this park in a city centre, alone on an early autumn morning. He wondered what truths had been obscured in that land he used to inhabit as he drove the best deals forward, tested them against the law, found them watertight and collected his fee from companies so large they never challenged his gold-plated commission.

A dog brushed past him barking. He looked up and saw a Staffie bull terrier run at a girl's Papillon. She bent to scoop up her lap-dog, his little butterfly ears flapping in the breeze as he barked at the Staffie barrelling towards him. 'Don't pick him up,' Archie yelled. He ran towards her. 'Drop him,' he shouted, but the Staffie had reached her and was springing at her arms, snapping at the small dog. The bull terrier caught her sleeve, turning into a wild beast focused on its prey. The switch had flicked – pet/wolf, wolf/pet. Archie reached her and struck the Staffie on the back of its neck with a clenched fist, kicking it hard as it fell, and grabbing its collar.

An old lady was approaching. 'Well I never,' she said. 'He's normally so sweet. I'm walking him for a friend in hospital.' She clipped on the dazed dog's lead. 'Are you quite alright, dear?' she asked the dog, and pulled him away, ignoring the girl.

'How about an apology?' the girl shouted after her. 'He could have ripped me to shreds. What are you going to do about my jacket?'

Archie watched the old woman retreat. 'Just leave it,' he said. 'She's not worth it. Didn't anyone ever tell you not to pick up a dog in an attack?'

'Or jump into water for a drowning man?'

He smiled, and looked down. He didn't want her to see his eyes. He didn't want her to shrink away if she glimpsed his inner landscape on this bright day.

'Coffee?' she asked. 'As a thank you?'

He nodded. 'So what are you doing out so early,' she asked, as she led him towards a café on the edge of the park, 'if you're not a dog walker?'

'Thinking,' he replied. 'Trying to clear my head.'

'Any luck?' she asked.

He looked at her for a second. 'Not yet, no.'

'You're quite the macho man,' she said. 'Like Tarzan. Thanks for saving me from Granny and her killer mutt.'

'You're welcome,' he replied. He felt peaceful, as if the violence had cleared something in him, a tension that lived in his muscles, roasted at the back of his head.

They had reached a small café. 'Greasy spoon, okay?' she asked, pushing open the door. 'It's my usual stop for sustenance.'

'Luxury,' he said, and meant it. 'I was on my way to St Philomena's.'

'Oh,' she said. 'Isn't that where they feed the homeless?'

He nodded, embarrassed, as he sat down.

'How long have you been volunteering there?'

He paused, wrong-footed by her assumption. 'Not long,' he said, picking up a menu covered in photos of eggs, bacon and sausages. The picture-book mushrooms dripped butter and the tomatoes were grilled. Tea and toast. He swallowed the saliva that had flooded his mouth.

'Have the full breakfast,' she said, 'if you like. I owe you.'

He shook his head, afraid to show her his hunger. 'I'll have what you're having,' he replied.

She wandered over to the counter and exchanged a few words with the man behind it as he put two egg rolls on a tray and added two mugs of tea. She paid him and wandered over to Archie at a small table by the window.

'So what do you do?' she asked, stirring sugar into her tea. 'When you're not feeding the homeless?'

'I'm into … fitness,' he said.

'Like a personal trainer?'

'Yes.'

'So that's why you're so buff.'

'I run classes on the Meadows,' he continued, marching with the lie.

'Oh, I know someone who's looking for one. She's fighting the flab but losing the battle. What's your company called?'

'Slim … Slim for Jesus,' he said, spotting a picture of Jesus baring his beating heart on the wall behind the till. 'Slim for Jesus.' He hoped it would put her off. 'I have a Facebook page if she wants to sign up, but it's two hundred pounds.'

'Well, it's going to take a miracle to get her fit,' she laughed. 'I'll let her know.' Her dog strolled over to the plastic tub of water by the door and spooned it up with his pink tongue. Archie watched him, remembering the dogs who had run in among the troops as they cleared the ghost towns on their patrol, and adopted them with hopeful barks, whining as they moved off towards the Green Zone. A strange sing-song of regret.

The girl finished her roll and stood up, wiping her lips. She hadn't seemed to notice his eyes. 'Maybe see you again,' she said, and raised her eyebrows. 'What's your name?'

'Archie,' he said.

She held out her hand. 'Nice to meet you, Archie. I'm Sooze. Short for Suhaylah.'

As the door closed behind her, he turned over a paper and read the front page. President Assad was smiling in his sharp suit, happy that Russia had extended him a lifeline following his alleged use of gas against civilians. Obama wasn't going to launch a strike against him if he decommissioned his chemical weapons, the weapons Obama said crossed a red line. A red line that demanded action from the international community. The House of Commons had voted against another military action. Thank fuck, he thought. There's a 'Russian plan for Syria,' the paper announced, but Obama wanted it in days or weeks, and Putin and Assad said it would be months. So the old tick-tock of diplomacy that took Syria closer to America's strike, which Obama said would not be a pinprick, chuntered on, and Archie wondered if anyone remembered the people on the ground: the ants scurrying for the borders before they closed, before the water dried up in desert lands, groaning under the weight of refugees sliding on the dunes. He tasted the sand in his mouth, smelled the odour of unwashed bodies, and of rotting corpses torn by dogs. He swallowed. 'Another tea, mate,' he called across the room before he remembered he couldn't pay for it. He stood up and pulled out his empty pockets. 'Sorry,' he said. 'No change.' The guy behind the counter brought the pot over anyway. 'It's probably a bit stewed,' he said, pouring a dark stream of liquid into Archie's cup. 'Put in a bit more milk and it'll taste fine. Unless you want mint?'

Archie shook his head.

'Didn't think so,' said the man with a smile. 'I'm Karim,' he said.

'Archie.'

'Bad business,' he said.

'Bit of a bun fight,' replied Archie, 'especially now Al Qaeda seems to be in the mix.'

'I meant with the dog,' said Karim.

'Oh,' said Archie. His finger was resting on a picture of a statue of the Virgin Mary looking down on the ruins of the town of Aleppo.

'John the Baptist's dad Zachary is buried there,' said Karim.

'I really don't care,' said Archie.

Karim stepped back. 'Three things,' he said. 'I overheard you talking – I thought you were into that Christian kick with your Slim for Jesus gig; second, I'm Syrian; and third, your attitude leaves something to be desired.'

'Sorry, mate.' He downed the cup of tea.

Karim pointed to another picture. 'The Voyager spacecraft has left the Solar System. They launched it in 1977. Kind of puts it in perspective, doesn't it?'

'Does it?' asked Archie. 'Is that how this works? Men in flares build a floating camera and push it off the planet, and we're meant to think nothing matters here.'

'Do you have any better ideas?' asked Karim. 'Do you know how to kill the pain when you're tied to your country, and it's going down the tube, and there's nothing you can do to break those ties because they're wrapped tight round your heart?'

'Woah,' exhaled Archie. 'Let's turn the page.' He stood up. 'I have to go,' he said. Karim's emotion was unsettling him, tightening up the release he had felt after punching the dog.

# 3

ARCHIE WANTED TO SAY THAT the nuns at St Philomena's were nice to him, but they patted him on the arm and made him feel small again. He felt guilty having a second breakfast and ate it too fast, stuffing toast down his throat. 'God bless you, son,' said a nun, patting him on the back as he choked and spat the bread back up in a soggy bolus. He put it on the corner of his plate and then dropped it under the table.

'That's clarty, man,' said a young guy opposite him.

Archie stood up and then sat back down, trying to slow his breathing.

'That's like a weapon of fucking mass destruction, man. Germs. You can't be too careful.'

'Funny,' said the nun, coming back over and pulling the young guy's ear. She spritzed diluted bleach from a plant spray over the table and rubbed it in with a cloth. Her bust shook beneath her tight, blue top, and the cross dangling from her neck swung over the food in blessing. She bent down and picked up the chewed food in a green paper towel before firing it across the room into a bin. 'I never miss,' she said, and looked at Archie. 'Bull's-eye.'

'Do you have a copy of the Bible I could have,' he asked, thinking of his bogus Facebook page, and added, 'please, Sister?'

She smiled and said, 'There are some through the back.'

He followed her along a corridor to a room lined with wooden panelling. There was a space on the wall above the fire-place where a picture had been removed. He assumed it was the Cardinal who had resigned. He remembered seeing the spokesman for a gay campaign group stoning him with words outside the cathedral. He remembered other stonings. He was trapped in the sand of his memories, his death's head face staring out across the barren landscape of his life bled dry. 'Where is he now?' he asked, pointing to the bright patch of wallpaper on the faded wall.

The nun looked over to the space and pursed her lips. 'You wanted a Bible,' she said. 'You could have this one. It's in good condition. Try and keep it that way.'

He nodded and flicked through the pages. An inky hand had written, 'To dear Moira on the occasion of your reception into the Faith.' It had a capital F. 'F for faith,' he said.

The nun nodded and locked the cabinet again. 'God bless you,' she said, making the sign of the cross over him. His eyes followed her finger, a target sight. The criss-cross hairs were across her face. The shot would be her lips. He saw the blood spray out of the back of her head. No one would notice it on the plum, flock wallpaper, a red miasma soaked up by those furry, little faces that stared from old walls in the night and woke the sleepers.

'Is something funny?' she asked.

'No,' he replied. 'Not at all.' He turned on his heel and swung away down the corridor to the blinding light of the day. Another one. The thoughts tumbled after him, escaping under the door of the convent, pressing themselves flat to slide after him. He tried to out-walk them. 'I don't need to do this,' he said to himself. 'I don't need to think these things. I am in control of my own mind.' But they raced along with him laughing, clinging to his shoes, which became desert boots on the grass, which became sand. He reached a wall round the new development of flats, looked up at the old hospital balconies where patients used to smoke looking out towards the Meadows, over the Pentland Hills to the south, contemplating their treatment and the short hand Fate had dealt them. He looked at the stone blocks in the wall, the crumbling mortar. Moss clung to the pitted surface: grey-green lichen glued in moon craters. The thoughts were climbing back into his mind. He placed both his hands against the wall and banged his head hard. It began to bleed. Someone behind him screamed.

'What?' he shouted, turning round. 'Fucking what?' He drove his forehead into the wall again, and staggered away, up Middle Meadow Walk. A woman was on her mobile phone, one hand on her buggy with a child squirming round to see the funny man with the red face. She moved her hand to her child's eyes, and covered them.

He passed a man playing a guitar, danced a few steps, and the music followed him along the path, past university students who stepped onto the cycle lane to let him pass. 'Sorry,' he said. 'Sorry.' He stopped, wiped his head on his sleeve and looked at the blood, there on his arm, an old friend. He licked it, tasted the salt and iron on his tongue and ran it over his lips. There was a gents' toilet at the top of the Walk, and he slipped down its mossy steps into a dark den that smelled of pee. The white tiles were cracked and an enamel sign above the single sink read, 'Others may be waiting.' He splashed his face with cold water and tried to clean his jacket with a wet, green paper towel. There was no soap left in the dispenser. He remembered the bars of soap his wife, Hannah, used to buy, with rosemary leaves trapped like lice in glycerine; the sharp scent of tea-tree oil. He pressed the flaky, metal bar of the dispenser again as if it were a slot machine, and pressing it fast enough would deliver the jackpot. The word 'yes' had been stencilled onto one of the tiles, and underneath it read 'to Scottish Independence'. Yes. If yes is the answer, he thought, what is the question, and he looked in the mirror. 'Am I a worthless, fucking dick?' His eyes flicked to the stencil. Yes. 'Am I a fucking criminal?' Eye-flick. Yes. 'A bad husband?' Yes. 'A shit reservist?' Yes. 'Is life worth living?' Yes. 'No. No,' he said. 'No, no, no. Wrong fucking answer.'

The police were waiting for him when he came out, blinking like a mole, a surrendered soldier from his bunker. He put his arms in the air. 'The answer is not yes,' he said to the officer who cuffed him.

'Whatever you say, sir. We're not arresting you, but you understand that you have caused these good people some alarm. The cuffs are just a precaution. We'll get them off as soon as possible.' A small crowd had gathered. 'We're going to take you down to the station and get you sorted out.'

'Sorry,' he said, as he was put in the car, and his blood dripped on the seat. 'Sorry.'

He blew his last breath into the breathalyser.

'Negative,' the officer said to his partner.

'Negative, Captain,' Archie parroted, and spiralled away, to the sound of the chopper-blade car engine, the siren wail.

# 4

THE DOCTOR AT THE STATION was young and black. 'Shall we start with your name?' he asked.

'Forbes. Archie Forbes.'

'Archibald?'

'Are you fucking kidding? I still have my own hair.'

The doctor's pen stopped moving. 'The custody officer is concerned about you and called me. I'm part of a trial quick-response team. I need you to cooperate.'

'Yes,' he said. 'Archi-bald.'

'Now, Mr Forbes,' the doctor said. 'My name is Dr Clark. I'm going to give you a statutory medical and take a short history from you. I'll need to take a little blood to do a more thorough alcohol test, but we can do that at the end. Is that alright with you?'

Archie nodded.

'So, we'll do urinalysis, blood pressure, height, weight, audiometry, spirometry, visual acuity, skin assessment, lifestyle screening, and I'll give you a few stitches for that head wound before it dries out too much. Is that acceptable? Paper stitches should be fine. We'll also think about some medication to keep you on an even keel. Help you out a bit, till things settle down. OK?' He lifted his pen. 'Address?'

'None,' said Archie.

'Emergency contact?'

'You could try my ex-wife, although I doubt she'd care if I copped it.'

'Divorced?'

'Separated.'

'When did that happen?'

'Oh, about a month after I got back from Afghanistan.'

'Service record? Army?'

'No shit, Sherlock.'

'Rank?'

'Lieutenant. TA Reservist. Weekend warrior called from my desk by Queen and country.'

'So you saw service?'

'You could call it that.'

'What do you call it?'

'I don't call it anything. I call it ask Bradley.'

'Bradley Manning.'

'Chelsea Manning.'

'Right, the whistle-blower. Moving on,' said Dr Clark.

'Yeah, let's do that,' said Archie, 'Let's move on, except it's not so fucking simple is it? Moving on. Bet you've seen some shit. Where are you from? Zimbabwe, Rwanda?'

'Peterborough. Let's talk about you, okay? Parents?'

'One dead, one indifferent.'

'Date of birth?'

'Thirty-two in April. Sixteen, four, nineteen eighty-two. The litany of numbers. Life's lucky dip. Dip, dippity dip. Born in the marvellous era of Mrs T and her glorious naval battle for a rock in the South Atlantic. It's all about controlling the sea. Empire, you know. You should know all about that. Fruit of the vine ...'

'Let's stick to the point,' said Dr Clark.

'Shame she's not here for Gibraltar,' said Archie.

'I'm going to get you a cup of tea and leave you to calm down. I want you to try to focus while I'm gone. You want to get out of here, don't you?'

Archie looked round the walls of the cell. They were thick, shut out a lot of stuff. 'I don't know,' he said. 'I like it here. Bed's not too bad.' He squashed the blue, plastic mattress. 'Could do with a few more springs, a bit of spirology.'

'If you mean spirometry,' said Dr Clark. 'It's about lung function.'

'What's your name again?' shouted Archie, as the doctor closed the door behind him.

# 5

'STICK IT TO ME, DOC,' said Archie, rolling up his sleeve for a second injection the next day in the cell.

'Sorry we couldn't find an emergency bed for you last night,' said Dr Clark. 'There will be one for you at Greenford Hospital later today, and we'll do a full assessment of your needs and balance your medication. I'm based there and would like to take on your case, so, in the meantime, I'd like to try a technique on you that has had some success with PTSD sufferers. It's called The Counting Method – originated by Dr Frank M. Ochberg in 1989 at Michigan State University.'

Archie nodded. Whatever had been put in his arm was working.

'It's maybe a bit early in our relationship, but I think it's worth a try following our chat yesterday. So this is how it works – I'm going to start counting, and you are going to recall a troubling memory. This will take a count of one hundred, so your memory, your remembering, will be restricted by a time parameter, giving you a sense of containment, of safety.'

Archie's heart rate increased and he rubbed his chest. The doctor noticed his gesture, read his body language, and continued. 'This will help you, Archie. I can call you Archie, can't I?'

'You can call me anything you fucking like,' said Archie, grinning his death's head grin.

'Language, Archie. There will be a beginning, a middle and an end,' continued Dr Clark.

'That's what you say,' said Archie. 'I'm still stuck in the middle.'

'Just listen,' said Dr Clark. 'My voice will anchor you to the present as you enter the difficult waters of the past. You may experience feelings of terror, of horror, of helplessness – I don't know the exact nature of your memories, or what is unsettling you.'

Archie tipped his head back in his chair, exposing his throat and breathed in through his mouth.

'Can you look at me, Archie?'

He looked at the doctor through his pinprick eyes. The doctor looked very far away.

'You'll find that you can begin to control the memories by revisiting them in this controlled way – gain mastery over them.'

'Yes, Massa,' said Archie.

Dr Clark took a deep breath. 'Do you want me to terminate this session?' he asked.

Archie looked up from his hands. 'No,' he said. 'Sorry.'

'That's better. You can't push me away, Archie. I'm here to help you.'

'Sure,' said Archie.

'This is going to take several sessions. I'm not promising you a miracle, but you should find that next time the memory pops up, you gain some control over it. I hope I might also have your permission to write up my findings about early intervention using this method for a government study I'm involved in?'

Archie nodded.

'Shall we begin?'

'I already have,' said Archie.

'In a moment I am going to start counting,' said the doctor. 'Try to fill the one hundred seconds with your memory, letting the worst memories come in at the forties, fifties and sixties.'

'Do-wa-be-bop,' said Archie. 'A shang-a-lang-a-ding-dong.'

The doctor continued, a smile hovering about his lips. 'Letting yourself gently out through the nineties.'

Archie opened his mouth. 'Don't go there,' said the doctor. 'Joke's over. Do you think you can do that?'

'Yes,' said Archie.

'Now settle yourself comfortably.'

Archie stretched out his long legs. His feet scuffed Dr Clark's chair and he pulled them back. His heart was racing so fast it seemed it would bounce through his T-shirt, cartoon style, like Road Runner. He wondered about getting one printed with Jesus's heart, or tattooing a sacred heart on his chest and letting its raw pulp jump and dance. 'Boing, boing, boing,' said Archie, 'Beep, beep.'

Dr Clark clasped his hands together and began to count. He was a talking head, a side-show fortune teller, a wise man, turbaned, in the desert of this tile-lined cell. 'One,' he said, 'two, beat, three, beat, four …' The counting continued, a caravan of numbers, inexorable. 'Five, beat, six…' – the pause between the numbers a void – 'seven, beat.'

The memory was growing closer: the open door, gaping, flapping, no bolt to close it, his steps taking him closer to that dazzling place of horror.

'Ninety-nine, one hundred,' the doctor said. Archie's eyes were tight shut. 'Archie? When you're ready, become aware of the room. Let your awareness of the space around you increase. Listen to the sound of the cars passing outside, and hear my voice here, with you, now that the counting has stopped.'

Archie opened his eyes. 'I need a drink,' he said.

The doctor passed him a bottle of mineral water. 'In your own time, what was the first thing that came into your mind?'

'Chicken tikka,' said Archie. 'I'm fucking starving.'

Dr Clark typed on the notebook balanced on his knee.

'With a side of naan,' said Archie, 'if you're taking orders.'

Dr Clark looked up. 'What thoughts came to you at ten?' he asked.

Archie shook his head.

'At twenty?'

'I'm in a boat.'

Dr Clark remained silent.

'I'm in a boat,' said Archie. 'And it's cold.'

'Cold?'

'Very,' said Archie. 'We've been holed. There's a siren going, and it's inside my head. Whoop, whoop, whoop …'

'At thirty,' said the doctor.

'We're being towed into the bay. I can see land, a port. The sky is dark but there are flames on the water from the oil that's pumping out. Burning water. How fucked is that?'

'What's happening now?'

'The other corvette has gone. It wasn't meant to take us in. They were to keep going. I'm in a lifeboat. Our ship's going over. It's turned turtle. My mates are still inside. No one is coming to rescue us. We can see the houses on the shore, but no one's coming.'

'Where are you, Archie?'

'Russia.'

'Russia?'

'Murmansk. There are U-boats. Two channels on the approach. Take your pick. They're sitting pretty in one of them, but you might be lucky. You might pick the lucky one. The one they didn't target.'

'Where are you at ninety?'

'I'm with my grandpa. We're in a hospital. He's dying. He was the navigator who picked the wrong channel.'

'So this isn't your memory?'

'It's my memory of what he said. Of what he told me, seventy years after it happened, because after seventy years of saying nothing, about anything, it was the first, last and only thing he wanted to talk about before he died. The last thing he wanted to talk about was always the first thing. It was roasting right here,' Archie touched his forehead. 'Roasting right here with his men in the black water; water so cold they froze before they burnt. Crispy enough for you, Doc? Is that how you like your memories? Toasted? A wee side of horror? Terror? The words are easy, but they don't fit the truth. They aren't big enough.'

'It has obviously elicited a lot of emotion from you, Archie,' said Dr Clark.

Archie noticed he had pressed the bell.

'And we can explore that next time,' he continued.

'Will there be a next time, Doc?' he asked.

The doctor closed his notepad. 'God willing,' he replied. 'As I said, I'll ask for your case to be assigned to me.'

'I'm not going to any fucking looney bin,' shouted Archie. 'Tony Blair is why I'm here, George fucking Bush … why aren't they in the bin? I'll go if they go.'

'I'll see you soon, Archie,' said Dr Clark. 'I'll try and get someone to bring you a cup of tea.'

'What about the tikka?' shouted Archie.

'Two sugars?'

'Just shoot me,' said Archie. 'I'm dying here.'

# 6

ARCHIE HAD SEEN the Greenford Hospital's central tower from walks on the Blackford Hill. It sat like a sugar cube in the valley that ran from west to east, caught between the wind bowling in from the Atlantic past old pitheads, and the Forth – tranquil and cold, a grey finger of the North Sea – poking into the land. A quarter of the building's windows looked south, bathed in the sun that crept along the Pentland Hills, separating Edinburgh from the Borders and England beyond. To the north there was a green slope of trees and mansions: happy families who rode the crest of the wave. He remembered seeing the patients on Morningside Road, their tongues swollen with lithium, and he remembered waiting in the corner shop while their most able representative bought their fags with sweaty fivers and loose change, under supervision, from the Indian bloke behind the till. Now he was on the inside looking out.

As a change from sitting on the staircase with the other patients, Archie wandered into the felt-making class run by a woman with a nose-piercing, who introduced herself as Petal.

'Is Petal your real name?' he asked.

'Does it matter?' she asked. 'What's yours?'

'Archie,' he replied, 'but you can call me Flower.'

He took a seat at the table where he could cover the window and the door; see anyone trying to sneak in. The woman next to him had on a pair of pink rubber gloves and was rubbing washing-up liquid into a mass of wool trapped under a bit of netting. She was tall and loose-limbed with dyed blonde hair.

'Could you pass Archie a pair of gloves, Joy?' asked Petal, placing a tray of dry wool in front of him. 'Add a little water and washing-up liquid,' she said, 'and rub vigorously through the net to felt the wool. When you have a good base then we can felt on some colour.'

'What for?' asked Archie, enjoying Petal's perfume and her bare arms with the tiny blonde hairs sticking up. 'I bet you grow your own,' he added, looking at the daisy chain tattooed round her wrist.

'Veggies?'

If that's what you want to call it,' he said, pretending to smoke a joint.

'I'll ignore that insinuation.'

'Doesn't fit with the picture,' he said.

She smiled. 'We make our own pictures,' she said. 'That's why we're here.'

'Does there always have to be a reason?' he asked. 'Why we're here?'

'Quite the philosopher, aren't you?' said Joy.

Archie ignored her, and began to rub the wool under the net; small bubbles appeared. 'I'm forever blowing bubbles,' he sang. 'Shut up,' said Joy. 'I need to concentrate.'

'Sorry,' he said.

'I'm hungry,' said Joy. 'I want some crisps.'

'You can eat at break-time,' replied Petal.

'I'm hungry now.'

'At break,' repeated Petal.

'I could eat your bodies,' said Joy.

Archie laughed and held out his arm. 'Tuck right in,' he said. Then he stood up and bent over, 'Or some rump?'

'A word, please, Archie,' said Petal, indicating the door.

He followed her into the corridor, a naughty schoolboy.

'Take it easy,' she said. 'You're agitating Joy.'

'Sorry,' he said on his default setting. 'So what's wrong with her?'

'You're smart enough to know I can't tell you. Patient confidentiality. But I can tell you that the stories here are like felt squares, Joy's especially. You think you get the picture. It looks simple, two-dimensional, but underneath there is a tangle of a thousand different threads and they're all hooked into their neighbour. The problems become homogenous. It's not easy to unravel.'

'No,' said Archie.

'All I can do is give people some expression for that tangled place. Let images come to the surface and be seen, actualised, and that gives the patient some sense of control. Perhaps one day it will lead them towards an understanding of what is troubling them, what's driving the delusions and the voices. Let them tease it all out. Do you understand?'

'Yes,' said Archie, although he didn't.

'If you come in and start joking around, you unsettle people like Joy. The control goes. The sense of calm that lets the troubling image come to the surface where it can be seen and tackled – that sense of calm is destroyed.'

'I thought it was a felt workshop,' said Archie.

'It is and it isn't,' said Petal. 'Shall we leave it there?'

Archie sighed. He longed for the desert; the miles of emptiness peppered with stones and the night skies salted with stars. It hadn't been all bad. He looked up at the polystyrene tiles on the ceiling and the strip lighting. He rested his hand on a water fountain sponsored by a drug company, a name like a cleaning fluid emblazoned across it. He began to spell the letters out in his head.

'Do you want to go back in?' asked Petal.

He looked along the corridor; the polished lino gleamed, embedded with strands of pink that could be flesh, and something that sparkled. Flecks of metal. 'Yes,' he said.

'Take a deep breath,' said Petal. 'One, two, three.'

'Don't start that,' he said, and opened the door.

'You're back,' said Joy. 'Had a little word with Miss?'

'Yes,' said Archie, sitting down in his place.

'Did you sneak a kiss?' asked Joy, puckering up her lips. 'It's good to get some loving. Have you ever had good loving?'

Archie nodded, remembering his wife's arms clasped round his waist on lazy Sunday mornings in bed. The seamless days of deadlines at the office forgotten.

'You're quite good-looking, aren't you?' said Joy, moving closer.

'I like your brown hair. It's kind of wavy.' She pulled a strand through her fingers. 'What colour are your eyes?'

He kept them fixed on the table.

'Don't be shy. Do you want a massage?' She stood up and slid her hands down over his shoulders.

He tensed. Her thumbs brushed the back of his neck, meeting over the vertebra, pressing down, then releasing, her fingers sliding forward towards the hollow in his neck, the soft point between his clavicles.

'Hands, Joy,' said Petal.

Joy released him. He breathed out and closed his eyes. 'Remember what we talked about,' said Petal. 'Personal space.'

'Outer space,' said Joy. She looked towards the window. They were on the third floor, sliding above the trees. 'I can't go out there,' she said, turning to Archie. 'There's a bad ghost.'

Archie looked down at the bubbles melting on the fingers of his pink gloves. 'Would you mind if I leave now?' he asked Petal.

She was teasing strands of coloured wool into long, thin shapes. 'You'll miss adding a motif to your square,' she said.

'I'll cope,' he replied.

* * *

He edged along the corridor to the common room. Nick Clegg was talking on TV about his leadership of the Liberal Democrats being secure, saying there wouldn't have been any economic recovery after the 2008 crash without them and the coalition. Archie saw the pressure ooze from his brow, the tension in his eye bags, and recognised his own face there. 'What about the bedroom tax?' shouted a reporter.

'The single room supplement,' said Clegg.

Archie flicked the channel just as he spotted the doctor from the police station walk in looking at a clip board. 'Dr Umbogo,' he shouted, waving.

'Dr Clark,' replied the doctor.

'Just kidding, Doc,' said Archie. 'Lighten up.'

'I fail to find your humour amusing.'

'Well, you can't be good at everything.'

'As I said, you're not going to push me away,' he replied.

'I'm not trying to,' said Archie.

'And the band played believe it if you like?' asked the doctor.

'Touché,' said Archie.

'I'm preparing your care plan for your release,' continued the doctor. 'You'll come once a week for a review of your medication. SSRIs should be appropriate: serotonin specific re-uptake inhibitors. I'll start you on them today, and you can come for a weekly session with me up to a maximum of five. We can fit one in now.'

'One of your counting games?' asked Archie.

'If you want to call it that.' Dr Clark unlocked the door behind him. 'If you'd like to step into my office and make yourself comfortable.'

Archie marked out a soft-shoe shuffle across the room and lay back on the couch near the window. It was covered with a length of paper towel that wrinkled under his body as he tried to move up the bed.

'Now close your eyes,' said Dr Clark, 'if that's okay for you, and let's see where this session takes us. Beginning at one, hear my voice.' He began to count as before, a metronome to a tune Archie tried not to remember. An ear-worm of a memory eating into his brain: the brass band on passing-out day, the last post at the monument to the fallen at Camp Bastion, the disco in Cyprus, the pipes on the home-coming parade, the squeeze-me-tight jingle buried in the belly of his son's toy bear – his personal juke-box of blast from the past played on a loop. One, two, miss a few, ninety-nine, a hundred.

'And when you're ready,' said Dr Clark's voice, 'open your eyes. Feel your lids rising up, opening to the present, leaving the past behind.'

Archie sighed.

'Where were you, Archie?' asked Dr Clark.

'A graveyard,' said Archie, closing his eyes again. The room was silent. He opened his eyes. The doctor was still there, looking at him, waiting. The silence continued.

'Is this what you're paid to do, Doc. Sit in silence?'

'This is your space,' replied Dr Clark.

Archie bent his chin forward and rubbed the back of his neck. 'I'm in the garden at the Abbot's House in Dunfermline. I'm six.'

Dr Clark didn't move. Archie thought maybe he sighed, blowing the air out in an imperceptible exhalation over dry lips.

'Who do you speak to, Doc?' he asked.

'I have a supervisor.'

'For difficult patients like me?'

'Something like that. Let's try to focus. Where are you at twenty?'

'I'm sitting on the grass looking at the graves the archaeologists are excavating. They're brushing round the skulls with paint brushes, dusting the earth from the bones. They're peaceful, these sleepers, not creepy.'

'And at forty?'

'One of the men is calling someone over and pointing into the hole at the far end. I run over and stand by the path. There are chains round the feet of the skeleton. They say it's facing the wrong way. Its head isn't in the west.'

'Why is that important?' asked Dr Clark.

'It's a Christian site. He won't be able to rise with the dead on the day of resurrection. He'll stay in the grave. I hear them talking. They say they'll leave him that way. I want them to turn him, to be like the others.'

'And did they?'

'What do you think?'

'I don't know,' said Dr Clark, 'I'm guessing not.'

'Got it in one. That poor sod is still back-to-front under the bush they planted on top of him. They wouldn't, couldn't turn him, out of respect for the others. They upheld their judgement on him. So he's lying there unforgiven. His feet chained so he can't climb out of the grave.'

'That's in the formal garden at the back? Near the cathedral, where they buried Robert the Bruce.'

Archie nodded. 'Those buggers sat there afterwards, among the day-trippers, and drank lattes, and admired the flowers and the ornamental shrubs and box hedges, and kids chased each other on the paths, racing over the dead. They're still doing it today. No one remembers him. He'll be outlasted by his chains.'

'And where were you at eighty?'

'I was afraid.'

'And at ninety?'

'Afraid.'

'Of what, Archie? This isn't your story.'

'Isn't it?' he asked. 'How would you know?'

Dr Clark leaned forward. 'Do you remember we said we would begin to leave the emotion behind at seventy, eighty at the latest?'

'I don't have that much control,' said Archie.

'But you can shut the real memory off completely,' replied Dr Clark. 'The one that's digging at your foundations.'

'Not completely,' said Archie.

Dr Clark nodded. 'No,' he said. 'So I see.' He closed his notebook. 'We'll stop for today.' A seagull flew past the window. 'We need to find out why you hurt yourself.'

'I don't know why I did it,' said Archie. 'It was a spur-of-the-moment thing.'

'I think you do know,' said Dr Clark.

'Are you calling me a liar?' said Archie, his voice, rising. 'Is that how this goes? You say I do, and I say I don't. You say I will and I say I won't. We're like fucking Tweedledum and Tweedledee.'

'We're not going to battle,' said the doctor.

'What are we doing now, then?' asked Archie. 'What are we doing now?'

# 7

ARCHIE LAY ON HIS BED in the ward for three days and waited for his personal action plan. He was good at waiting; action and inaction. He tried to go to happy places in his mind. His wife riding pillion on their bike trip to Lewis. He had parked his Honda Pan-European at Callanish and they had danced round the standing stones with the summer light gleaming on the shining, red paint of his motorbike and his wife's lips. He had proposed that day, among the giants, and in the silence of the moment after she had said yes, he was the happiest man alive. Part of him still stood there, his happiness caught on the stones like sheep's wool. It had been a million miles from the place they had first met, at his company, Forbes, Stock and Wilson. Was this one of Petal's images detaching itself from his mind? He floated with it. Hannah had been batting for the other side. He had anticipated that Dr Grüber would be a crusty, middle-aged bloke. She had blown him away. As she had passed the glass partition leading to his office in the penthouse, she had been laughing into the phone pressed to her ear, and something in him had dissolved and reassembled itself so that he was open to her. He hadn't believed in love at first sight. She ended the call and pushed open the door with her hip, dropping the phone into her bag. He stood and reached out his hand across his glass desk. 'Hannah Grüber,' she said. 'Pleased to meet you.' Her coat had been soft when he hung it up for her – wool and cashmere. Good label.

'Great view,' she said, seating herself at the meeting table that ran the length of the window. 'Let's get started. My company has agreed your board's terms for a thirty per cent controlling share in their online business. As you know, I am a senior player in the operational business team. If we are agreed that you can define risk as the possibility of incurring a misfortune or loss, then can you confirm that the usual checks and balances are in place to mitigate against any such eventuality?'

She sounded like a robot, he thought. It must be her PhD; too many hours talking jargon in the tiny studies of bearded academics. He tried to reply in kind, on automatic, but all he could think was what extraordinary grey-blue eyes she had. They sparkled as she spoke. He cleared his throat. 'I have prepared a report on our policies and procedures as approved by our directors, an external auditor and the FCA. They regularly review risk policies, test them and review outcomes of actual losses in comparable projects. I'm pleased to report that in view of the directors' low appetite for risk, we have an exemplary record.' It was a dance of words, rich and formulaic.

She matched him step for step. 'That's why we were attracted to your offer,' she said.

'We continually update our strategies and mitigants,' added Archie.

'Delighted to hear it. As you can imagine, by selling you such a large controlling share, our primary concern would be loss of reputation and business interruption in the unlikely event that it all goes down the Swanee. So naturally we require a suitable level of professional indemnity.'

'All approved by our board,' said Archie. 'I head up group legal and I can give you my personal guarantee that we have a strong framework in place to deal with the concerns of your board, shareholders and customers. If you could action your marketing department to promote the rebranding of the company to include our logo in a prominent position, then I'd be happy to sign off on this one.'

'I guarantee you a positive market impact – all singing, all dancing, balloons and champagne.'

'Talking of which,' said Archie, 'there's a great tapas bar round the corner for a quick lunch if you fancy it, to celebrate? The cava is more than halfway decent, and while we're there I'll get my secretary to print out the draft contract.' He emailed his secretary with a clatter of keys.

'Is that the place with the honey-grilled aubergine?' asked Hannah.

'The very same,' said Archie, getting to his feet and holding her coat open for her. As she turned her back to him to slide her arms into her sleeves, he saw that the nape of her neck was slender; a gold chain lay against the bones visible under her skin.

He opened the door for her. His secretary was at her desk. 'You want to watch that one,' she said to Hannah as they passed. 'He's been single for a year now. Too much time spent running around with toy guns at weekends with the TA.'

Hannah smiled.

He made a throat-cutting gesture as Hannah turned to go, but his secretary laughed. 'You're not scary, you know,' she called after him. 'Not scary at all.'

\* \* \*

On the last day of his incarceration, he was released with a box of pills, his care plan and an appointment card. He made his way to the job centre at Tollcross as instructed by the hospital's resident social worker, a fifty-year-old woman who smelled of fabric conditioner.

There were two security guards on the door. He could take them both out, no bother, he reckoned. 'Morning,' he said, as he made his way past to the desk labelled 'Enquiries' in the middle of the floor. It was unmanned. A sign above it said, 'Our employees have the right to be treated with respect.' Beyond it, people sat opposite advisors. A man behind him baa'd like a sheep, and grinned when Archie turned round. 'It's a market, pal,' he said, 'but we're not the ones making the money.'

'Can I help you, sir?' asked a girl of about eighteen, coming over.

'I've come to sign on,' he said.

'First time?' she asked.

'Yes.'

An advisor will be with you in a minute if you'd like to take a seat over there in the waiting area. You'll be one of the first to try the new Universal Credit. It has already been trialled in the North of England and will be rolled out by 2017. It's all done online. You computer literate?'

He nodded. The man behind him bleeted again.

'No problem then,' she said. 'As long as you can budget monthly. It's up to you to allocate your own expenditure. Think you can do that? You'll need to set up a direct debit to pay your landlord.'

He nodded again. His head felt light on the drugs, like it would keep going up and down in slow motion. He shook it from left to right.

'Which is it?' she asked. 'Yes or no?'

'Yes,' he said.

'If you come this way, I'll let you see the YouTube video released by the DWP – that's the Department for Work and Pensions – which explains how you can improve your situation. Work pays,' she said.

'Depends on the work,' observed Archie.

She turned round.

'Sorry,' he said, his default setting. 'Sorry.'

She pulled up a blue, padded nylon chair for him in front of a screen and clicked on the link: 'Who is eligible for Universal Credit?'

An orange, cartoon man appeared on screen to upbeat music like false teeth clacking together. He was orange – not black, brown or white. 'James is a single person, aged twenty-two, who becomes unemployed,' said a voice. Archie tried to put the volume up, but it was already at the maximum. He leaned forward to hear. The orange was distracting, head to toe Guantánamo. No escape. A bus went past outside. '… and is due to pay rent of £261 a month,' continued the voice. An arrow shot across the screen to a pink house. 'Universal credit of £580 a month,' it said.

Orange James, the good citizen, appeared in the next shot carrying a tool bag and, to a trumpet fanfare, rose to the heights of £693 per month for twelve hours' work on the national minimum wage. Archie pressed pause. 'Please watch it to the end,' the girl said. 'It's important.' She slid the red dot back to the beginning.

Archie rested his forehead on his outstretched fingers and took a deep breath, then flexed his hands and cracked his knuckles. He looked straight at her. 'I get the picture,' he said.

'We require our clients to watch the information video from the beginning to the end.' She stopped speaking as her eyes met his, then flicked a glance at the security guard who was looking away. 'Never mind,' she added. 'Please, follow me.' She led him over to a male advisor, who brought up a new screen on his computer and turned it part way to face Archie.

'Right then,' he said. 'Let's get you started.'

The tick boxes were all being ticked: National insurance number? Yes. Aged between eighteen and sixty years and six months? Yes. Single? Yes. No kids living with you? No.

'Fine,' said the adviser leaning forward. 'We can proceed with your claim but I should tell you that this is not an unconditional award, a something-for-nothing benefit. You will be expected to sign a Jobseeker's Agreement and work on your CV with a personal advisor, as well as attend training with one of our approved service providers.'

Archie nodded.

'If you fail to attend for any session as advised, I have to inform you, and I say this with your best interests at heart ...' He lodged the mint he was sucking under his top lip with the tip of his tongue, which was white and furred, 'then sanctions will be taken against you. Seven, fourteen or twenty-eight days, which will be enforced unless you can provide a good reason for your non-compliance. For example, you had to take your mother to hospital.'

'Why would I have to do that?' asked Archie.

'Well, you might,' said the advisor. 'That was just an example. These low-level sanctions are for things we expect you to do. This is new territory for us too, but the good news is that once you comply with the request, then the sanction will be removed. Do you understand? It's very straightforward.'

'Yes,' said Archie, 'but what if you have a mental health problem, or something like that?'

'Do you have a mental health problem?' asked the advisor.

'No,' said Archie, looking round. 'I'm not a nut-job, a bampot.'

'Exactly,' said the advisor. 'That's fine then. All perfectly reasonable and above board. The high-level sanctions would be enforced in the realm of things that can't be remedied, for example ...' He paused to crack the mint between his teeth. 'For example,' he repeated, swallowing, 'if you don't accept a job and comply with our request.'

'Like Syria,' said Archie.

The advisor sat back in his chair. 'I don't understand,' he said.

'Sanctions,' said Archie.

'The point is this,' continued the advisor, 'compliance is the cornerstone in the edifice of the Jobseeker's Agreement. It has supported our labour market performance in this recession. We're on the case. We're making people do things. These are not isolated changes on the margins, but a move to reduce the national deficit through equipping people to work, moving the shirkers to centre stage and putting a spotlight on them. For the good of the nation. So who was your previous employer, Archie?'

'Mr Forbes.'

'We're all on first-name terms here. One happy family,' said the advisor, turning the plastic ID card on the end of his lanyard round. His photo looked out like a face on a bus. 'Pete,' he said.

'Okay, Pete,' said Archie. 'Her Majesty's Government in the person of the British Army.' He saluted. 'Lieutenant Archie Forbes of the TA, seconded for duty in Afghanistan from my company – Forbes, Stock and Wilson.'

Pete looked up from paring his nails with a pencil. 'Why don't you go back to Forbes, Stock and Wilson?' he asked.

'I was shafted,' said Archie. 'Long story. When can I expect to get my first payment on your Universal Credit?'

'It won't take more than a month to check your claim,' Pete said, unwrapping another mint from the tube in his pocket, a cartridge of green and silver paper.

Archie heard the cartridge drop into place, saw the rifle snap back up. 'Pull,' said a loud voice in his head and he saw his best man raise his gun and shoot the clay pigeon; the disc exploding against the sky to hang there; shards of a jigsaw flying out in the air, sketching the shape of its own destruction. First barrel kill – three points.

'If that is a problem,' said the advisor, 'then we can put you in touch with the Scottish Welfare Fund. I think it's up and running.'

Archie stood up and stepping to the side, pushed in his chair until it was hard up against the edge of the desk. He adjusted it and ran his hand along the top edge.

'I'll need your bank account details,' said the advisor, but Archie had already passed the guards and was standing in the street. 'Go back in, son,' said the older of the two. 'Get yourself sorted out.'

'What's the point?' said Archie. 'They don't want to help me. It's just another bloody assault course and I'm too damn tired to get over it.'

The street outside was grey. He began to walk but had nowhere to go. Uneven cobbles stretched past the Justified Sinner pub. Pole-dancing bars advertised their opening hours and he crossed the street, leaving the three-sided block of strip clubs locals called the pubic triangle. A drunk was mooning the window of a café where students pored over iPads. His cracked and hairy arse was pressed to the glass, fleshy like a snail where it made contact with the smooth surface. The manageress was heading for the door. All hell was going to break loose. Archie walked on past the fire station and the art school, crossing the road to the Meadows. He reached a bench and sat down. He was thirsty. He pulled his jacket closer round his chest and tucked his arms under his armpits, bowing his head. He was a beetle. He remembered seeing the desert beetles skate to the tops of the dunes in the Namib Desert, and turn their back to the fog that rolled in from the sea. Had he really seen that? Was it on telly? Had there been a narrator's voice, words on desert wind? The water from the air condensed on their shells and ran down in clear drops to envelop their heads and arms. Such a long drink. They were detritivores feeding on seeds blown from distant, green places. 'I'm a detritivore,' he thought, 'trying to suck food and moisture from this land. Suck, suck – sucker.' His brain was a barren blank. How to change channels?

'Hello, stranger,' said a voice. He looked up to see Sooze standing there, her dog sniffing a nearby tree, his lead at maximum stretch. The dog rooted under leaves, around the bulging, fungus ball of extruded bark, reading the history of the squirrel that had crouched there, the child trailing its hand round the trunk in a game of hide and seek. 'I couldn't find the Slim for Jesus website,' she said. 'Are you still running classes?'

He nodded, his lie appearing on the horizon of his mind. 'I'm redoing the site,' he said.

'Got your Bible with you,' she said.

He glanced down at his pocket, surprised to see it sticking out. 'Yes,' he agreed.

'So how about I bring my friend here on Thursday. You could give her a trial lesson?

'What day is this?' he asked.

'Wednesday the eighteenth of September. A year to go to the referendum. How could you not know that? It's a big day.'

'For some,' he replied.

'You a Unionist?' she asked.

'Never thought about it,' he said. 'Ex-army, queen and country, face on the coin, coin in my pocket – generic, comfortable, easy-peasy, or so I thought.'

'And now?'

'There's always a hidden cost, Sooze. No such thing as a free lunch.'

Her dog came over and snuffled round his feet. 'Hello, pal,' he said, scooping him up. 'Still in one piece?'

The dog tried to lick his face, diving at his lips, spilling from his hands. Archie laughed.

'He likes you,' said Sooze.

'Glad someone does,' he replied.

'So tomorrow, here, at two pm? That suit you?'

'Affirmative,' he replied.

'Twenty pound okay for a trial lesson?' she asked.

'Yes,' he said. 'No problem.'

He sat on after Sooze left. He watched the people cross the

Meadows in waves along broad paths that dissected the grass, and pass out of sight under the whale jaw-bone arch, green with moss. Jonahs – reborn at the next street corner. These were the daylight people – pensioners, mothers, schoolchildren, teenagers and students; and later the night people would come – shouting – party-goers in search of a laugh and a shag. His eyes were fixed open as they marched across his retina, a meaningless parade, spot-lit by the SSRI tablet hanging like a winter sun over his frost-bleached landscape.

* * *

This time the road to Leith had been longer, his shoes heavier. He had caught up with Mike at the writers' group and now lay on the bed in his spare room, sublet with promises of paying his bedroom tax. It was no more than a box room with the misfortune of a small window that looked into the kitchen above a glass-brick partition. He supposed it had once been a sleeping alcove with a box bed. The door made it a room, and now it was an asset of the State. The ceiling was decorated with black vinyl discs. He lay on the single bed behind the glass bricks. Through them, he could see the wavy shape of Mike supervising a baked potato in his micro-wave, which sparked. The cooker was a burnt-out shell. Mike had assured him that he was on the anti-booze and there would be no more fires. 'One sip of alcohol and it's like the fucking *Exorcist*,' he had said, miming vomit spouting from his mouth. 'The disulfiram reaction is not a good look. And I've stopped putting my fag ends in the plastic bag on the back of the door. Got a bin out of Oxfam after the last visit from the fire brigade. Fire Safety Man, that's me. Dry as a bone.'

The microwave pinged. Mike knocked on his door with a dish-towel over one arm and said, 'Dinner is served.' Archie walked through to the kitchen. A bag of tins from the food bank lay unpacked in the corner. 'Take this, mate,' said Mike passing him the baked potato on a plate. You need it more than me.'

'I can't,' said Archie, trying to smile.

'We'll go halves then,' said Mike. 'There's some beans in that food bag at your feet. We'll add them. Tomorrow can take care of itself.'

After the meal, Archie opened the Bible in his room. 'Thank you, Moira,' he said, as he turned to the Concordance at the back for references to food. 'And now to business.'

'In these times of social austerity,' he wrote in a notebook from Dr Clark to chart any 'unsettling incidents', 'it is a social imperative not to squander resources. This is as true for the individual as for the society in which they live. The society that feeds them.' Then scored it out.

'Ladies,' he wrote in capital letters, 'Slim for the Lord! You want to be in the best possible shape when you reach the Pearly Gates. He doesn't want to see you there early, girls.' He added, 'And boys.' He scored that out too.

'Loving,' he wrote, 'starts with yourself. How can you spread God's love if you don't start at home? Real love is nourishment for body and soul, and nourishment is goodness. That's natural food, untainted by the processed world of manufacturers and big business. Jesus cast them out of the temple, the usurers who profited from over-consumption. Why let them into the temple of your body?' Archie wondered if the drugs were inspiring him. 'Man, this is good,' he thought. He went through to the kitchen for a snack. There was only one banana in the bag. 'Mike,' he shouted through the hall. 'Do you mind if I eat the banana?'

There was no reply. He walked through the hall. Mike had his headphones on, plugged into the telly, watching the news. A TV diet of horror. Assad's picture rode above a red line of newsfeed saying that Putin expected he would sign up to the Convention on Chemical Weapons. One hundred thousand dead since 2011, as civil war reaches stalemate. Archie waved the piece of fruit in the air. Mike looked at him. 'Be my guest,' he said.

Archie cut it into a bowl of kids' cereal and added milk. He returned to the Bible. It fell open at Jeremiah. Chapter 22, Verse 3. He read, 'Do no wrong to the stranger, the fatherless, nor the widow, neither shed innocent blood in this place.' He flipped over the page, Verse 16. 'He judged the cause of the poor and the needy: then it was well with him, was this not to know me? saith the Lord.'

'Fuck knows,' said Archie to himself. He flipped back to the Concordance. 'Can I use your computer, Mike?' he shouted as his new landlord lifted one ear of his headphones on seeing him at the living room door again.

'As long as you treat it with respect,' he said. 'Dinnae dis' it man.'

The computer sat in the hall on an old dressing table. He slid his legs underneath and tried to ignore his reflection in the mirror. He could see the sides of his head in the wing mirrors that were splattered with black patches where the silver paper had flaked away. As the computer loaded, he pushed the mirrors flat so that they reflected the wall behind him. Through the open door he could see that Mike had fallen asleep, his ears still connected to the world of the television, the woman shouting at her partner in the soap opera that played out in daily episodes, her scripted misery emptying itself piecemeal into the room.

The computer was slow to load. The monitor's fat, beige body still boasted charity shop and electrical testing stickers. He scratched at them with his nail and then went to look for some scouring powder he had spotted under the sink. When he came back the screen had loaded. There was a picture of a tropical paradise. It was password protected. 'Password,' typed Archie. It opened. He created a new email address and joined Facebook, his eyes skimming over their stock price. He clicked on a new page and typed in 'Slim for Jesus'. He added a picture of a smiling Jesus with arms outstretched, and put in a picture of the trees on the Meadows. 'Looking for pastures new?' he typed. 'Are you martyred to an unproductive way of life? Join me on Tuesday and Thursday mornings for a new approach to personal fitness.' Then he added, 'This class is aimed primarily at those with a persistent weight problem. Learn to distinguish between need and want.' Archie smiled. He flicked to the back of his Bible, looked up the account of feeding the five thousand and added, 'Look out for my forthcoming recipes based on a Mediterranean diet known to promote good health. Eat the food Jesus himself would have eaten; walk in

41

his shoes.' He skimmed through a few recipes online but began to feel hungry and logged off. He sat down in front of the telly and stared at the wall. His mind was racing.

Mike stretched and walked towards the bathroom, yawning. There was a sound of splashing water, tooth cleaning and spitting, and he emerged in a tight T-shirt and black jeans. Archie noticed they were split at the back. 'There's a hole in your jeans, mate,' he started to say and then stopped. 'For God's sake, Mike,' he said. 'Don't do that.'

Mike shrugged.

'It's not safe,' he said.

'Safer than pulling them down,' said Mike. 'Get caught with your keks round your knees and the wrong kind of dick up your hole, and I'm telling you, man, it's not going to end well.'

'You don't need to do that,' Archie repeated. 'You don't know who's out there.'

'You'd be surprised,' said Mike. 'There's quite a high class of client. There's knobs and there's nobs. Lube up and think of England. Easy.'

'I'm not laughing,' said Archie. 'Sit down, mate, and we'll talk it over. Find you something else.'

'No can do,' said Mike. 'I'm late as it is.' He opened the front door. 'Don't you break my computer,' he said. 'Or do anything I wouldn't. I don't want the police round here because you're a fucking terrorist paedo.'

'No worries,' said Archie, saluting. 'I'm ex-army, remember.' And he tried not to remember, as he heard Mike's feet echoing on the stairs, growing fainter, winced at the bang of the door at the foot of the stairs as it closed. He walked into the kitchen and put the tins in the cupboard, turned all the labels to the front and then lay down on his bed. He banged his head on the pillow seven times so that he would wake up at seven, and closed his eyes, willing himself to believe he would sleep. The moon swam through the glass bricks, having let herself in at the window, and someone, somewhere, laughed.

# 8

SOOZE AND HER FRIEND were waiting for him as he ran up in a pair of joggers he had borrowed from Mike. They were a bit tight, but he was pleased at the way they showed off his thigh muscles. It made him look the part. He had an old whistle round his neck over a T-shirt. The women waved as he drew up with that strange shoulder-high, tick-tock hand gesture they reserved for friends. He nodded. 'Alright?' he asked.

They looked sepia through the sunglasses that he had found in the drawer of the dressing table. He hoped they didn't smell of old lady face powder.

'This is Louise,' said Sooze.

He held out his hand, saw her wondering at the sunglasses and looking up at the sky. The sun was back-lighting the flat, grey clouds. 'I need to protect my eyes,' he said. 'Sun damage.'

'Sun damage?' parroted Louise. 'In Scotland?'

'Afghanistan,' he said. The word was rocky.

She smiled a sepia smile. She was fat. Doll-like. 'Okay, Doll,' he said. 'Ready to start?' She opened her mouth. Her skin was good, he noted. Soft, like her brown hair.

'Don't call me Doll,' she said. 'Unless you want me to call you something I'll regret as a good Christian.'

'Sorry,' he said. 'The client is always right.'

'No, I'm right,' she said. 'There is no client about it.'

'Well, let's get started. We'll do a trial lesson and you can tell me if you want to continue.' He stretched his arms up and rolled his shoulders. 'Time and tide wait for no man.'

'What about a prayer?' she asked. 'Your page said each session starts with a prayer.'

He hadn't remembered typing that bit. 'Dear Lord,' he began, clasping his hands together and trying to remember the nun's blessing over the food at St Philomena's. 'Please reach out your loving arms over this, your servant, and make us truly thankful for what we are about to receive.'

'What are we about to receive?' asked Louise, opening her eyes.

'The gift of health,' he replied, enjoying the internal sunshine of Dr Clark's potion. 'The gift of eternal life.' He wondered if that was overdoing it and, grasping his ankle, pulled his calf up to meet his thigh. 'Let's warm up,' he said. 'Put one hand on that tree if you feel wobbly,' he said.

She stretched out her hand. Her nails were painted green, shellacked and shiny; beetles.

'What do you do, Louise?' he asked.

'I'm a hausfrau,' she said. 'A homemaker, a domestic engineer, a mum.'

'And when are you going back to work?' he asked.

'I've got three kids,' she said, 'under ten. That's work. W-O-R-K.'

He grimaced, thinking of his son. He must be one now. He wondered if he had missed his birthday. Wondered if that made things better or worse with his wife.

'I've got a son,' he said.

'How old?' asked Louise.

'One,' he said. He pulled up his other leg. 'We're going to warm up and then run along that path. I want you to follow me. Keep your arms level with your ribs and tucked in. Don't let them flap.'

'I can't run,' she said.

'Then we'll walk to the first tree and jog to the second. Walk to the third, jog to the fourth. When I say jog, it's optional, we can increase the pace to a faster walk if that's easier. The trick is to get your heart rate up. Do you want to do this?' he asked.

'Yes,' she said. 'Let's do it for the Lord.'

'Hooah,' he said, American army style, then changed it to, 'Hallelujah.'

She started walking. Her pink bottom wobbled through her joggers. He drew level with her. 'We'll up the pace in three,' he said. His stomach rumbled, but she didn't seem to notice.

'This is better than I expected,' she said, as they reached the children's playpark ten minutes later. A spray of sand flew over the railing from the sand pit. A few grains hit his lip. Kids were screaming in a swinging dish, small bodies lying under the sky. His eyes rolled; he felt them flickering behind his glasses and drew a deep breath.

'Are you alright?' she asked, touching his arm. The beetles crawled up his sleeve.

He bent over. 'Cramp,' he improvised.

'I thought you were the tough guy,' she said, and passed him a plastic water bottle from her pocket. The water was warm on his lips. Body temperature.

'Let's go a different way,' he said. 'We'll cut over there.' He began to run.

'Wait,' she shouted. 'I can't keep up.'

He stopped, and jogged on the spot until she caught up. He was on the parade ground.

'I don't know if this is going to work,' she said. 'Maybe I'll stop now. I'll still give you the twenty pounds.' Sooze wandered over from a nearby bench.

'No giving up, Mrs,' she said to her friend. 'Remember what you said about the website last night? You thought it might help to work out with a group a few times a week.'

Louise nodded. 'I'll start properly next time.'

'I'll post something tonight,' said Archie. 'Just for you. Something motivational.'

'Okay,' said Louise, passing him the twenty-pound note she had scrunched up in her pocket. 'You can promise me a miracle, if you like, but you had better deliver.'

Archie wondered what the 'or what' might be on the end of that sentence. 'Or what?' he said, but she had already turned away with Sooze.

'I'd invite you to the café,' Sooze shouted, 'but you might give us a row for the sin we are about to commit.'

He laughed. He could give Mike the £14.95 for this week's rent and still have a baked potato from the spud shop at the foot of the

Walk. A real business lunch, he thought. Paid for by yours truly. Eat your heart out, Orange James.

*  *  *

The TV in the baked potato shop was shouting from a shelf. Armed gunmen ran round a shopping centre in Nairobi firing at people crawling away, cowering behind aisles.

'Those terrorists are animals,' tutted the woman behind the counter. 'No better than that lot in the hotel in Mumbai the other year. Nowhere's safe now,' she said.

The newsreader showed a map of Somalia, explaining the war against terror for Orange James, if he was watching. 'African Union troops drive out the Al-Shabaab terrorists daily.'

A map of Somalia flashed up on the screen.

'What can I do for you?' asked the woman.

'Your finest baked potato with cheese, please.'

She snapped on a pair of plastic gloves. 'Any extra toppings?'

'How much are they?' asked Archie.

'Fifty pence.'

'No, thanks. Just cheese.'

'Go on,' she said, 'a big lad like you? Treat yourself. Try some tuna.'

'Just cheese,' he repeated. He propped himself up on one of the bar stools along the wall. African Union troops loaded into trucks were rattling across the sand in the goldfish bowl of the television. 'The Al-Shabaab attack on the centre is thought to be motivated by revenge for the presence of Kenyan troops in Somalia,' said the newsreader.

'Would you like tea?' asked the woman, balancing a white plastic fork on top of a polystyrene container that hadn't closed over the potato.

'UN mandate,' said the telly.

'No, thank you,' said Archie.

'Help yourself to a napkin,' she said.

Archie pulled a white napkin out of its steel container. It was a paper sail. He thought of the Somali pirates with their strings of tankers, tried not to think of the microcosm of his Facebook page, and its tangle of religion and cash.

'We're all to blame,' he said to the woman.

'What?'

'Money,' he said. 'At any price.'

She laughed and walked across the shop to hold the door open for him. Best to get the cranks out pronto. 'Have a good day,' she said. 'And splash out on tuna next time. It's good. Dolphin friendly.'

\* \* \*

He logged on when he got back to the flat to shut his site down. He felt like a fraud. Mike was floating in the peach-coloured bath with the door open, snoring to music on a waterproof radio that was taped round the edges. There was a new message in his newsfeed. A businesswoman looking for a thirty-minute early-morning session. Monday, Wednesday, Friday. Sixty pounds a week at the introductory rate, he calculated. Too good an offer to refuse. His scruples would have to wait. He heard the splosh of water running onto the floor as Mike woke up with a start and climbed out of the bath. There was the sound of deodorant spraying and then an 'Oh, fuck, man' as it stopped.

'Have you been using my deodorant?' he shouted through the door. 'It's fucking dead.'

'Sorry, mate,' said Archie. 'I ran out.'

'You never had any,' replied Mike.

Archie ignored him and, with a change of heart, pressed reply and fixed an appointment for the following week. He opened the Bible and typed a message to Louise. 'Please reflect on this passage. Think about donating to charity the money you could save by indulging in fewer treats. The satisfaction your soul gains will enhance the progress your body makes.

'St Luke: Chapter 16

The Rich Man and Lazarus

19. There was a certain rich man, which was clothed in purple and fine linen, and fared sumptuously each day:

20. And there was a certain beggar named Lazarus, which was laid at his gate, full of sores,

21. And desiring to be fed with the crumbs that fell from the rich man's table: moreover the dogs came and licked his sores.

22. It came to pass, that the beggar died, and was carried by the angels into Abraham's bosom: the rich man also died and was buried;

23. And in hell he lift up his eyes being in torments, and seeth Abraham afar off, and Lazarus in his bosom.

24. And he cried and said, Father Abraham, have mercy on me and send Lazarus that he may dip the tip of his finger in water, and cool my tongue for I am tormented in this flame.

25. But Abraham said, Son, remember that thou in thy lifetime receivedst thy good things, and likewise Lazarus evil things: but now he is comforted and thou art tormented.'

A message was fired straight back from Louise. 'I have got three kids clasped to my own bosom, you self-righteous prick,' he read. 'My problem is glandular. Stuff your website, and stuff you.'

'Sorry,' he typed back.

'You're so full of crap,' said Mike, towelling his hair dry behind him, his eyes on the screen.

'Please don't stand behind me,' said Archie.

'Or what?' said Mike. 'You gonna break my neck or something?' He skipped away. 'You're not a big man now.' He sang a few bars of an American army camp training cadence: 'Met superman and had a fight; I hit him in the head with some kryptonite.'

Archie jumped up, knocking over the chair. Mike backed into the living room. 'I hit him so hard that I busted his brains,' he continued, stumbling over the sofa. 'And now I'm dating Lois Lane.' He fell back onto the green velour cushion and lay there laughing. Archie looked away, stared at the wall and saw jellyfish Chinooks blossom on the wallpaper, supplies dangling on wires below; in the far distance, a snowy mountain was growing out of desert sand. The supermarket siege played on a loop on the television, which had been left on. 'It's so fucked,' he said. 'It's all so fucked.'

Mike stopped laughing as Archie snapped off the TV, his thumb on the detonator button. He threw the remote across the room. 'Watch it,' shouted Mike. 'That's my new remote. It's not paid up yet.'

'Sorry,' he said, and walked into the hall. Picking up his hoodie, he stepped out into the street. It was just beginning to get dark, the tracer lights of cars making their way up the Walk, a long avenue of red. At the top, he turned off past a pet shop onto an old Victorian path and climbed up to the top of Calton Hill. 'All day,' came the memory of US troops singing in his head. 'All day,' he sang. 'Running, running.' Call and answer. 'All night'; 'All night,' he answered. 'Running'; 'running'; 'All night,' the voices called. 'All night,' he echoed. 'Fighting'; 'Fighting.' A car back-fired somewhere in the streets below him and he jumped, pressing himself into the wall. A man with his girlfriend at the top of the path spotted him, put an arm round her shoulder, and turned back to take the other way down. He whispered in the girl's ear and she laughed, glancing back at him. 'I'm not a nut,' Archie shouted after them, stepping back onto the path and holding his arms wide. 'It's fine. I thought we were under fire.'

Walking past the old observatory on the crest of the hill, Archie sat on a bench looking out over the Forth. A man walked past him wrapped in a Saltire from a tourist shop. Archie missed his son. He missed his wife. He wondered how they were doing without him, wondered if his child had cut his first tooth. Did the tooth fairy come for that? Was that how it went, he wondered – in other lives; in his other life that played out somewhere in the might-have-been?

# 9

HE WOKE UP ON THE BENCH in the morning stiff and cold. All around him in the grass he could see the detritus of the Independence March that had gathered there to 'fill the hill' the day before: cigarette butts, mini saltires and, winking at his feet, a Yes badge. He picked it up. When did the independence debate reduce itself to a yes/no vote, a game show choice? It would be televised with the shopping mall murders, the soaps, the TV schedule that churned real life into bite-sized pieces to be swallowed with food by the fire, and then turned off, as if turning it off made it stop, made it go away, kept it tidy. He thought of Mike, wondered if he had noticed he hadn't come back in the wee, small hours. Leith lay in toy-town rows of tenements by the Forth. He felt nothing. The view was a criss-cross scratching on his retina – inconvenient, meaningless. The numbness scared him. His disconnectedness was growing. He began to walk with the jerky legs of an automaton down the hill to the road. If only he could make those connections again. Join his brain to his legs, his mind to his feelings, and not fear that they would engulf him in a tsunami of regret, churning with the flotsam of his old life.

Out of habit, he walked down Broughton Street towards his old home in Trinity. His body began to warm up as the light grew, and he walked faster. He pumped his arms up and down to get the circulation going, moved his jaw from side to side – mandibles, snapping on air. His clothes were damp and he sucked his sleeve, tasting the bitter dew on the cotton of his sweatshirt. Fog beetle. He stopped at his old garden gate. The front door had been painted a different colour. He checked the number – ten – it was the right house. Ten – still feeling okay. Forty to go to the start of the bad memories. Today he would stick on ten, count backwards to one. Start from the beginning with new memories, new sensations, not seen through the prism of the warped past, the distortion of his broken life. He rang the bell. Through the glass of the door panel he saw the shadow of his wife approaching. She stopped and he saw her eye recognise him through a gap in the flowers etched onto the surface with acid. Her eye was very blue, the pupil small and black, imploding in on itself, a distant black hole. 'Hannah,' he called. 'I only want to talk.' He held up his hands. 'No tricks.'

She opened the door on the chain. His son was in her arms, and Archie looked at them through the crack in the door, a Madonna and Child on a narrow altar panel. Perfect. Remote. 'How are you?' he said.

'We were fine,' she replied. 'You're not meant to be here. Margaret is to call the police if you come within five hundred yards of the house. You know that.'

He looked across the fence to the neighbour's bay window. 'No sign of the Twitcher,' he said.

'Don't joke.'

'I never meant to hit you,' he said.

'You knocked me unconscious,' she said. 'It was like being hit by a train.'

'I'm sorry,' he said. 'Really.'

'Why are you here?' she asked.

Margaret must still be sleeping, he thought, or she would be knocking on the window by now, and miming dialling for the police. 'I couldn't remember when Daniel's birthday was,' he said, looking at his son, who turned his face into his mother's shoulder.

'It was the first,' she said. 'The first of September. How could you forget a date like that? It's not difficult.'

He nodded. 'I was on a tour of duty,' he said, 'when he popped out.'

'He didn't pop out,' she replied. 'As you would know if you'd been there.'

'It wasn't my fault.'

'So whose was it? Who arranged your life? I thought it was you.

A personal secretary and tablets and iPhones and yet, somehow, Mister Smart Guy missed the birth of his first child.'

'I was called up,' he said.

'You volunteered. It's different.'

'I wish I could go back in time and make different choices, but I can't.'

'So why are you here, Archie? Do you want to go to jail? Breaking a restraining order is an offence. You should know that.'

'It's worth it to see you,' he said.

She shut the door. 'Discussion's over, Archie,' she said. Her voice was muffled behind the glass. 'You have three minutes and then I'm going to call the police.'

'Okay,' he said. 'Just get me my training gear and my old smartphone, and I'll leave you alone. You can call me if you change your mind. He's my son too. I still want to be his dad,' he said.

There was silence and then, as he backed away to the gate, the upstairs window opened and a bag flew out onto the grass. It was full of clothes.

'Thanks,' he called, but she had already pulled out her mobile and was looking at the watch on her wrist. 'Three minutes,' she mouthed.

He gave her a thumbs-up. The bag made him feel human, the loss of his possessions at the hostel less pointed. He swung it up onto his shoulder and marched along the road, whistling. He put it at his feet at breakfast in St Philomena's. The regulars had backed away from him as he came into the room, and he sat alone at a table that could seat six. 'Alright, big man?' said a volunteer collecting the dirty dishes.

He nodded. He tried to switch his phone on to confirm his appointment with the businesswoman but the battery was flat. He found the charger at the foot of the bag covered in dust. He wiped it off with a finger: his wife's skin cells, the fibres from his carpet, the grease from his skin. 'Can you charge this for me?' he asked the volunteer. 'Please? I think it's still about fifty quid in credit.'

'I'm not really allowed to,' he said.

Archie's hand trembled as he put the phone back in his bag.

'Give it here,' said the volunteer. 'Who are you going to phone anyway?'

'A business contact,' said Archie.

'Ooh, get you,' said the volunteer, 'A business contact, and here's me frying your bacon and eggs, while you're living the high life.'

# 10

AFTER A DAY CATCHING UP in the hospital studio, Petal was phoning the inbox of the only hot man in the newspaper's lonely hearts column. 'Cupid Calling connects you to your perfect date,' said an automated voice. 'Put the passion back into your life, but remember to meet in a public place and let someone know where you are going. Cupid doesn't accept any responsibility for adverts placed in this paper. Please speak after the tone.'

'I'm a forty-five-year-old community health arts worker,' said Petal, 'and looking for lurve.' She paused.

'Remember to press the hash tag when you have finished recording your message,' purred the mechanical voice. 'If you want to change your message, press two.'

She pressed two. 'I'm a thirty-five-year-old community health arts worker,' she said, 'looking for a serious relationship. I have a good sense of humour, GSOH.' She laughed, 'And OHAC, own house and car. Please call me on my mobile.' She read the number out from a sticker on the wall-mounted phone. 'I look forward to hearing from you,' she added, and hung up. She didn't play it back. As she passed the mirror in the hall, she smiled and tried piling her hair on top of her head. Then she shook it down, and went into the bathroom. As she lay in the bath, she remembered Archie. He had been nice, troubled but nice, and handsome. She imagined drawing him, tracing the lines of his face in charcoal and healing his eyes, smudging in dark centres, relaxed and dreamy. If only he didn't stare in that fixed way. Maybe Dr Clark could work a miracle and she could resign and gallop off with Archie into the sunset. A knight in shining armour. He was muscular, maybe ex-army, like the guy a few years ago. The one who had lost his arm. She looked at her body floating in the water. She was a mermaid. Her hair was seaweed. The water ran off her skin as she lifted her arm up into the light, and saw the water droplets clinging to the tiny hairs. Where were the desiccated limbs of the injured soldiers now; dried fingers pointing at the sky; chattering bones in the desert; bright skull houses for scorpions. She remembered the small, amorphous statuette the one-armed soldier had shown her. He had found it in the sand in Iraq. It lay in the palm of his good hand, its round stone breasts and strong thighs pock-marked by the wind. 'Maybe you should give it to a museum?' she had suggested, but he had already tried that. 'It didn't fit with their collecting policy,' he said. 'Said it wasn't local.'

She had laughed at the understatement. 'Try a national?'

He had shrugged and put it back in his pocket. 'I don't want to get into trouble,' he said. 'We were walking over the Queen of Sheba's palace. It was still there, under the sand. I saw this sticking up and I trousered it, but now it doesn't feel right to have it. It lives in a shoe-box under the bed. I swear it walks around in there at night.'

# 11

ARCHIE SLEPT ALL WEEKEND and woke on Monday morning from a dream about his conference trip to Vancouver. In the happy book of his past life he was standing on the bus to Granville Island with Hannah. The driver had looked Middle Eastern. Tourists packed onto the bus. 'Would all the cute and the beautiful move to the back?' shouted the driver.

Hannah squeezed past Archie. 'For those who don't speak English …' the driver added.

'Here we go,' said Hannah, smiling at Archie, and her smile grew wider as the driver made the same announcement in five languages. 'I got the French,' said Hannah.

'Is that all?' replied Archie with a laugh. 'I'm a polyglot.'

'You're a comedian,' she said. The bus jolted as it moved off and Archie caught Hannah's elbow to steady her. 'Sorry,' he said. 'Reflex.'

'It's alright,' she replied, and looked into his eyes.

He held her gaze. 'Are you enjoying the conference so far?' he asked for something to say.

She nodded. 'Intelligent Eco-Investments … mmmm. Not to be missed, but I'm glad the afternoon session was cancelled. I enjoyed our lunch in Edinburgh that time.'

'Yes,' he agreed.

'Fancy another at the marina?' she asked. 'An aunt took me last summer.'

'Contrary to appearances,' he said, indicating his suit. 'I only came for the world-famous shrimps.'

'And curly fries? You can admit it to me. That's the great thing about Canada. No one looks down on you if your order curly fries.'

He laughed and through the window saw wooden houses in

candy colours give way to multi-storey apartments with trees in pots on their balconies. Yachts were moored at pontoons.

'Granville Island,' shouted the driver. 'Give a big cheer if you're happy.'

Archie cheered. There was a smattering of whoos from the teenagers at the front. 'That was not a big cheer,' said the driver. Hannah whooped.

'Lucky the big boss isn't here,' said Archie.

'Where did you tell him we were going?'

'The Museum of Anthropology. I saw an advert for it at the airport. Smart and cultural.'

'Good call,' said Hannah. 'Sounds a lot better than a bar.'

'Not if he asks me about it,' he replied.

'I was there last year,' she said. 'Great carvings. Tell him about the winged bird men in cases, or the legend of the man whose wife was swallowed by a whale. You see pictures of it everywhere. He rode its back clinging to its fin to rescue her.'

'Difficult to hang on, I would think,' he said. They had flown into the city over Vancouver Bay and seen whales drifting deep under cockleshell boats on the surface. They had looked no bigger than melon pips from the air.

'It's a metaphor for the tenacity of true love,' said Hannah.

'Very metaphorical,' he said.

'Very,' she replied. 'I'll see if I can get you a postcard of it.'

'To lend authenticity to the lie if we bump into Charles.'

'No. To remind you of a great story.'

'Don't get all deep on me,' he said. 'I'm still thinking about the curly fries.'

\* \* \*

He could smell them as he woke. He staggered to the door of his alcove. Mike had frozen chips heating in the microwave. He could smell the fat rising off them. It made him gag. He grabbed his towel and headed for the bathroom.

The radio burbled from its perch as Archie cleaned his teeth. President Kenyatta had ordered a day of national mourning in

Kenya for the shoppers killed in the shopping centre. He switched it off, afraid that the sound of gun-fire would play as the reporter recapped on the events recorded from the next block by journalists crouched in the road – gathering their stories; feeding the media machine; fresh mice dropped into the gaping throat of their pet serpent. In the silence after noise, he could believe himself human again as he shaved, and put on his favourite old T-shirt and joggers from his bag. He added the sunglasses and walked out. 'Breakfast?' shouted Mike as he passed the kitchen, where bacon was sparking in its own universe in the microwave.

'You'll need to get that fixed,' he said.

'It's in hand, my friend,' said Mike. 'My social worker promised me a new cooker in August. Should be here any day. Any day now.'

*   *   *

Archie found the businesswoman waiting under the statue of the unicorn on the old gate-posts to the Meadows. 'You're late,' she said. 'I made it with almost no notice, so should you.'

He had run up the Walk, but tired more quickly than he expected and had had to stroll the last mile. Three miles used to be a warm-up, he thought. 'Hooah,' he said.

'Don't give me any of your American army training shit,' she said, and he knew then that she was going to be a real ball-breaker.

'I've adjusted it to reflect the Christian ethic of the training,' said Archie, wishing he had had enough money to buy a bottle of water.

She stared at him. 'Why are you wearing sunglasses?' she asked. 'It's not exactly bright.'

'Sun damage,' he said. He held his arms up, palms facing upwards like a preacher he had once seen on telly. 'Let's start with the Lord's prayer.'

'No time,' said the woman. 'Let's skip that bit.' She put her foot up on a bench and pushed her thigh forward.

'Don't extend past ninety degrees,' said Archie, 'to protect your knees. Drop your pelvis down towards the ground to feel the stretch. Gently.'

Her clothes were expensive. 'Messenger,' she said, following his gaze. 'Best brand on the market.'

Archie nodded. 'Have you run before?' he asked.

'These aren't new,' she said waving at her training gear. 'I can do twice round the Meadows,' she said. 'I just need some motivation to keep going.'

'I'll give you a meditation to repeat to yourself as you run,' he said. 'Rather than a chant. Let's try ...' he paused, trying to remember what he had typed on his Facebook page last night. 'Let's try ... "Oh, Lord thou art our Father; we are the clay, and thou our potter; and we all are the work of thy hand." Isaiah, 64:7.'

'Eight,' she said. 'Isaiah 64:8. 'I looked at it this morning.'

'Good,' he said. 'Just testing. The idea is that you must make yourself into good clay. Not fill yourself up with crap.'

'I don't eat crap,' she said. 'Just one too many business lunches.'

In his mind's eye he saw a table laden with food: his wedding buffet, the guests breathless from dancing, the ceilidh band drinking cool glasses of beer before the second set. So much laughter – then. So many good things, and Hannah held close; the small bump of her pregnant belly invisible beneath her wedding dress. He dismissed the thought. 'Let's go,' he said.

They began to run. A light mist dripped from the trees. There was a smell of damp leaves.

'Watch you don't slip,' he said. 'You okay with intervals?'

She nodded.

'We'll start with four minutes moderate, one minute fast and repeat. Slower up the hill over the Links. The faster pace in the minute interval will boost your calorie burn.'

He increased the pace. 'Don't let your hands flap across your body. Keep them facing forward in a light grip. He's the potter, I'm the clay,' he chanted.

She glared at him and he fell silent. 'You're the client, hope you'll pay,' he said into himself, and grinned.

'You're loving this aren't you?' she said.

He looked over at her from behind the filter of his glasses. 'What?' he asked.

'Running fat ladies round this hamster track and collecting cash from them, like an ant milking aphids for sugar.'

'Sugar's not good for you,' he said.

'You know what I mean,' she replied. 'It's a power trip for you. Just like the board room. You know what the suits said to me on my first day? Just write your wee name in the book. I mean how fucked is that? I'm top of my field.'

'What field's that?' he asked.

'I'm an actuary,' she said. 'You can thank me for your pension plan later.'

He increased the pace. 'Pump your arms up and down at this point,' he said. 'Burn more calories. Get a better return on your investment.'

He slowed down as a cyclist sped across the path in front of them. Arthur's Seat seeped into view through the mist.

'I've got a stitch,' she said, clutching her side. He stopped. 'Stretch it out,' he said, reaching up. She put her hand in the air and he took it and lifted her arm higher. 'Better?' he asked. 'Keep breathing.' He released her and she took a drink from her bottle.

'Aren't you thirsty?' she asked.

'I tanked up before we started,' he lied. 'Best practice – a drink an hour beforehand, on top of fruit, or an energy bar, consumed two hours before the training session. And don't forget calcium for strong bones. A thousand milligrams a day for your age group. Fifteen-hundred after fifty.'

Fifty. That number, the mid-point of remembering. The man with chained feet, the sinking ship. How long could he hold it back? He wished his mind could become clay – stop jumping and leaping in his head, throwing unwelcome pictures up on the shadow wall inside his skull. He had forgotten to take Dr Clark's pill. 'We'll stop there for the day,' he said to the woman. He couldn't remember her name. 'Let's walk back to our starting point, fit in a plank to strengthen your core muscle and hope that puts paid to stitches in the future. We'll build it into your training regime.'

'How do you know I'm going to hire you?' she asked, plugging in her headphones. 'You must think you're pretty hot.'

He waited, bit his lip with disappointment. 'Just kidding, you bozo,' she said, punching him on the arm.

Hunger had robbed him of resilience. He had nothing left. She tossed her half-empty bottle into the bin when they reached the gate-post with no gate, and walked off. The weathered sandstone unicorn crowned a list of Scottish burghs carved below. Prince Albert's exhibition palace of industry had long since gone, leaving only its gate-posts. 'See you same time Wednesday,' she said over her shoulder. 'And my name is Brenda, since you've obviously forgotten.'

He re-tied his shoes then picked the bottle out of the bin. He was parched. 'Hey,' her voice said behind him. 'What are you doing?'

He turned round, the bottle in his hand.

'I never had you down as a scrounger,' she said.

He looked down at the green plastic bottle, at the liquid inside. The hot surface of his throat contracted. 'Recycling,' he said. 'Can't bear to see all that plastic go into the earth. There's a recycling point over there.' He waved in the direction of the new flats. 'I'm going that way.'

'Okay, man of clay,' she said. 'I wanted to ask you about charting my progress. It would be nice to see the weight dropping off. How about a chart, or something?'

'I'll send you one tonight for you to download and fill in. If it goes well, you might want to put it up on my page to testify, to bear witness for others that ...' he took a deep breath, '... you can slim for Jesus.'

'Amen to that,' she said. 'I'm glad you've got faith.' She pulled forty pounds from a roll in her pocket. 'Here's a small advance. See you next time.' She turned on her heel and jogged off.

He put the bottle in his pocket and walked towards St Philomena's, hoping he hadn't missed breakfast.

# 12

HE GOT BACK TO THE FLAT with a bag of shopping, courtesy of Brenda's money, and climbed into a hot bath filled from the electric shower and three kettles. He poured in two handfuls of Dead Sea bath salts from the health shop and sank down into the slippy water. His muscles softened and he fell asleep. Not dreaming. Floating. Floating out of the past, out of the present, slipping by the promontory of his appointment with Dr Clark, drifting on the sea, a dark, internal sea, the current off-shore.

He washed up at the community garden a mile across the hospital grounds that afternoon. There was no sign of Dr Clark. Petal was there, digging up a line of potatoes. Her flowery dress clung to her back, which was more muscular than he expected. She was wearing green wellies with tiny rhinestones and sequins glued to them. 'Jazzy,' he said, pointing at them, 'Not standard issue.' Picking up a hoe, he marked out a few defensive Tai Chi moves in the air; strike head, right, ribs, left, knees, throat, press down. His sunshine pill shone behind his eyes. He pushed up his glasses. It was brighter inside than out.

'Good to see you,' she said, and he hoped she meant it.

'I'm here to dig for the five thousand,' he said. 'Like that minister in Leith who's trying to feed the hungry.'

'I hear he's run out of food,' she said. 'One of the food banks is empty.'

Archie thought of Mike's hand-outs drying up. 'There's always the pound shop, if you like instant mash and chocolate biscuits.'

She didn't reply and bent to shake the earth from the potatoes' thin roots. 'Autumn is my favourite time,' she said. 'I'm a root veg girl.'

'Five a day?' he asked.

'Minimum. I'll need to introduce you to my beetroot smoothie.'

Archie grimaced. He didn't want to hear the roar of the blender's blades, see the steel cut into the red flesh. 'A cup of tea, and you've got yourself a date,' he replied, trying to smile, but it wasn't working.

'Are you alright?' she asked.

He nodded. 'You know how it is,' he said.

'I don't,' she said. 'You haven't told me.'

'I haven't told anyone,' he said.

She leaned on her spade.

'Where's Joy?' he asked, looking round.

'She's away for an op,' she replied. 'They picked her up this morning. Women's troubles.'

Dr Clark was picking his way between the veggie beds towards them. 'Hide me,' he said to Petal, moving behind her, but Dr Clark was already calling his name and waving.

'You missed your appointment, Archie. That's the bad news, but I have time now. That's the good news.'

'It depends on your point of view,' said Archie.

'What's your point of view?' asked Dr Clark, stooping to pick a nasturtium flower and eating it.

'I'm happy here,' he said.

'No one is happy here, Archie. That's why you're here. Happy is what they do outside this place. Healing is what we do here, and that takes effort.'

Archie passed Petal his hoe with an exaggerated sigh.

\*　\*　\*

Dr Clark's office was just as before. The TV in the common room was blaring. Something about a handshake between President Obama and the new Iranian leader, Rouhani. He remembered his translator in Afghanistan telling him how the Iranians and Syrians hated each other. How the Persians called the Syrians Arabs, and spat. Their governments were friendly but the people were not. Nothing was simple, and now this new détente between America and Iran over Syria: Obama and Rouhani tweeting.

'Nothing to do with putting pressure on Assad,' he said to Dr Clark's back.

The doctor shrugged. 'I don't pay much attention,' he said. 'There's enough going on here.' He waved at the room with its beige walls, like the bank. Neutral.

'I hate beige,' said Archie. 'Everything is wall-to-wall beige.'

'Take a seat,' said Dr Clark. 'How's life?'

Archie shrugged. 'As a closet racist?' he asked, to fill the silence.

'Are you a closet racist, Archie?' asked Dr Clark.

'No, but I might be a fruit-cake.'

'Let's move on, Archie. Keep it professional. You were a professional man, weren't you?' He looked at Archie's notes. 'A financial services lawyer. A lieutenant in the reserves.' He picked up his pen. 'How are you finding the medication? It kicks in more quickly in some people than others. A fortnight is average. It can take a month. No side effects, I hope?'

'Helpful, I think,' said Archie. 'When I remember to take it.'

'Is that difficult?' asked Dr Clark. 'Are things difficult at home?'

'I'm not at home.'

Dr Clark raised his eyebrows and scanned the notes. 'Of course. Forgive me. So where are you staying?'

'The Ritz,' said Archie. 'Also known as The Alcove, 8/6 Skid Row.'

Dr Clark leaned back in his chair.

'Why are you staring at me?'

'I'm observing you. We're going to try something new today. It's called EMDR – that stands for Eye Movement Desensitisation Reprocessing. It was developed by the rather wonderful Francine Shapiro, who posted a study in 1989, in the *Journal of Traumatic Stress*.'

'Couldn't you subscribe to something more cheery?' asked Archie. '*Homes and Gardens, Anglers' Weekly*?'

'She noticed that bringing eye movements under control during the recall of a traumatic event reduced anxiety in the patient, especially when it can be evidenced that PTSD or depersonalisation disorder might be the root problem.'

'What's depersonalisation disorder, Doc?' he asked to slow down the approach of the therapy, but he already knew. It was his body looking out over the Forth on an early morning; it was his figure at the door of his old home; it was the restless sleeper behind the glass wall; it was the calls he had deleted without answering.

'It's very effective,' said Dr Clark. 'We move slowly from Preparation to Desensitisation to Closure.'

It was walking through a minefield. 'I don't really fancy it,' he said.

'I know you are being avoidant, Archie, and that is entirely understandable, but could you at least give it a go? Let's try with a memory you can handle. Nothing approaching the memory you have locked away, but still something upsetting. Something difficult. Perhaps something you trained for?'

'There's no training for the things I saw, Doc,' he said. 'Sticking a bayonet in a straw man is seventy years out of date. We're talking clinical strikes here.' Even as he said it, he saw the ground that had exploded; the sandy road with big slabs of toffee tarmac; toy cars at crazy angles; the boy with the tiny bird on his arm, the black bird on his white arm, stock still, smiling, watching them pass. 'You can't ask me to go there,' he said, 'and then come back here as if it were a holiday and shop in supermarkets, and ride on buses and sign up for the Universal Bloody Credit in your world of abbreviations where everyone has forgotten how to talk to each other, and no one wants to listen.'

'I want to listen,' said Dr Clark.

Archie fell silent.

'If you want to talk,' added Dr Clark. He walked over to the water cooler in the corner and poured Archie a paper cone of water. Archie drank it, then put it between his lips and sat staring at the doctor over his beak.

'Not funny,' said Dr Clark. 'Is this bird ready to sing, or not?'

Archie balled up the paper cone and fired it into the bin under the window. 'Do your worst,' he said, moving to the bed and straightening its paper towel. He lay down.

After thirty seconds of silent recall, he tried not to laugh as

Dr Clark waved his pen from side to side in front of him. He described the ruined road and then replaced his negative cognition with a positive one, as instructed. He saw the road healing itself. The tarmac fitting itself back together in a seamless jigsaw and, by the time he had mentally scanned his body for areas of tension, he had tarmacked a path the length of Afghanistan to Kabul. 'I'll give you a couple of relaxation exercises to practise in tandem with these sessions,' said Dr Clark. 'Remember to replace your NC, negative cognition, with a PC, positive cognition, if this unwelcome memory should intrude at an inappropriate moment. This is about empowering you.'

Archie's eyes flickered.

'You don't look quite so staring,' said Dr Clark. 'Not quite so fixed.'

Archie got up and checked his reflection in the mirror positioned above the sink. It was the same. 'Thanks anyway, Doc,' he said.

Dr Clark passed him a piece of paper. 'I think you should contact this veterans' support group in town,' he said. 'They might be able to help you. You could be eligible for a WCA, Work Capability Assessment, and that might get you off JSA, or Universal Credit, and onto DLA, in the short term at least.'

Archie put it in his pocket. 'Is gobbledegook all anyone speaks nowadays? Gobble. Gobble. Gook. Gook. Gook.'

# 13

AFTER A LONG DAY AT THE HOSPITAL, Petal logged on to her gaming account. Her avatar leapt on screen with her bow on her back. Behind her, mountains spread out in pink and blue. Petal scrolled through the money and weapons in her account, and selected a quest. Negotiations to find the lost mine of Nazar would be difficult with so little gold to bribe the white elves, and the forest was full of serpents. She looked at her map and decided to consult the wizard at Delphium. The Oracle of Hath was too far. Crossing the swamp would be difficult, but if her health was good, she could leap from tussock to tussock. Her fingers flew over her controller and her avatar did a back-flip, landing on the first grassy tussock, sure-footed. Cupid would have to wait. Two hours later she checked her phone. There was a message. 'Great to hear from you,' it said. 'I am a self-employed businessman, forty years old, a bit of a foodie, no ties, and if you would like to meet up for a drink, then text me on this number and I'll see you at The Byzantium Bar at six thirty pm tomorrow.'

'No problem,' she texted back. 'See you there.'

\* \* \*

The guy wasn't what she expected. He was completely bald. Hairless. He stood up as she came into the bar, and held out his hand. 'Calum Ben,' he said, 'of Ben Organics.'

'Petal,' she replied, 'of nothing in particular.'

He put a hand under her arm and steered her to a table at the back. There was a bottle of Chardonnay open. 'Wine okay for you? It's from Burgundy, none of your sweetie water trash. I thought I'd let it breathe.'

She nodded and watched him pour her a glass. He topped up

his own. Not spiked then. She smiled and raised her glass.

'Cheers,' he said. 'I must say your dress looks lovely.' He put the glass back down on the table. 'So what do you do, Petal?'

'I'm an art therapist,' she said. 'I'm working on a felted wall-hanging at one of the local hospitals.'

'Really,' he said. 'Don't think I've ever met an artist before.'

'It's not as glamorous as it sounds. I spend half my time digging in the community garden. Health and food are intertwined, don't you think?'

He nodded. 'I built my fortune on it. Just secured a deal to supply a well-known hotel chain. The dirtier the vegetable the cleaner the money.' He laughed. 'I'm thinking of moving into a range of juices.'

She noticed his nails were very short. 'What about the sulphites in wine,' she asked. 'How far do you take this health kick?'

'Everyone's allowed one vice. Otherwise we'd all be saints.'

She laughed. 'Here's to you, Mr Saintly. Was there ever a Mrs Saintly?'

He nodded. 'Sadly it didn't last. I'm a fallen angel. Thought she could do better elsewhere. My new business venture was slow at first, and she wasn't the most patient of women.'

'I'm sorry to hear that,' said Petal.

'You?' he asked, leaning forward.

She swirled the wine round her glass. 'Never seemed to meet the right bloke,' she said. 'Still single. I mother the people in my classes. That keeps me going.'

'So you want kids?' he asked.

She was surprised by the directness of the question. 'Yes,' she replied. 'I suppose I do.'

'Me too,' he said. 'I'm looking for something serious. A long-term commitment.'

'Let's drink to that,' she said. 'And a second date?'

He clinked her glass. 'I'll take you to a nice little restaurant I know. They build the menu around foraged foods in season. We're talking about a new, joint range called Forage.'

'Like Nigel Farage,' she quipped.

He didn't laugh. 'It's a big market since the horse-meat scandal. Organic produce used to be left on the shelf because it was more expensive. Those were the golden days of freeganism: executive, dot-com hippies raking in designer-supermarket bins at night, feeding themselves and their green principles for nothing on discarded stock.'

Petal smiled. 'You're painting quite a picture.'

'Don't tell me you were one of them?'

'No, I'm a primary gardener,' said Petal. 'You'll find me at the sharp, pointy end of a garden fork. I agree people are prepared to spend a bit more for organic, if they can afford it.'

'Correct,' said Calum, 'and it goes into the pocket of yours truly, now that the hungry customer has been persuaded that antibiotic-saturated meat, factory eggs and pus-filled milk really do sit at the wrong end of the safe-to-hazardous spectrum.'

'Stop,' said Petal. 'That's disgusting.'

'But true. The scary food stories that the media delight in publishing cater to the apprehensions of the amygdala, your radar for danger, and humanity's primary instinct kicks right in: "Avoid what might be dangerous". No rational thought required. It's now an emotional decision. What's safe to eat? It's a whole new field of neuro-economics. "Eco", "green" and "organic" are the magic words that drive our purchasing decisions and make me very rich, even if deep inside the consumer knows it's perfectly okay to eat the shit they always ate. The new golden rule is better safe than sorry whatever the price.'

'As I say, if you can afford it.'

'Don't tell me you're a bleeding heart liberal?'

'No,' said Petal, 'but I do believe in community initiatives. They used to grow veg along the sides of the roads in housing estates in Communist Yugoslavia. I saw it on holiday years ago. We could do that here. Transform our council estates. Plant fruit trees instead of those hellish, hairy green leylandii. Create an orchard city.'

'Careful,' said Calum, 'you'll put me out of business.'

'I thought you said you were marketing yourself to the designer end of anxious foodies?'

'I am.' He drained his glass. 'I have very particular tastes myself. I like to go against the flow; fugu is a favourite, it really gets the amygdala shrieking. Blowfish tetrodotoxin is not for the faint hearted, but I've had the luck of the devil so far.'

* * *

That night at home she googled his company, but there was no sign of it. She tried spelling Ben with two 'n's. Perhaps it was registered off-shore, or was a subsidiary? She wasn't sure how these things worked. He wasn't on LinkedIn or Facebook either. Maybe that fitted with the alternative, organic kick. Well, it wouldn't hurt to go for a meal in a public place. She drained the beans in her slow-cooker and put them in single-portion sizes in her freezer. It would be nice to have male company.

# 14

Archie was standing at the end of his garden among the shrubs, his back pressed to the wall. He could see his wife through the window of the extension. She was feeding Daniel, swooping a spoon of baby-mush into his mouth as he played with a piece of chopped apple. The baby reached out to her and she lifted him out of his high chair and put him to her breast. His legs kicked as he drank. She opened a magazine on the table and paused while reading it to stroke his hair. He could see her lips moving as she sang to him. His son looked up at her and laughed. It was the last feed before bath-time. Above him a bird chattered. All was well but not for him. He was lonely. He had treasured feeling the weight of his new son strapped to his chest on the way to the paper shop on Sundays; the shape of his floppy limbs; the feel of his tiny foot cupped in his hand as he walked. Hannah had often been too tired to come with them to their favourite café on the shore after the birth. He had missed their small rituals: the office stories she told him to make him laugh; her impressions of her golf-mad boss.

Archie emptied the peanut feeder into his pocket and slipped back out through the gate into the alley. He had told her to get a padlock to secure the hasp, but the gate still flapped. He walked down Ferry Road towards Leith and into Great Junction Street. He fancied a beer to go with his peanuts, but the supermarket would only sell him a four pack. He paid with the money from Brenda and reckoned that still left him enough to pay Mike his rent. He would get more money from Louise in their session tomorrow. If he went to bed early, maybe he wouldn't feel hungry. When he got in, Mike groaned at the sight of the beer shining through the plastic bag. 'How could you, man?' he said. 'I told you what happens to me on the anti-booze if I take even one sip. Do you want to see my face go beetroot, and my blood pressure fall into my boots? Do you want to see me crashing into the furniture because I don't know which way is up? And a word to the wise, you'd better dive for cover when I start spewing unless you have a bloody huge umbrella. Get that fucking beer out of here.'

Archie backed out into the stair and sat on the top step drinking his cans and nibbling his peanuts. He had a bit of small talk with himself, for old times' sake. The party guests were standing in his head, holding glasses of champagne. He mingled among them hiding his beer behind his back. 'Yes, we had a great holiday in the south of France; it's a gite we take every year, but we thought we might book Cambodia this year. Yes, fabulous food from the floating markets. You haven't tasted fresh fish until you've shopped for it on Lake Tonlé Sap.' He was warming up. 'A great squid ink reduction at that new restaurant on Morrison Street? Five star? Yes, lunch? I'll call you. Is that the time? I really must go. So sorry to cut our evening short – early flight tomorrow. Business in Vancouver.' He tucked the last can into his jacket, and opened the door.

'I'm clean,' he said to Mike as he went back in. He lay on the bed in his alcove. The glass bricks were a turquoise waterway. He picked up his phone and called his old home number. 'Hello,' said Hannah.

'Hannah, it's Archie. Don't hang up.' His speech was slow and slurred. He drew a deep breath.

'What do you want?'

'I want to ask you a question.'

There was silence.

'About Vancouver.'

'Couldn't you google it?'

'What was the mountain called?'

'The one with the cable car?'

'And the lumber-jacks shinning up poles in that cheesy show.'

'Grouse Mountain.'

'That's it. I couldn't remember.'

'Look, this isn't a good time.'

'Do you remember the sign we saw about the bear on the loose? The one we saw after we'd been through the woods.' He laughed.

'Why are you asking me this, Archie?'

'I was thinking about our happy times.' He could hear Daniel crying. 'Why is Daniel crying?'

'Mum's trying to settle him.'

'Is he okay?'

'Yes. Look, I need to go.' He heard her draw a deep breath. 'Archie? I don't know how to say this any other way. I don't think you should call again.'

'I didn't mean to bother you,' he said. 'I was ...' he paused, '... at a party and I wanted to hear your voice.'

The line went dead.

'Hannah?' He swung his feet over the edge of the bed and pressed redial. It went straight to the answering machine. 'I'm sorry, no one is available to take your call and you cannot leave a message.' He hung up and opened the last can under his cover to muffle the sound from Mike.

# 15

'Here comes the man of mystery,' said Louise as he ran up, out of breath. He had slept in. It had taken him longer than he thought to design Brenda's training plan, and Bible-dip to find this morning's quote for Louise. Ed Miliband had been on the telly proclaiming, 'If you can't tell the difference between me and Cameron, just remember he's the one who brought in the bedroom tax. I'm the one who's going to abolish it.' There was a shot of the conference floor, Ed Balls looking dewy-eyed.

'Where's Sooze?' he asked.

Louise shrugged. 'We're not joined at the hip. This is Benjy,' she said, indicating the two-year-old in the buggy behind her. 'I had to bring him with me today. My mum's sick.'

'Hey, Benjy,' he said. He turned to Louise. 'How's this going to work?' he asked, hoping she might cancel. His head was foggy after the beer.

'I'll fast walk, and push him. It'll be more of a work-out,' she said. 'Like those yummy-mummies with their running groups and jogging buggies.' He thought of the mums' army he had seen on a circuit round the Meadows, chatting, a brisk woman running alongside them with a whistle.

'So what's today's quote?' asked Louise.

'He took the seven loaves and the fishes, and gave thanks, and brake them, and gave to his disciples, and the disciples to the multitude. And they did all eat … Matthew 15:36.'

'And your point would be?' said Louise.

'We can all eat if we share?' said Archie, his voice going up at the end.

'Are you saying I'm eating more than my fair share?' asked Louise. 'Because I am this close to dumping you.' She pinched her fingers together.

'I don't know what I'm saying,' he said. 'I was thinking of the food banks in Leith.'

'What's that to do with you?' asked Louise.

'Nothing,' he lied, picturing Mike's tins. 'Food is a resource and we need to understand our place in relation to it.'

'Are you going all eco-righteous on me?' she asked, 'because I've got my own multitude to feed here.' She waved at the pram. Her son had fallen asleep.

'Why don't we do some body conditioning?' he suggested. 'There's no point in busting a gut when you still have to push His Majesty home.'

She smiled. 'Let's get started,' she said, 'and then I'll take you for a coffee if you behave. You look like you could do with one.' She tried a star jump and then clutched her groin.

He helped her up. 'Follow my lead,' he said. 'Marching on the spot.' He began to pump his arms and feet. He looked along the path, narrow, stippled with sunlight, then stopped. He saw the man ahead of him sweeping for mines, watched him place his feet; sweep, step, heard the ping of ... a bell. Archie turned too late. A cyclist swerved to avoid him. 'For Christ's sake, man,' he shouted at Archie, and gestured. 'Are you crazy, or what?' He straightened his bike and pushed off.

Archie watched his helmet receding and, in a time-slip, saw him fly through the air, silhouetted in the light of an explosion; a starfish spinning; saw his limbs detach and catch in the trees. He felt for his belt pack to find a bin bag to put the body parts in. Take them to the freezer back at camp. Nothing. The feel of his own belly.

He looked down to see Louise touching his arm. 'Are you okay? Why don't we have that coffee now?' she asked, 'and come back to this?'

He nodded.

'I'll still pay you,' she said. 'I really just fancy a chat. Anyway, you've got a face like a sheet. You're not much of a superman.'

They sat at a table outside Sooze's usual café, squeezed against the wall, cyclists and joggers rolling past. He supposed they looked like a family: mum and dad enjoying a day with their son, his hair cherubic, gold and curling. Benjy was nibbling an egg roll, the yoke running down his chin. Archie leaned forward to mop it up with a thin paper napkin. 'Just leave him,' said Louise, 'he's a fussy eater. This is good.' She smiled at her son. 'Wish I had his problem,' she said. 'I'm thinking of having my stomach stapled. Save me all this effort.'

He drew a deep breath. 'It could be hormonal, as you say. Or a food intolerance,' he added. The coffee was calming him down. He drew another breath. The air smelled of damp grass and mouldering leaves.

She shrugged. 'The doctor tells me I'm borderline diabetic. How's that for a sticky end? Killed by a bun.'

'Don't get surgery,' he said. 'I've heard fasting is good. You can drink fruit juice so it's not too painful.' He thought of the weight he had lost since coming back. 'It really works. Why not try it once a week to start and build up from there?'

'Or why don't I just tie a really huge rubber band round my middle? That should suck it all in and then I can forget about it. I won't need to wrestle with myself.'

'You're not alone,' he said. 'I go ten rounds with myself every night.'

'But you're so thin,' she said. She passed Benjy a carton of juice and stood up. 'Well, I'd love to stay and chat, but I have to get this bundle of fun to the park before he goes nuts.'

Archie wondered why it made him feel lonely. 'What about the rest of your session?' he asked.

'Too full. We'll start properly next time. Promise. Don't tell Sooze. You should try and get a few more clients. I'll see you on Thursday.'

He watched her walking away, saw her open the gate to the playpark and release Benjy from his pushchair. A woman waved to her from a bench and she sat down beside her. He tried to put the call with Hannah out of his mind, but he heard her voice replaying: 'I don't know how to say this, Archie.' It echoed in his head. 'Say this any other way.' He leaned back in his chair and tipped his head up to look at the sky, as if he could dislodge the hard pebble of the sound. 'Don't call' – and then the hard click of the answering machine: 'I'm sorry, you cannot leave a message.'

'Fuck,' he said, under his breath. 'Fuck. Fuck. Fuck.' He closed his eyes. When he opened them again, the women had gone from the park.

Karim came out to wipe the table. 'I'm seeing you around here a lot these days,' he said. 'Sooze is still so grateful to you for saving her ridiculous dog. Want anything to eat?'

Archie nodded.

'Fancy a change from the usual fry-up? A little house speciality? Kebab karaz?'

'A kebab?' said Archie.

'Not just any kebab,' said the man. 'My mother's special recipe from Damascus.' He waved at the sign above the door. 'The City of Jasmine, aka Damascus. Lamb meatballs cooked with cherries and cherry paste, pine nuts, sugar and pomegranate molasses.'

Archie remembered the pomegranates he had eaten staking out the Green Zone, sheltered from the burning sun but not the eyes of the dickers. Eyes like pips.

'Sure,' he said. He thought of his promise to include recipes on his website. 'Is that a recipe you could share?'

'I'll see,' said Karim. 'If you clean your plate, you can have my recipe. It was good enough for St Thomas, one of our most famous Damascene residents, so it'll be good enough for you. Guaranteed.'

Somehow Archie had always pictured the apostle tucking into a dry crust. Karim passed him a menu. 'This is for special customers,' he said. There were no pictures. Just names, a long list of spells: kibbeh, wara'enab, tabbouleh, fattoush, and ingredients that spoke of an oasis – orange, rose water, dates, pistachios, tamarind sherbet, mint lemonade.

'No sparrow's tongue?' he asked.

Karim took out his pad and sighed.

'Just joking,' he said. 'You could contribute recipes to my fitness website and I'll advertise your café. What do you say?'

'What's your website called again?' he asked.

'Slim for Jesus.'

Karim raised his eyebrows. 'You know that's one of the signs of the end of the world, trading faith for gain.'

'Do you think so? Is it Gog and Magog?'

'Keep your hair on,' said Karim. 'I'm just saying.'

'I'm doing what I have to do to survive.'

'You're a bit touchy today,' he said.

'Anyway, you've got a picture of Jesus on your wall. What's that all about?'

'I never got round to taking it down when I took over this place,' said Karim. 'It reminds me of mum. Christian. Caused a few ructions when she married my dad, I can tell you. He died a few years ago now.'

Archie sank his chin onto this chest and breathed out. A tear dripped onto the table. 'Sorry, mate,' he said. 'I've got a lot on.'

Karim touched his shoulder. 'You wait here,' he said. 'I'll get you sorted out.'

\* \* \*

Karim's food had spread an unfamiliar warmth through Archie's limbs, and he wandered over to a bench on the Meadows to enjoy the moment. Beneath Prince Albert's sundial, three students with long hair waved wooden swords at each other. One appeared to be called Frost-light, and he blocked his opponent's blows with a round shield cut from a piece of hardboard. They circled each other in a slow-motion imitation of a film fight, balancing on the balls of their feet. A blow landed on the shield and a bit of the Celtic knot painted there flaked off. Frost-light wiped at it with his index finger. 'You'll pay for that,' he said, and ran at his opponent, who stabbed him in the gut.

Archie thought of the ANA recruits fixing bayonets to their SA80s. The top of the blade was blunt like the students' swords but could slide between the ribs and part them, leaving the heart a sitting duck. The sharp point would pierce the beating muscle, emptying the blood from its chambers to rush in a chaotic water-fall into the gut. He had seen the veins of the victim become flaccid and close, their vital energy fatally disrupted. He had seen the lassitude of death glaze their eyes.

'Frosty,' shouted a voice.

Archie opened his eyes. Frosty was staggering about pretending to die, his legs taking stagey strides as he dropped to his knees and rolled over onto his back. His eyes stared up at the sky.

Archie stood up and clapped. The dead Frosty threw him the bird. Archie took a step towards him. Frosty's friend raised his sword above his head, its point towards Archie. 'Come on then,' he said, 'if you think you're hard enough.'

Archie dropped into a crouch. There was something in his eyes.

The student straightened up and dropped his sword arm to his side, 'For fuck's sake, man,' he said. 'It's just a game.'

Archie stood up, pushing his thighs upright. He was growing taller, gigantic; his head shot into the trees; the height was dizzying. 'Sorry,' he said, holding his arms out, palms up. 'Sorry.' He was the wrong size. What had Dr Clark said about side effects? He tried to laugh but it came out as a groan.

Frosty grabbed his bag. 'Let's get out of here,' he said to his friends.

# 16

AFTER COUNTING THE FIFTEEN RECORDS on his ceiling for the third time, Archie sat up in his bed behind the glass wall and dialled the first help-line number he had googled. His memories were flying down the line in the shooting game of his mind: big purple shapes, dismembered limbs, pink regrets. He couldn't hit them out of the air – zero points for a miss; twenty-five birds and counting. No score.

'Good evening,' said a voice. 'FCC – Frontline Compassion and Care is committed to your well-being. Jo speaking. How can I help you?'

Archie was silent. 'If you could give me your name, in your own time,' said Jo. 'There's no rush.'

'My name is Archie.' It was all he had left.

'Hello, Archie.'

There was that silence again. The listening silence. He didn't know how to fill it.

'How can I help you?' Jo asked.

His throat felt tight.

'Would you like to give me your number in case we get cut off and I can ring you back?' Her voice was Bitchin' Betty on a good day, clear and measured, leading the Apache into attack.

He gave her the number, numbers like coordinates. He saw his finger tracing on a map at school. What is at map reference 159, 261? A church? A post office? An ancient monument with old ghosts, their faces turned up to the stars? More coordinates – fast air, explosions, danger close and deadly.

'I'm having a few problems,' he said. His voice was rough. His nose was filling with water and he began to cry. He lay back on the mattress, the tears pouring down his face, running onto the sheet.

'Just let go, Archie,' said Jo.

'That's what I am afraid of,' he said. 'Letting go.'

'Are you getting any help at the moment?' she asked.

He nodded. The glass wall swam. 'Yes,' he said. 'A bit.'

'Can you tell me where that is?'

'The Greenford Hospital in Edinburgh with Dr Clark. I have three sessions left.'

'And are you on any medication at the moment?'

'SSRIs.'

'Serotinin specific re-uptake inhibitors?'

'Yes.' He wondered when he had begun to speak the language.

'And is that helping?'

'I can't tell,' he said. 'I don't know what it would be like without them.'

'I'm assuming you're ex-army as you chose to call this help-line, so I am inferring that you might have been prescribed SSRIs for a traumatic injury, or PTSD.'

'Yes,' he replied. 'PTSD.'

'Then I can tell you that Lady Justice Hale set out sixteen propositions relating to an employer's duty of care in her judgement on four cases of stress-related psychiatric injury in 2002. This means that you are entitled to help. I would strongly recommend that you get in touch with Combat Stress Now, the veterans' support group.'

It was the one that Dr Clark had recommended. 'Okay,' he said.

'Do you have anyone at home to help you, Archie?'

'No,' he said. 'I'm alone.'

'Can you tell me more about that?'

'I can't talk about it.' He pressed the red phone symbol to end the call. The phone rang back, but he didn't answer.

Behind the glass-brick wall, the microwave floor show began again, sparks flying. He could see Mike shadow dancing to the music on his headphones, sketching the outline of a figure in the air, and singing, 'Hey, angel.'

# 17

By morning Karim had emailed him his mother's recipes, along with a picture of her outside the Grand Mosque in Damascus where John the Baptist was buried. She was smiling at the camera. He wondered where she was now, if she had left Syria, like Karim. The pictures of the shattered cities of Homs and Aleppo had vanished from the news. There were no more pictures of civilians choking on gas. Perhaps she was in a desert camp. Perhaps she was trapped somewhere. He wondered whether, if Obama bombed Damascus, John the Baptist's head would blow right into the air like a football. American style. Would anyone be there to catch it? Touchdown in the end zone with no interception. The end of an era.

He got a drink of water from the kitchen, then came back to the computer and deleted half the sugar from Karim's recipes, credited the café and set out for his appointment with Brenda. 'It's 07.05,' she said, when he ran up. 'You're late.' The sky was pink and blue with thin wisps of cloud drifting across its face.

'I'm sorry,' he said. 'It won't happen again.'

'You're lucky I'm in a good mood.' She pulled her ear-plugs out and pocketed her phone. 'The best news: it looks like Miliband is going to lose Labour the next election. He's gone all Red Ed, freezing fuel prices and stopping the swing voters in their tracks. Until his conference speech, they were all set to vote him back in. He's sent the seventeen per cent drift from the Con–Dem coalition running back to Cameron with their tails between their legs. Cheers, Ed.' She gave a mock salute. 'Shall we get started? I know, shouldn't mix politics and pleasure. Just had to share.'

He tried to smile, moved his lips back over his teeth and then looked down, unable to relax his cheeks. He drew a deep breath. 'I want you to pretend you're exercising in water,' he said. 'Take the warm-up slow, and stretch through the length of the muscle.' He jumped his feet wide, raised his arms in a starburst across his face in slow motion and lifted his chest up. 'Lift the chest to open. Chin to chest and then open your arms out to the side and repeat. Now, drop the heel of the back leg to stretch the calf.'

'Let's skip the warm-up,' she said, 'I have a meeting at eight thirty.'

Archie ignored her comment. 'Imagine the water is up to your chest.'

She folded her arms. 'I don't buy this water metaphor. It's fitness class not a rehearsal for global warming. Talking of which, did you see that intergovernmental report, the IPCC; claims we're ninety-five per cent responsible. The sea will be up eighty centimetres by the end of the century. Lucky we won't be here.'

A picture of his son floating past in orange arm-bands popped into his mind. He laughed. He had been the only dad at the water babies class.

'Sometimes I wonder about you,' she said. 'You don't seem quite right.'

He stopped waving his arms about. 'Let's run,' he said.

'Amen to that,' replied Brenda.

# 18

THE NEXT DAY ARCHIE WAS SURPRISED to see Petal standing with Sooze and Louise beneath the unicorn pillar. 'Hello, stranger,' he said to Petal as he came to a halt beside them.

'Oh, God,' Archie,' she said. 'I never thought you ran Slim for Jesus, not in a million years. This was the only local class that fitted in with my time off.'

'Yeah,' he said. 'Part-time nut-job, part-time personal trainer. It's a balancing act.'

She took his arm and leaned forward to whisper. 'I can't stay. It's against the rules. Professional distance.'

'How about one session now you're here? You don't need to pay me.'

She stepped back. 'I suppose that might be alright,' she said.

The women smiled at her. The Papillon pushed his head out of the rucksack on Sooze's back. 'Couldn't you leave him at home?' Archie asked. 'If you're serious about this?'

'I'm not serious about this,' she replied, 'I'm here to give Louise some moral support.'

He sighed.

'But I could leave him with my cousin at the café, if it's bothering you,' she added.

'You know Karim?' he asked.

She nodded. 'I'm sure I told you, he's my cousin.'

Archie felt like he was missing so many connections these days, simple social connections that everyone else could see. His brain was still hard-wired into the past; searching for tell-tale movements as he walked down streets, the shadow of a raised arm that heralded sniper-fire, half-glimpsed, before the red-hot searing of a bullet passing too close. He saw Sooze's lips were still moving in a slow-motion continuation of their conversation. He had tuned her out – '... so no clever-clogs stickers for you,' she finished, and smiled. 'Like at school.'

He stared at her, her allusion clear now, and remembered Prince Charles pinning a medal to his chest last year, when he still found sand between the pages of books he had read in Afghanistan; and he saw Birkhall over the Prince's epaulets, its gingerbread-house perfection iced in white; its gardens; its old-world order; the smiling monarch-in-waiting presiding over it all. There on the Meadows, as the women waited, re-tied shoe laces, fussed over the dog and stretched, all the while watching him, his own home came into focus, just as it ever was, and he wondered why he didn't fit in there any more; which piece of him was missing; what event had fired that key connector out of his life so that everything was jumbled?

Petal was rubbing the dog's ears and it yelped and tried to lick her hand with a small, pink tongue. 'Get down,' Sooze said, reaching behind her shoulder to push him back into the bag. Archie flinched and crouched, throwing his arms over his bent head – the trip-wire of words triggering small and deadly explosions of memory that continued to maim him. There were so many pitfalls. He dropped his arms and touched the ground. The women were staring at him now. 'Just checking the going,' he said, drawing a deep breath. 'It's fair.'

'We've not had rain for ages,' said Petal, frowning.

He jumped up. 'Let's start with a thought for the day,' he said. 'Let's try "He knew me in my mother's womb", and let's think of our perfection before we were born into the complicated choices of this life and ask when did we begin to make the wrong choices.' He looked at the group of women: Faith, Hope and Charity. 'The wrong food choices,' he said, correcting himself. 'You two aren't too bad,' he said to Sooze and Petal.

'Oh, thanks,' said Louise.

'Sorry,' said Archie.

'You've got a lot to apologise for,' said Louise.

'You're probably right. Intervals?' said Archie, and they began to jog on the timings he had introduced in Brenda's session. As they slowed to a walk behind him, he heard the women chatting, Petal saying something about replying to a lonely hearts column. 'For God's sake, don't do that,' he said over his shoulder. 'He could be anyone.'

'I wasn't talking to you, nosey,' said Petal.

He turned back to the path and increased the pace, glancing at his phone. One minute would take them to Middle Meadow Walk. His mind drifted back to his wife. Hannah had looked so beautiful on their first real date; walking up Schiehallion, picking the first of the brambles on the way down and putting them in his mouth. They had stopped at the world's oldest yew tree near Glen Lyon. Its roots had self-renewed for two thousand years, tangled snakes coiled in the black, crumbly earth.

Louise's voice was shouting something on the margins of this happy place, and he looked back to see the bike crash into Petal. She fell in a tangle of arms, legs and wheels. The guy was picking up his bike, rubbing his knees and shouting, 'It's a fucking cycle path, you morons. You have to give way.'

Archie ran over and punched him; felt his fist connect with his chin; enjoyed the flesh giving way under his knuckles, the contact.

'Archie. Stop,' shouted Petal. She was clutching her ankle. 'It was an accident.'

'Yeah, get the facts right,' said the cyclist, swinging his leg over his bike and cycling off. 'I could do you for assault.'

Archie pulled Petal to her feet. Her ankle buckled and he lowered her back onto the grass. 'Do you think it's broken?' he asked, pressing gently along the line of the bone. 'Is that painful?'

'I think it's just sprained,' she said.

'You'll need to ice it,' he replied. 'The sooner the better.'

'If you could help me home,' she said, pointing to the flats of Warrender Park Terrace, 'I'm just over there, and there are lots of bags of peas in the freezer. Organic, of course,' she joked.

He looked at Sooze and Louise. 'Do you mind?'

They shook their heads. Sooze lowered her rucksack to the ground and let the dog out. Archie hoisted Petal onto his back.

She laughed. 'I haven't had a piggy back since I was five,' she said.

He enjoyed her warmth as he straightened up, his forearms under her thighs. Sooze and Louise wandered off to the café. 'No charge for today,' he called after them and they waved, the dog running at their feet, his little ears flying.

* * *

Petal lived on the ground floor; her flat was reached by a tiled path that crossed from the pavement over the concrete garden of the basement flat below. Plant pots full of sunflowers, with beans twisting round their stems, lined the path. Small plastic figures hiked up their stalks, roped on with garden wire. 'What's this?' he laughed, pointing to a green, plastic elf no bigger than a pea-pod.

'It's a modernist twist on the garden gnome,' she said. 'I'm a gamer. Frankie the Conjurer after the wonderful Francine Shapiro, the therapist, you know?'

He nodded at the tiny figures climbing towards the sun. 'Blink and you miss them,' he said.

'Something like that,' she replied.

Her flat was full of antiques, old throws and felted wall-hangings. 'How can you afford a place like this?' he asked.

'It was my Granny's,' she replied. 'I looked after her at the end of her life and she left me this. The family are loaded, so no one objected.'

'So the fluffy, green thing is just an act?' he said.

'No,' she replied. 'Are you really that stupid?'

He put her down on an old blue velvet recliner in the bay window and propped a cushion made from a faded shirt under her foot. 'I'll get that ice,' he said.

Her kitchen was full of pots of herbs and windfall apples, their green skin mottled with black spots. In the garden, two hens scratched round a plastic igloo.

'You must have fun keeping them safe from urban foxes,' he shouted through the hall. He heard her laugh.

'The neighbours are more of a pest. I have to bribe them with eggs so they don't report me to the council.'

He carried the ice, and some painkillers he had found in a cupboard above the sink, through to her.

She had a controller in her hand and was logging onto some kind of game. Options scrolled up the screen. Luminous green numbers flickered and bleeped as she selected them.

'Would you mind turning that off?' he asked, rubbing his forehead.

'I thought it might distract me from the pain,' she said.

He waved the paracetamol and extra-strength codeine at her. 'No thanks,' she said. 'I prefer not to take anything unless it gets unbearable. Those were for a disc I slipped two years ago. Classic gardening injury.' She popped on the news channel. David Cameron, the prime minister, was at his party conference, talking to camera about hard-working people. A huge banner behind him proclaimed 'For hard-working people'. 'Maybe they should put a comma after hard?' suggested Petal.

He laughed. In America, the federal government was paralysed, its offices closed, unable to agree a budget with the Republicans over their protest at the Democrats' ObamaCare health plan. Chemical weapons inspectors were going into Syria to disable chemical weapons. 'Could you switch that off too, please,' he said. 'I hate politicians.'

'Picky, aren't you? I can't believe they shut the Statue of Liberty to visitors,' she added, snapping off the images.

He looked round the room. 'I suppose I should go,' he said, unsure where to sit in the clean house, full of the relics of a long family life: the photos on the mantelpiece, the side-board full of crystal sherry glasses, the book cases and patchwork cushions. 'This is paradise,' he said.

'This old stuff,' laughed Petal. 'It's flotsam. I always think I should thin it out and de-junk, but somehow it works just the way it is.'

'It does,' he said. 'It's a rare pearl!' And he wished he had a photo of his grand-parents and his son so that he could stand in his place between them, tying them together through the years with the simple things that mattered: the forks they'd eaten with, the glasses they'd drunk from, the books they'd read and laughed over, the piano they'd played. He wondered when the digital age had got hold of everyone, eaten into their every waking moment so that there was no time to sit by the fire and reflect on the whole picture, thinking backwards and forwards, before taking decisions. The thing he missed most, standing in this snapshot of an old world, was the time to talk things over with family, sitting on well-worn sofas, in flickering firelight that invited secrets and ancestral memory of longer passages of time – like seasons, or stars growing in their nurseries, or planets in their orbits. This press-button society, with its phoney, first-name intimacy; this remembering with strangers and therapists, to counts of one hundred; kindness and time measured out, quantified and paid for somewhere, by someone, didn't work; and the cost, the real cost was unacknowledged, flaring briefly in support groups and chat rooms – thin, typed lines of isolation, grief and remorse for decisions that snapped, crackled and popped.

'I need to go,' he said.

'Yeah, that would probably be best,' she replied. 'You're still a client.'

'As opposed to what?' he asked. 'A friend? A good Samaritan?'

'You know what I mean. I have to think of my job.' She paused.

'Maintain that professional distance?' he suggested.

'Got it in one,' she replied.

'Understood, Ma'am,' he said, saluting. 'You're the boss.' He turned on his heel and marched on the spot, set off across the carpet in slow time, arms swinging up to the level of his chest.

'Stop taking the piss,' she said. 'I'll see you at the hospital.'

'For another session with the woodland folk?' He tapped the side of his head.

She stopped laughing. 'Show some respect,' she said. 'Is that so difficult?'

'Sorry,' he mumbled. 'Sorry.'

# 19

PETAL LAY BACK on her chaise-longue in the bay window. She could see Archie through the scratched glass walking across the grass to the Meadows with the castle high on its rock behind him. His arms still swung in time to a march only he could hear, although he seemed unconscious of it, and then, without breaking stride, he began to run; slow at first, then faster. He ignored the lights and ran straight across the main road dissecting the park, and onto the track worn between the trees. He increased his pace and became a flickering zoetrope – man, tree, man, tree, as he passed between the trunks. She saw him pass her view-point twice in the distance; a running man, dwarfed by the castle rock and lazy Arthur's ghost on top of his mountain. She knew almost nothing about him, or what he was running from, what pursued him – hobgoblins from his shattered mind jumping and leaping along the path behind him; goblins who knew he would never outrun them because he was connected to them by strings of remorse, long and sticky – perhaps with human blood. She couldn't imagine him – this ex-lieutenant – as a killer; couldn't connect his evident humanity with lifting a gun, pressing his eye to the sight, and firing down the cross-hairs of his decision to take a life in that single instant when it somehow made sense. She saw from her sofa in the bay window of an Edinburgh flat, remote from the conflict, that the decision to take a life, or lives, still burning and smouldering in him, had never been his, but had already been framed, remotely, by players at computers. He was their avatar but he carried the burden of choices that looked different now because they were reviewed from a distance without the catalyst of the heat and the panic, and the fear and the smell, and the noise. How did he feel now, without Death pulling a finger down the back of his neck to chill him, about those decisions made in a hot desert with the breath of the grave-mouth condensing on his back? Now, alone on the planet of his daily life, his insignificance in the scheme of things was apparent, and his right to have been so mighty a player in question. She guessed that his first doubts were revolving in the finite universe of his mind, where he stood – a lonely Adam – the apple in his hand a time-bomb.

Her eyes closed and she dropped off, a small figure in a large room, and she woke only when her neighbour's voice and a dog barking sounded in the common stair. The front door banged shut behind them. Mrs Robb upstairs was looking after her friend's dog while she was in hospital, and Petal had become familiar with the scrabble of his claws on the floorboards. He wasn't the friend-liest-looking animal. He had been muzzled since some incident of the Meadows the week before. Mrs Robb passed doggie treats through the plastic bars of his muzzle, which gave him the look of a four-legged and very tiny Hannibal Lecter, his eyes velvety and reproachful.

Petal's ankle throbbed as she stood up and tried to put some weight on it, so she crunched up two of the old painkillers and swallowed them with a glass of water. She wasn't going to miss her first second date in three years, even if it was with Baldilocks. They could always talk gardening if conversation ran out: how to mulch strawberries, encourage worms in compost and whether his business venture could take some of the hospital's produce.

She put on a vintage silk dress from a charity shop along with a shawl, and grabbed a stick from the back of the wardrobe. It had an elephant's head carved on it. Granny had said it was Ganesh.

The taxi driver dropped her off outside the restaurant Calum had mentioned on their first date, but there was no sign of him. The street was empty and the place was closed, a padlock on a metal grille fixed over its door. She read the menu stuck in the window. He drew up five minutes later in his car and called her over. 'Sorry,' he said. 'Bad choice. I forgot they were shut for refur-bishment. I know another place just round the corner. His eyes took in her stick and he smiled. 'Jump in,' he said, 'I'll drive you round.'

The car door swung open. Her foot was throbbing after standing on it. 'I'm really sorry, but would you mind just taking me home?' she said. 'I've sprained my ankle. I thought I could ignore it but being out is making it worse.'

'Okay, no problem, granny.' He climbed out of the car and helped her slide into the passenger seat. 'Your wish is my command,' he said, a Prince Charming. He shut the door and, walking round the car, settled himself in the driver's seat. He patted his knee and smiled. 'Put your foot up here,' he said. 'I'll take a look.' He leaned over and guided her foot over the gearstick to his knee. His aftershave was dizzying. He pushed the hem of her dress back up her leg to her knee. His hands were warm as they slid down her calf to her foot. He cupped her heel in one hand and stroked the puffy skin of her ankle with the other. She tried to pull it away.

'Trust me, I'm a doctor,' he said with a laugh. 'Can you move it?' Grasping her toes, he moved her foot clockwise and then anti-clockwise. His fingers were very strong. 'It's a bit stiff and swollen,' he said.

'No shit, Sherlock,' she replied.

'Permit me to kiss it better.' He lifted her foot up to his mouth and bent to kiss the top of her arch.

'Don't,' she said, pushing her dress back down her leg. 'I hardly know you.'

'Your feet are so beautiful,' he said. 'So much nicer than mine. I couldn't resist.'

'I really need to get home,' she said.

He released her foot and stared at the road ahead. A Halloween pumpkin dangled from his rear-view mirror. Its gaping eyes swung round to stare at her as the car reversed. 'I'm disappointed, of course,' said Calum, putting the car into first gear, 'but your wish is my command.' He glanced over at her and drew a deep breath. 'I don't suppose you would agree to a short detour? We could park up on the coast at Longniddry Bents and admire the view over the Forth. It would feel like less of a wasted evening and you wouldn't need to put any weight on your poor foot. Just sit back and sip the best champagne money can buy. I've got a bottle in the back.'

'I'm flattered,' said Petal, 'but I think I should go home.'

He turned the corners of his mouth down and slumped his shoulders. 'I'm crushed,' he said.

She looked at him. The first man she had dated for years. She liked his hands. The way his strong fingers gripped the steering wheel. His touch had warmed her. It was odd how little physical contact she had with anyone these days. It amazed her that she could live in a city full of people and only really be touched by her hairdresser, or friends as they met at the pub. The number changed on the clock on the dashboard, another minute gone. Time passing in a series of digital numbers, and another night alone in front of the telly, or gaming, ahead of her. 'Okay,' she said, 'one glass.'

He turned to her and smiled. 'I know the perfect place.'

# 20

ARCHIE TUCKED THE TEDDY he had bought his son as a belated birthday present into his sweatshirt and walked over to his old house. He was feeling better after an afternoon snooze and one of Mike's sparky bacon butties. He slipped into the garden by the back gate, still unlocked, and pressed himself against the wall as before. It smelled of leaf mould. At his feet a woodlouse crawled past. A blackbird tossed over some dry leaves, looking at the ground with a sunshine-yellow eye and turned over the next leaf; a diner making informed choices in his black tuxedo, which glistened green.

Through the window, Archie could see his wife carrying dishes to the kitchen sink and then she opened the back door and let their son wheel out in his walker onto the patio. He had small cubes of cheese on the tray on the front. His tiny legs pushed forward and he rolled onto the grass, pushing faster, moving across the lawn towards Archie's hiding place beyond the border. Archie slid to his knees and lay down along the base of the wall, the leaf mould pressing into his cheek. A smell of cat pee, or fox, made him gag. His son came closer, taking tiny steps, pushing the walker forward with his chest until he stopped at a shrub and reached out to pull a leaf. His hair was blond now, curling round his ears, and his cheeks were red with teething. He pulled at the leaf and the shrub above Archie rattled, some wind chimes ringing, the hollow tubes clashing together in an alarm call. He heard his wife's quick footsteps. She bent to scoop up their son and kissed him on the cheek. 'Not the laurel bush, Mister,' she said to him. 'That's not for eating,' Daniel laughed, reached out for the bush again, set the chimes ringing. Archie closed his eyes, aware that the force of his gaze could alert his wife to his proximity; that her radar as a mother to the presence of a watcher would be acute – the primitive woman breathing just under the skin of her civilised sister's designer clothes.

He couldn't face her inner cave-woman today. He held his breath. She turned away singing to Daniel, 'Bath-time, gorgeous boy. Swim. Swim.'

'Dada,' said Daniel, pointing towards the bush.

'No Dada,' said his wife. 'Dada's away. Say Mummy. Say hello, Mummy,' and she rubbed her face in his chest to tickle him, and made him wriggle and laugh.

Archie lay in the earth with the creatures who lived there moving past in their evening routine. They crawled over his hand; something was buzzing. He pillowed his head on his arm and watched the light in his son's room, watched as it was dimmed for sleeping and the curtains drawn. Pins and needles spread down his right side, and he sat up and pulled the bear out of his pocket. It was damp and had absorbed a stain of leaf mould or earth through his sweatshirt. He stood up, slipped through the gate and threw the toy in a bin in the alley before walking back to Mike's flat, pumping his arms to try and warm up.

He climbed the stairs to the flat two at a time. Mike was going out. He was wearing his special jeans. Archie put his arm across the front door. 'Don't, Mike,' he said. 'I'll get you the money. We'll work something out.'

'It's another bloody sanction, man,' he said, and shrugged. 'I missed my reassessment. I went to the wrong place. It'll be months before I get any cash.' On the telly behind him David Cameron was talking about hard-working people again. Archie snapped it off with the remote that was lying on the sofa. When he turned round, Mike had slipped out. He threw his muddy clothes into the washing machine and stood under the shower. Water ran down his back and pooled round his ankles. His stomach rumbled.

# 21

IN THE MORNING, Brenda was waiting for him as usual beneath the unicorn. He could see the regulars going for their *Sound of Music* breakfast, drifting up the street to St Philomena's. She had her headphones on and waved. 'Just catching up with Cam's conference speech,' she said. 'Loving it. A real crowd pleaser. Build a land of opportunity. Great stuff.'

'Almost biblical,' he said. 'The promised land.'

'Talking of which,' she said. 'promises, that is. There was nothing new on your website last night.'

'No,' agreed Archie. 'I was … out.'

'Alright for some,' said Brenda. 'I was up to my eyes in a report. Some worries that the American government isn't going to agree to raise its debt ceiling and will default on its loans. It's contingency time for us, I'm afraid. Could be apocalyptic for the markets, I kid you not.'

Archie thought of the work that would roll into his old firm, suit and counter-suit, and he remembered his lean year without pay in the 2008 crash. It could swing either way. Recovery had been slow. Recovery. Brenda poked him with a manicured finger. 'Quote for the day?' she said.

'You choose,' he replied. 'Is there anything meaningful for you that you could relate to yourself?' Petal's counsellor-speak was rubbing off on him.

'Something about milk and honey?' asked Brenda.

'Yeah,' said Archie. 'Good for the skin.'

'Sometimes I think you are completely bogus,' she said. 'You don't seem very religious.'

He clasped his hands and unclasped them, searched back in his memory of school days, sitting cross-legged on the floor in

Assembly in the gym while a minister in a white dog collar thundered at them.

"'I will rain down bread from heaven for you, and the people shall go out and gather at a certain rate every day, that I may prove whether they walk in my law, or no." Exodus, 16:4,' he said. 'It's about bread and fair shares, but also about balance. You can't complete your spiritual journey if your body is out of balance. The two go hand in hand.'

'I don't really want a whole sermon,' she said. 'To tell you the truth, Archie, I have a confession to make. I'm not a church-goer. I picked you because you're a good price.'

'Right,' he said, laughing. 'I forgive you. Let's stretch our legs. Fancy more of a challenge? We could just about fit in a circuit through the community garden at the Greenford Hospital, past Watson's School and back along the canal to Tollcross.'

'A community garden?' said Brenda. 'What's the point in that? You can get all the veg you want delivered online. No need to waste time digging.'

'It's a bit of an Eden,' he said. 'You'll see.'

They set off across the Links golf course, dewy with a mizzle of rain, and ran down Morningside Road with its parents dragging toddlers to breakfast club at nursery and buses groaning on the hill. There were no payday loan companies or pawn shops here. Everyone had credit cards and expectations of climbing property and career ladders in the game he used to play round polished tables with pots of coffee and trays of pastries served by middle-aged women in shapeless, janitorial white coats. Who had they been? Anonymous, smiling and reverential. The boardroom was hallowed ground and he had been one of its brightest stars. Now his feet carried him over the pavements of the entrance to the Greenford Hospital, past the sugar cube, the stable block mortuary, the young people's unit, and along a narrow lane. Brenda was breathing heavily behind him. The path opened out onto a wilderness and they stopped. The nettles were waist-high; scrubby willow trees and a broken wooden bench framed a view of distant hills, soft, blue-grey mounds rising behind the old

Craiglockhart Hospital for shell-shocked servicemen of the First World War. He imagined them lying broken in starched white beds, missing limbs, or pieces of their minds, their pale faces at the window, trying to reconcile the purposefulness of the doctors, who repaired them in these clean rooms, with the trench they might yet die in. He remembered seeing his second lieutenant with his new steel leg, machine-tooled and jointed, a gleaming, high-tech robo prop – efficient, ergonomic, tailor-made – and he wondered if someone could tool him a component, bright and shiny, that would calibrate his mind; prop up the pink-curled mine-shaft of his brain, and let him switch off the bad thoughts that drizzled earth through the gaps in the boards.

'Is that hospital empty now?' asked Brenda. 'Great location. Ripe for redevelopment.'

He took a sip of water, and, as he swallowed, wanted to hit her with the bottle he refilled each night at Mike's. The raised plastic ridges were the contours of a grenade. He fought down the thought. Tried not to think of the bottles and bodies they had retrieved from the sand after the Warrior in front of them was hit.

'Let's go,' he said. They ran on past the wooden gate to the community garden: raised beds of strawberries and kale, brambles trained upwards on trellises and the ancient orchard, one hundred and fifty years old, where apples fell under the stars with a soft thud. They reached the main road through the back gate and arrived back at their starting point with five minutes to spare. Brenda tapped her watch. '07.55. Great timing,' she said. 'Spot on.' She stretched out her legs and looked up at him. 'I'm curious,' she said. 'How did you find out about that place?'

'Oh, you know,' said Archie. 'Once you run off the beaten track, it's amazing what you discover.'

'Meaning?'

'Nothing,' said Archie.

# 22

PETAL WOKE IN A DARK ROOM. Her foot throbbed. She lay there remembering the plastic champagne glass Calum had passed her as they parked up on the coast. It had been very dark and quiet, but he had put on some music. The jazz and distant city lights dancing on the water had made it seem alright. She had a memory of him popping Turkish Delight into her mouth after a second glass, and laughing. The pills and alcohol had made her woozy. Perhaps she had passed out. Calum must have brought her here, not knowing where else to take her. Had she told him her address? She swung her legs over the edge of the bed, tested her foot and put a bit of weight on it. Not too bad. She hobbled to the door. The light didn't seem to be working. Perhaps there was a power cut. She tried the handle. The door was stuck. 'Calum,' she shouted, 'Calum. The door's stuck.' There was no answer. She crouched down. Between the edge of the door and the door frame she could see the metal rectangle of the lock had been shot.

'Help,' she shouted. 'Help.' The word scared her. Confirmed a new reality. In the faint lamplight from the grille high up in the wall she could see her hand. It was grey and ghostly. Suddenly her granny's flat seemed so bright and precious, and her patients waiting for her at the studio table, sitting among the rainbow colours of wool and bubbles, so unutterably fragile. They needed her.

She watched the daylight hours pass through the window grille, thin shafts of light pressing through the holes. Searchlights that missed her. She lay on the bed trying to keep warm, but her feet were growing cold and the chill had reached her knees. There was a taste of rose water at the back of her throat and something bitter.

She was woken by a tapping at the door. She looked up to see that it was chained on the outside and Calum was peering through the gap. A light was on in the hall behind him.

'I'm going to come in,' he said, 'but I want you to stay still on the bed.'

She sat up. 'Where have you been? Why the hell am I here?' she shouted.

He put a finger to his lips. 'Shhh,' he whispered. 'Calm down.'

Her throat was dry and she had a headache.

'If you're good,' he said, 'then you can improve your situation.'

'Improve my situation?' she said. 'Improve my situation? Get me out of here now.'

He shut the door.

'Come back,' she shouted.

'I was hoping you'd be a bit more cooperative,' he said, through the closed door.

'I need the fucking loo,' she shouted. 'I don't want to pee on the floor again.'

'Okay,' he said. 'Calm down, and I'll let you use the toilet and bring you a light bulb. And every time that you are good, I'll bring you something else.'

'Okay,' she said. 'Just be quick.'

He peeped round the door and came in, locking it behind him. He had a torch on an elastic round his head – the kind cyclists or mountaineers use. He screwed a bulb into the light fitting. 'It's an economy bulb,' he said. 'Eleven watts but gives fifty. Not too bad. Bright enough.'

Petal looked at this poor sun. Calum's bald head gleamed in the light. 'This must be some kind of a mistake,' she said. 'I want to go home now and I promise I won't say anything to anyone. Please just let me go.'

'We both know you'd go to the police,' he said.

He passed her a bottle of mineral water, waited until she had taken a sip and then walked across the room and unlocked a door in the back wall. It led to a loo with a tiny sink. 'En suite,' he said.

She lowered the bottle. 'You're fucking insane,' she said.

'That's not very ladylike,' he replied. 'I'm not being rude to you.

I could be rude, but I'm not being rude. So I expect the same standards of behaviour from you.'

She screamed.

'I told you to be quiet,' he said, taking a step towards her. The lamp on his head was a huge eye. She pushed herself to the back of the bed. He looked down at her, then went out and locked the door.

She hopped over to the bathroom and used the loo. There was no mirror. She splashed her face with water and wiped her hands dry on her dress. The plaster on the walls was erupting in small craters. The air smelled damp and mouldy. Her stomach rumbled. She walked over to the door to the room and pressed her ear against it. There wasn't a sound. 'I need something to eat,' she shouted, through the door. She heard his footsteps coming down some stairs.

'I said no shouting. If you're quiet, I'll bring you something. Are you going to be good?'

'Yes,' she said through the wood. It was a whisper.

He returned with a freezer tray of food. 'Sweet potato casserole with aduki beans and silken tofu,' he said. 'Mood enhancing.' There was a disposable wooden fork riding on the vegetables.

She didn't reply. Accepting it made her shudder, as if this could become a new way of being.

'It will be alright, Petal,' he said. 'I don't want to hurt you.'

'You are hurting me,' she said.

'No, I'm not. I'm your friend. I'm looking after you until you get better.'

# 23

Archie was sitting at the table in Petal's studio at the Greenford Hospital, but the room was empty. He watched the grey clouds drifting across the sky, watched the tree branches waving backwards and forwards, and seagulls gliding east on the wind, or flapping against it before tumbling back in a short collapse of wings. After an hour, he stood up and stretched. Dr Clark stopped at the door. 'I think you should just go home, Archie. She's not in. Must have called in sick or something.'

Joy paused at the door. 'Where's Petal?' she asked.

'Missing,' said Archie, and stood up to go. Joy sat down at one of the art tables and squeezed washing-up liquid onto her felting tray. 'I'm forever blowing bubbles,' she sang. 'That's your song, Archie.' Her voice echoed along the empty corridor behind him.

Outside the sugar cube, a three-year-old child was cycling its tricycle on the road towards the exit. A car was passing on the other side and the child's mother was strolling fifty yards away. 'Come onto the pavement,' he said. 'It's safer.'

The child stopped and stared.

'Come onto the pavement,' he repeated, 'and wait for mummy.'

The child still stared. The mother came level with him, pulled the child's bike onto the pavement by the handlebars and passed without eye contact. He followed them towards the exit and chose a different road from them to walk back to the Meadows. He hit the main path through the trees and walked, surrounded by students and tourists, who shuffled and stopped to take photos in a stop–start rhythm that left him no clear line of sight. His heart was beating faster. It was the marketplace crowd that hid death. He veered away towards the street overlooking the park, escaping over tree roots on a well-worn shortcut. He jumped a patch of disturbed earth out of habit in case there was an IED, and stopped. He was near Petal's flat. He walked forward along the pavement, looking at the doors. Petal's door was red with a thick rope carved in stone above it. He walked up the path and rang the bell. There was no reply. He tried the door handle. It didn't budge. The elves still climbed their sunflowers and autumn leaves had gathered in the dark well of the pots. One of the tiny figures and fallen off and he picked it up and put it in his pocket – a talisman, a souvenir. He rang again. Still no reply.

*  *  *

Mike was sleeping in front of the television when he got back. There was a faint shadow of bruises on the side of his neck, the imprint of fingers that had held him too tight. Archie threw a blanket over him and then sat down. The reporter believed that American Special Forces had grabbed the leader of Al-Shabaab in Somalia. 'Some voices have objected to the use of drones on past operations,' said the newsreader. Another guy had been bundled into a car in Tripoli. Since Iraq, the war on terror had become a high-tech game of snatch with high-value targets. Now there were no more decks of most-wanted cards, dusty with sand and gum, in the hands of American troops hunting Saddam Hussein. The Ace of Spades had died at the end of a rope, and dodgy dossiers sat photocopied in exhibitions on propaganda in the British Library. Archie wondered when the world had become a tower of Jenga bricks, piled high; wondered when a hand might slide a piece out, with a sideways smile at his companions, and bring the whole game tumbling down. The weather forecast woman was talking about warm and cold fronts, waving a manicured hand at blue air sinking over the United Kingdom – average for the time of year, but feeling colder in the wind. He switched it off. He walked into the kitchen and opened a tin of rice pudding from Mike's latest food-bank carrier bag, and, after a few mouthfuls, lay down on his bed. It was time to update his website, but he did nothing. He thought of the Jews walking across Sinai to the Promised Land, the parting of the Red Sea. He thought of the women running on the Meadows. He thought of himself alone in the wilderness of his mind and wondered where God was. Where were his miracles? Where was his great hand? His rage? His justice? It was a planet of curiously shaped beings with jointed limbs, a place of confusion. It was a Christmas bauble planet in a pound store universe. His Bible-dipping was getting him down – the half-glimpsed passion of the prophets, the words of Christ highlighted in red ink, skim-read. Where was this new world?

He pulled a leaflet Petal had given him from under his pillow. It advertised a charity cook-out next weekend on Leith Links for five thousand people, organised by the churches running the food banks. They wanted volunteers to cook and prepare vegetables from Edinburgh's community gardens to publicise their work. Some politician had said going to a food bank was a life choice. Mike had said it had kept him alive. Archie tried to imagine himself at the cook-out as a volunteer; he pictured the trestle tables, the buckets of muddy carrots and potatoes, and the knives laid in rows ready for use. Could he trust himself with them? Pick up one of the deadly blades, and not run his thumb along the edge with practised habit, slash the throat before him in rehearsal of the move that could save his life in that other world he knew where it was reflexive, expected, praised. It was all about context. It was all about control. He could picture the headline: 'Vegetables Fly as Crazed War Vet Runs Amok at Church Barbeque'. He couldn't risk it. Another quiet weekend then.

# 24

As usual, Brenda was curt with him when he met her on Monday for their session. She had on a new navy top and knee-length, skin-tight bottoms. 'Your website's flat,' she said. 'In fact it's flat-lining. If you're not going to update it daily, why have it? You'd be better to tweet. I'm sure you could get your message into one hundred and forty characters. In fact, I think Jack Dorsey was being generous with the word limit in your case.'

He nodded without answering and set off running with a measured stride. He could hear Brenda's footsteps behind him and she drew level, matching his pace.

'If you're not going to chat, you might be pleased to hear I did lose a kilo,' she said. 'As you would know if you had bothered to log on last night.'

'Congratulations,' he said. 'Let's check your BMI today and create an eating plan. Organic and Mediterranean are the watch words.'

'I need more feedback,' she said.

'You'll get it,' he replied. 'Honestly.'

It was as they stopped to cross the cycle path that he saw the picture of Petal taped to the lamppost. It was in a plastic stationery pocket. 'Missing,' it said.

'You'd think she was a cat,' said Brenda, jogging on the spot.

'Arabella Dexter, also known as Petal, failed to turn up for work. Family and friends are concerned for her safety. Please contact police on 101, or call Joy on the mobile number below if you have any information.' There was a picture of Petal at a party, smiling over a raised glass. 'I know her,' Archie said. 'She was at my last class.'

'So how can she be missing today?' asked Brenda.

'I don't know,' replied Archie, looking towards Petal's flat as if he might spot her at a window.

'Shall we finish the run? This is on my time, after all,' said Brenda, checking her watch. 'Big meeting today,' she said over her shoulder, running on. 'They're actually going to discuss getting more women onto the board – and ethnic minorities – maybe someone working-class. Bit like the Conservatives' ministerial reshuffle. Got to please the voters, not have too many moon-faced white men round the table; need a little crunch in the salad, some nuts in the crumble.'

He laughed, pulled out of his thoughts about Petal. 'You're really working the food metaphor.'

'Maybe I'm feeling hungry on your ridiculous diet,' she said. 'I mean, where am I meant to get reduced-sugar pomegranate syrup?'

\* \* \*

That night, Archie's feet took him to Petal's flat. He was curious to see if she was home safely, the poster a premature alarm call. Women weren't cats. They couldn't disappear on sunlit days, could they? The lights were off and the curtains drawn as he paused on the street. He rang the bell. No answer. The lion's head door-knocker smiled at him as he banged the brass ring clenched between its teeth. Still nothing. He tried the stair door next to Petal's front door. It was locked. He buzzed the service bell. A voice mumbled, 'Hello?'

'I'm delivering leaflets,' said Archie. 'Could you let me in please?' The door clicked open. Polished Victorian tiles bordered with acanthus leaves lined the walls. He walked past the bikes chained to the railings and down the back steps into the garden. It was brighter here after the dark street: kitchen lights were blazing. There was the sound of voices from open windows, steamy with the mist from boiling potatoes and damp washing hanging on pulleys. Petal's flat was unfenced, although the ground-floor flats often claimed a private patch of the common back green. Her patio was full of geraniums in pots. The hens were clucking in their coop. He put a shovel of grit and grain through the bars into their dish. He paused and scanned the building. Her bathroom window had been left open at the top and he pushed it down and climbed in. The bathroom was papered with golden carp swimming in black water and weeds. Their silver eyes stared at him as he walked across the room to the hall. He could hear her neighbour moving about upstairs, the sound of a child's tricycle on the floorboards, merry laughter, and a radio playing. 'Petal,' he whispered. There was no reply. He opened all the doors in the flat and peered in. Every room was empty. His whisper met silence. He arrived in the living room she had made so bright with her warmth. It was lit by the orange glow from the street lights outside. At her desk in the corner, he found her computer. She was logged on, her password remembered by the machine. Remember me. The box checked. How many people would remember him, he wondered – ex-everything, and his memories X-rated, an impenetrable barrier between him and his previous life, patrolled by himself. The only way he could move forward was to retreat. Why was he standing here uninvited in the home of a woman he knew only as a therapist? He sat down at the desk.

There was nothing in her emails that caught his attention. The first one read 'Five Thousand Cook-out', as if the loaves and fishes were a modern-day miracle that could be repeated, a hat-trick. The emails were peppered with smiley emoticons and 'yeah!' was typed over and over, by this cheer-leading campaigner, this good soul. Her name was signed off with loads of kisses and lots of love. He sat back. What he was looking for wasn't here. In the bin at his feet he saw a copy of the local newspaper and a smiling lip shape drawn round some text in red felt pen – a personal column ad. He tore the page off and put it in his pocket. Then he shut down the computer and walked to the front door. It had been double-locked with a key. He turned back and slipped out the hall door into the communal stair.

Granny and the killer mutt from the Meadows were standing there. She was holding a child by the hand. 'Oh,' she said. 'Is Petal back? I never heard her this morning and her curtains are still shut.'

'Eh, no,' he replied. 'Not yet.'

'I haven't seen you here before,' she said.

'No,' he agreed, moving towards the door to the street.

'Wait a minute,' she said. 'You're the man who kicked poor Hector – you're that Jesus nut from the park.'

'No,' he said. 'You must be thinking of someone else.'

'Don't give me that,' she said. 'I could report you for cruelty to animals. Hector was pretty sore, I can tell you. Bruised. I had to take him to the vet.'

Hector was sniffing round his feet, his plastic muzzle scratching on the terrazzo floor.

'Look, I don't have time for this,' he said. 'I'm sorry, okay?'

'That's right, just walk away when things get uncomfortable.'

He opened the door to the street and walked out. It banged shut behind him.

'Charming,' shouted the granny, her voice muffled. He heard something further about manners as he paused at the foot of the step wondering where to go. He walked towards Karim's café. Karim was playing backgammon with a customer and stood up when Archie came in, walking forward to shake his hand. 'What can I do for you, my friend?' he asked.

'I need a serious drink,' said Archie, 'and something to eat.'

'Not licensed, I'm afraid,' said Karim, 'but I have some lamb tagine through the back. I'll get you a plate. Thanks for the publicity on your website.'

Archie nodded to the other man and sat down opposite the counter. Hamid Karzai flashed up on the TV in his green striped robe. It seemed he didn't think NATO and the US and British actions had helped Afghanistan: 14,000 civilians had died. The Afghan people had suffered. Archie looked towards the man, who shrugged. Archie put his jacket back on and walked out. He sat down with his back to a tree near the door and put his head on his knees. He was numb. Karim walked towards him. 'Are you OK?' he asked, crouching beside him.

'No,' said Archie. It was a full stop. A dead end, a fixed point in the universe, which had stopped turning. 'No,' he said again, because it was the only true thing in his life.

'Sooze said you were in the army?' asked Karim. 'Did you see service?'

'Service?' said Archie. 'I fought the Taliban. Now I'm fighting myself, and they're all talking about talks. It doesn't make sense any more. I don't know what happened.'

'It's all in God's hands,' said Karim.

Archie looked at him. 'Well, they must be red and bloody hands,' said Archie, 'because I sure as hell don't see him here.'

'Are you sure?' asked Karim, waving his hand towards the Meadows, with the trees standing in long rows under the clouds, stars visible in the navy-blue spaces between them.

'Believe me,' said Archie. 'I have never been more sure.'

'Come back in and eat,' said Karim. 'You're hungry. My tagine will put everything right. He who eats alone, chokes alone. Come on. You'll be as good as new.'

'Don't hold your breath,' said Archie.

Karim put a hand under his elbow and helped him to his feet. 'We're pals now,' he said. 'You saved Sooze from that mad dog. I still see it around here. It should be put down. Once they turn, you can never trust them again.'

Archie looked into his eyes. They were hazelnut – a Mediterranean brown. Warm. He looked away, afraid of seeing them change, then looked back. Karim was staring at him, frown lines appearing on his brow.

'How about that food?' said Archie, for something to say.

'Yes,' said Karim, releasing his arm and stepping back. He cleared his throat but didn't speak.

*   *   *

Archie washed up for Karim after the last customer left. He didn't want to be alone in his alcove, shelved and isolated from the world he used to know. Mike's vulnerability depressed him and when Mike smiled or made a joke about it, something in Archie twisted with pain, like metal under stress. This wasn't how it was meant to be.

The hot, soapy water grew greasy and Archie tipped out the basin to refill it. 'You're doing a good job,' said Karim. 'I might get home in time to get some sleep before I have to be back in for breakfast.'

'You're working too hard,' said Archie. 'You need to get a dishwasher.'

'Can't afford it yet,' said Karim. 'My priority is to get mum over here. That takes cash.'

'Right,' said Archie. 'How's that going to work?'

He paused. 'I'm in touch with the Syrian Embassy. They've got information on all the refugee camps.'

Archie remembered Camp Bastion, the long rows of tents in the sand, regimented behind perimeter fences. He heard the roar of the generators and air traffic. It had grumbled in the silence of the desert nights, a great canvas and steel hive. 'As long as she's safe,' he said.

'Let's hope so. I left mum in Damascus when I got my Chevening Scholarship to Edinburgh Uni just as the war broke out, and then got hitched to someone on my course and stayed. This place was my father-in-law's.'

'Where's your mum now?'

'She's stuck in a UN camp in Turkey. I want her here. There are a million like her. I'm not holding my breath. She wants to go home. They all do.'

'Home,' said Archie, 'is a precious place. It's not always easy to get there.'

'What's holding you back?'

Archie tapped his head. 'I'm bonkers. Hadn't you noticed?'

'You're not bonkers. The world is bonkers.'

'We know that, but it gets in the way. It got between me and my wife and I don't know how to stop it.'

'Give it time, Archie.'

'Any other clichés you'd like to throw at me? Something Syrian perhaps? The son of a duck always floats.'

'You're not being funny.'

'I'm not trying to be.'

'So I see. I'll finish the dishes, okay.'

'Are you mad at me?'

'I'm not mad at you, Archie. You can't blame a pot for being broken.'

'Is that one of your clichés?'

'No, I just made it up.'

'So we're still friends?'

'We're both in a tough place. We both know the world isn't always kind, so let's not add to the trouble.'

'You've got yourself a deal,' said Archie. He put the apron on the counter. 'I'll see you soon,' he said. 'Maybe help out again?'

'Maybe,' said Karim. 'We'll see.'

# 25

ARCHIE LAY IN BED the next day counting the air bubbles in the glass bricks after cancelling his class on Facebook. Thousands of trapped bubbles, thousands of burst lives. At 6pm, Mike brought him a bacon sandwich and a cup of tea. He sat on the end of Archie's bed, shaking his head. 'You're in a worse state than me, man,' he said. 'I'm positively full of the joys compared to you: a regular fucking comedian. I thought you were the rock.'

Archie shut his eyes again and pulled the duvet over his head.

'Why don't you get this butty down your throat, log onto the computer and cheer yourself up. Business is going well, isn't it? You're probably making more than me, and I've got a degree.'

'You've got a degree?' said Archie, sitting up.

'Yes. Why should that be a surprise?'

Archie waved a hand at the charred kitchen beyond the glass wall.

'Okay, maybe philosophy and the magic weed weren't the best choices for a future life course. I thought I could scale the heights and ended up plumbing the depths – no pun intended.' He slapped his rump and grinned. 'Why do you think there was a copy of Diogenes in the bog? Total shit misogynist bastard, of course. Hated women. Saw one drowning in a river and said an evil end for an evil bitch. Still, I couldn't bear to part with him when I sold my texts – not much money for second-hand books by prosaic Greek bastards.'

Archie sipped the tea, and took a bite of the food. Mike had put it on his best plate.

'I'm enjoying my new copy of Davidson's stuff on truth-conditional semantics.'

'What?' said Archie.

'Truth-conditional semantics. "Snow is white" is true if, and only if, snow is white. Get it? It's a big debate.'

'Life is shit only if life is shit. I get it,' said Archie.

'Not exactly,' said Mike.

There was a knock at the door. Mike looked at him. 'Are you expecting anyone?' asked Archie. Mike shook his head, and then went to answer, smoothing his hair back.

'Archie Forbes,' said a voice at the door. 'Police.'

Archie grabbed his jeans and sweatshirt from the floor.

'No. I'm Mike …'

'We have reason to believe he's residing with you,' said the voice. There was no answer.

'So do you mind if we come in?' asked the voice. 'We'd like a word.'

'It's not convenient,' said Mike.

'It'll just take a minute of your time, sir.'

'Okay, then.'

Archie had a vision of himself in Petal's flat and the poster on the tree. They probably wanted him for breaking and entering, or abduction or worse. He moved towards the kitchen window, pulling on his trainers. He heard Mike take the police into the living room and then excuse himself. He came into the kitchen, nodded his head towards the back window, then took a travel-sized bottle of mouthwash out of his latest food-bank bag and winked. 'Cheers,' mouthed Mike, 'you're my Judy.'

'No, Mike,' whispered Archie, making a swipe for it. It wasn't alcohol-free.

Mike downed it in one and grinned. His face began to flush and he went back through to the officers. Archie heard vomit splatter onto the vinyl in the hall, as he climbed through the window and lowered himself onto the flat roof below. He dropped onto the ground, edged past the bins and an abandoned sofa, and began to run. When he reached the main road, he slowed to a walk. He wasn't sure where to go. He walked along the edge of the industrial estate past the cat and dog home towards Portobello and up London Road to Abbeyhill. He skirted along the foot of Arthur's

Seat, and made his way through the walled streets of the Grange with its mansions tucked up tight behind high walls and automatic gates. He had been to parties here. Events he thought boring, with small talk and crudités handed round by students working for elite caterers. The rooms were awash with nibbles for guests who weren't hungry. They ate to be polite, and exclaimed at the flakiness of the pastry, the tenderness of the shrimps, and the richness of the wine – its bouquet, its plum notes, its chestnut finish. When had there ever been time to do that? To stand with a glass and feel warm by a fire, and clean, and well-dressed, with his wife in her evening dress and the strappy sandals he had bought her in Italy. The sandals that were her favourites, and it had mattered to him, pleased him, that she was clothed in their shared history.

The gates he passed were closed now. The key pads of friends a magic sequence of numbers he no longer knew. The same cars were parked on the drive, and only his planet had been hit by a meteorite; somehow they had all survived in their own orbit and he was the one drifting, drifting away from it all. Everything he had ever valued and hated at the same time: the social concord swallowed with his peers and their tacit agreement that all was as it should be; his gilded bird-cage life shared with friends. He was alone now and he couldn't work out how it had happened. He had made all the right choices. The warrior going to war, his rifle slung on his shoulder, had been an honourable estate, evinced admiration in the eyes of his friends, who were still at their desks on another Monday as he strode out into the desert to save the world. He was the fearless warrior who embraced a war that was not as he thought it would be, should be. People died; people who also ate and shat and desired. He had seen the Green Zone become a killing field, the orchards full of death, bullets that shot like hornets from trees against the intruder – Afghan bees. He had seen the elders come to a jirga in army tents to ask permission to harvest their crops, which ripened and rotted yards from their deserted villages. They had all fallen from the garden into the desert. They all longed for peace and a full belly and love because, at the end of the day, what else was there? They had that in common.

He pulled out his phone, wondered about calling some of his old friends and scrolled down their numbers, but most had made it clear that violence against women was a bridge too far, even if combat stress might be a factor. He knew that, even should they still hold some affection for him, he would only bring trouble to their door. Position was fragile. People knew who you knew, and whispers could pull a business down overnight. He wandered on, skirting the walls of the Astley Ainslie Hospital, and crossed over to the mental hospital grounds via Comiston Road, away from the security cameras. He wandered past the playing fields of the private school and climbed over the wall into the community garden. It was dark and quiet. He splashed his face at the stand-pipe by the tool shed and took a drink. The water was cold. Under the starlight, he picked some peppery green mizuna leaves and some raspberries and ate them sitting in the circle of chairs laid out for the weekly lunch with volunteer gardeners and patients. It was peaceful. The chairs were all mismatched: old metal wait-ing-room chairs with canvas backs and flaking, grey enamel; wooden kitchen chairs with blistered paint; a park bench. It was a meeting place for memories and he presided over it alone. Near the hut there was a huge pile of wood and vegetation cleared for the hospital's redevelopment project, and scattered among the lopped branches and bits of old board were some timber palettes. Archie began to excavate himself a hole near the back of the mound and lined it with the palettes. They made a good platform, insulating him from the ground. He dragged over more old boards and branches to make a door and roof, and then lay down inside. The bed space was just long enough for him to stretch out. It smelled of rotting vegetation, but enough air filtered in to breathe. He found some old tin cans and filled them with a supply of water, then walked over to the orchard to collect windfall apples. Someone had pinned poems to the trees. He pulled the edge of the paper towards him and read: it was about joy in the harvest. The apples he gathered in his sweatshirt rolled together. He looked down at his crop, remembered shopping online; the apples that arrived in his house on plastic trays and tasted of nothing. He lifted his head – voices echoed over the gravel path that passed between his den and the orchard. There was a smell of cigarette smoke, a girl's voice and the rumble of teenage laughter. He dived across the path and walked down the side of the mound, trying not to stand on any branches that might crack, crawled into his hole and pulled the board into place. He held his breath. They were talking about gaming; some eejit had lost them the league and they were back to stage one.

'We ran double burst assassins last night to break the game,' said the boy.

'That's hilarious.'

'We converged into one death squad so people weren't expecting it, and couldn't counter us. It was fun. Fan-diddly-astic.' He laughed.

'Big old trollers.'

'It's almost not trolling because it works. We were losing pretty hard in the beginning, so we grouped up and started running team fights. It was absolutely mental. Doug kept overreacting, but we were all bigging it up. You'd be great. We need to talk strats.'

'I can't. My dad says I can't go online until after the exams.'

'Bummer.'

'I know, right.'

There was the sound of a can being opened and then the silence of kissing, the suction of lips parting, and a giggle. Through a gap in his branches he could see them looking at the view with their arms round each other. Bungalows and flats spread up the hill behind the old orchard.

'Have you played that idiot called Pete?' asked the boy. 'He's such a game tard. He invades all the games, gets on your team, walks onto the battlefield and refuses to shoot. I nearly wet myself the first time he did it, but it's not funny now.'

The girl shivered and looked round. 'Let's go. It's a bit quiet here,' she said.

'Stay,' he said. 'We've only just got here.'

She began to walk away. 'It's creepy.'

The boy pulled his jumper over his head and began to walk

towards her like a headless zombie, groaning. 'Stop it,' she said, laughing.

He grabbed her and picked her up, pretending to chew her neck. 'Stop it.' She tried to hit him and he dropped his lips to hers and kissed her again.

Archie closed his eyes, releasing them from the beam of his gaze, his longing. They were holding hands now, walking away. Their feet rolled on the gravel, a dust trail settling at their heels. The shadows folded themselves back over the path behind them. Archie pulled his hood up over his head and fell asleep to the sound of cars passing beyond the wall.

# 26

His phone rang at 7.05 am. 'Where the hell are you?' demanded Brenda.

'In bed,' he said.

'Really fucking professional,' she replied. 'You're meant to be here, with me.'

'I'm not feeling great,' he said, rolling on to his side, and sitting up. He felt in his pocket for his SSRIs, then remembered them lying by his bedside at Mike's. Each pill was a full stop on the daily monologue of his pain; without them the stream of consciousness that had carried him away would return in full spate.

'Can you make it for our next session?' she asked. 'Because I am this close to firing you.' He could see her squeezing him between her manicured fingers; bug squash.

'I really don't give a fuck,' he said.

'Pardon?' said Brenda.

'I'm sorry to fuck up,' he said. 'It's a bad line. I'll see you next time.' He ended the call and lay on his bed as the sun rose, watching the gardeners' portacabin. A man on a bike arrived and unlocked the door, carrying his bike inside. Archie could hear a kettle boiling and the sound of a radio. 'Syrian refugees have drowned trying to reach the Italian island of Lampedusa in the Mediterranean. The exact number of casualties and fatalities is not known.' The channel went silent and then there was the staccato music of channels being passed over: snatched words, the first notes of a Schubert piano sonata rising into the air. Archie rolled onto his back. His legs were cold and sore. He wished he had got out of his hole and stretched before the volunteers had arrived. After eating one of his apples, he watched the day unfold like a time-lapse nature programme, watched the gardeners hoe the beans, covering them with net balanced over silver poles. He saw them plant and mulch new seedlings, rolling white fleece over them like early snow. A girl picked berries from the raspberry canes and put them in a plastic tub, holding each one up to the light before adding it to her pile. He saw an old woman in a wheelchair sit with a nurse and gaze at the plants as if she would see them grow, witness each cell swell with light and sugar and pop out in its predetermined structure of stalk, leaves and seeds, moving through its brief life, immune from the tendrils of her thoughts, which kept her enslaved. Over the wall, schoolboys yelled each others' names in rugby matches, coaches blew whistles, and car doors slammed as kids were collected at the end of the school day. So many people passed in front of him, but there was no sign of Petal. This was her patch. He wished he had spoken to the police. He wasn't sure why he had run, what impulse had made him drop from the window. He turned the question over in his mind. The fact was, she was missing and his finger-prints were all over Petal's flat. He had a restraining order framed with his law membership on his virtual wall in the land of Orange James' masters; his head was closed with paper stitches and Dr Clark was his new best friend. On the list of bogeymen e-fits, he was damn near the top. It was simpler to stay here in limbo. As he stretched out, the wood was rough under his hands and splinters caught at his scalp.

From his den, he watched the gardeners pack up and lock the shed. At 19.00 hours by his phone, he decided to risk lighting a fire outside in an old oil drum. The flames would be hidden by the metal walls and the smoke would drift unseen on the night air. He kicked out a hole in the rusting base to vent it and added a piece of wire fencing mesh on bricks to let the ash drip through to the bottom. He was pleased with his new stove. He broke up bits of wood from his dung heap house and fed them into the fire as it caught. He laid four potatoes from a nearby vegetable patch in the ash cavity, ready to cook in the hot embers as they crumbled through the grille above. He could have two for supper and keep the others for breakfast. He wondered how his day would have been if his life hadn't lurched sideways into war. Maybe today he would have been evaluating his performance, sitting in his office with its view over the city to the Forth, the faint hum of air-conditioning playing in the background, the lights casting a sunshine glow over his mahogany desk, the stained-glass panels of clouds and sailing ships – commissioned from a Dutch artist at great expense – drifting in a centuries-old, fantasy landscape behind the workers on the open-plan floor beyond. They had built barriers round their desks, customised with pot plants and family photos. All of the pods abutted each other in a maze of tiny cells, each illuminated by the sun of a computer screen. Compounds. The sandy walls he had climbed on a ladder.

His mind leapt back to his last meeting in that office, as he was read the litany of 'it's time to step down', the creed of the parting of the ways. 'What are the quality indicators in the framework of your performance, Archie – in your professional judgement? Professional judgement that, in your case, has been sadly lacking. Aspects of your output have been less than rigorous, and while you undoubtedly have major strengths, Archie, and your strengths outweigh your weaknesses, don't get me wrong, you will concede that Forbes, Stock and Wilson are about market excellence, a benchmark that must be consistently applied across the board. Let me be quite clear about this, you have fallen short in critical areas and remedial action is required. It's not personal, you understand, but we must meet the needs of our stakeholders and clients. You can't underplay the legitimacy of their concerns and expectations. With all due respect, running round Afghanistan playing at soldiers doesn't fit with the consistency of our standards of performance, and coming on the back of the Fitzroy Ltd debacle just as we were trying to close the Chinese deal – well, I'm sure you understand.'

Archie remembered his own silence, the puff of an air-freshener releasing a hiss of sandalwood into the office as the chairman of the board pushed back his chair.

'It's all about reputation. Reputation fosters reward.' There was a pause. 'Of course, we are all very sorry about the difficulties you have been having with your wife.'

Still no reply.

'Have you thought about getting help, Archie? I don't want you to feel that when you step down, that you have been pushed … into a position … where you might feel that … well, as I say, the shareholders' expectations remain paramount … it's out of my hands …'

Archie closed his eyes. He opened them again on the twigs above his new home. He should try to salvage his reputation. Make a start. Petal was somewhere out there. He pulled the scrap of paper from his jeans pocket. His eyes rested on the highlighted number in the glow from the embers.

## 27

SLEEP WAS A CRUEL TRICK. In Petal's dreams her life continued as before but when she woke it stopped. Was sleep the sugar pill, the promised land of nod that made anything, everything bearable? A land where there was no God, a land where the only god was imagination, where wishes came true, where the prisoner could escape. When life was full of fear, the bogeymen in dreams lost their power; they became insubstantial: trolls who could be sent scuttling back under the bridge by saying the magic words – 'I'm dreaming. Wake up now.' It was life that was problematic – its puzzles less easily solved, its terrors more solid.

Petal opened her eyes. It was morning. At some point Calum had come into the room and covered her with a duvet, but she hadn't woken. She wondered if anyone was looking for her. Dr Clark might have noticed she wasn't in, but equally he might assume she was on annual leave, or had called in sick. She had been due to meet her friend last night and that was her best hope. No one else would be looking for her. She only called her mum fortnightly, so she wouldn't be expecting a call yet. No sign of her handbag or mobile.

There was the sound of a key in the door and Calum looked in over the chain. 'Good morning,' he said, in a cheerful voice.

She sat up and swung her legs onto the floor, but didn't stand up. Her foot was still stiff. 'Perhaps you could lie down again,' he said, 'while I bring in your breakfast?'

She lay back watching him. He put a tray with two croissants on the floor. There was a boiled egg and a small pot of honey, lumpy with broken hexagons of wax. 'Bon appétit,' he said, and rechained the door.

'Don't go,' she shouted. 'I need to talk to you. I need some clean clothes and some soap.'

'I'll see what I can do,' he replied through the door. 'As I say, it all depends how good you are.'

'I want to go home,' she said. 'People are expecting me.'

'Try to think of this as your home now,' he replied. 'I can make it nice for you. I've texted your mum and your friends for you. There are quite a number on your phone. Interesting threads. LOL.'

She screamed: a raw, animal noise. She did it again.

He came in and clamped a hand over her mouth. 'If you do that again, I'll tape your mouth and I'll tie you to a chair so tight that you'll wish you had never been born. Do you understand?'

She nodded. His hand was suffocating her. He lifted it off her mouth. 'That's better,' he said. 'I'm not a violent man. You're putting pressure on me and I don't like that. I just want things to be nice. To have a little company. That's not a crime, is it?' He looked at her and reached out for her hair. 'I felt we had a connection.' His eyes were dark, the pupils dilated so that their junction with the iris was lost.

'Don't kid yourself,' she said.

He tightened his grip of her hair.

'Please,' she whispered. 'I'll be good.'

He relaxed his fingers and looked at the strand of hair lying in his palm. 'I have to go to work now,' he said, releasing it. 'I'll see you later. I won't be late.' It was the kind of thing a husband said to a wife.

She sat up once he had gone, trembling. The breakfast tray lay just inside the door, a tray that reminded her of a bed and breakfast in Amsterdam when she was inter-railing. She decided to eat. If she kept her strength up, then she had a better chance of escaping. If she could only work out what made him tick. I am a tourist she thought, in an unfamiliar land. I am Francine. It's just a game. This trauma is navigable.

*   *   *

When he returned that evening, she smiled from her bed as he entered the room. 'Let's eat together tonight,' she said, as he laid her tray on the floor. He looked up, crouching at her feet. He was muscular. His suit well-cut, stretched tight over his thighs.

'Why the change of heart?' he said.

'It's a long day when there's nothing to do. I don't like being by myself.'

He smiled. 'I'll be back soon.' He returned with another plate of food. 'Thai curry,' he said, 'with a coconut and lemongrass base, dressed with raspberries. The ingredients are anti-bacterial and anti-ageing. Very good for you. Preserve your youthful beauty. I wonder if you could wash your face and hands,' he added. 'If we're going to have dinner.'

'It's not a date,' she said.

'Still,' he replied, 'it's nice to make an effort.' He passed her a linen napkin. 'I'll get you a fresh towel and some soap.'

When she came out of the bathroom, he had brought in a folding table and two chairs. It was a garden picnic set, white curled metal, as if they were sitting on the terrace of a hotel. 'Madam,' he said, getting to his feet and pulling out a chair.

'This is just a bad dream,' she said to herself. 'A quest.' She sat down.

He put her napkin on her knee with a flourish. 'I'll fetch some wine,' he said.

She watched him unlock the door and close it again, then she leaned over and spat in his food. The saliva pooled on the surface of the coconut sauce and she stirred it in with her fork. On an impulse, she switched plates.

'What are you doing?' he asked as he came back in. 'The food isn't drugged if that's what you're thinking. This isn't a movie – one of your horror films.'

'Isn't it?' she asked.

'Don't be silly, Petal,' he said, taking his plate back. 'As I say, I just want your company, that's all. For a short time. This is all a bit of misunderstanding, if you must know. It's moved a bit faster than I expected. I was going to take you home that night. It's not my fault that you passed out.'

'I don't understand,' she said.

'Me neither,' he replied. 'So let's make the best of it. See what develops. We both love good food. The organic things in life. We have that in common.' He raised his glass. 'To unexpected friendships. To the future.'

She stared at her glass. Her fingers were shaking as she reached out for it.

'First date nerves?' he asked.

'You're joking,' she shouted. 'You're just a sick fuck.' She threw the glass of wine in his face, watched it run over his cheeks and lips, drip into the gully of his mouth.

He jumped to his feet, swearing, and tipped the table over. 'Do you want to play like that?' he asked. A dog barked above the grille to the street. 'Don't push me, Petal.' He pointed at her with his index finger. 'Don't push me. I spent a lot of time over that meal. I was planning to try a seafood espuma for you for tomorrow. I even bought a new nitrous oxide cartridge for my gun. I'm a gourmet. A gourmand, if you will. If you insult my food, you insult me.' He walked out leaving the food and plastic wine glasses on the floor.

Petal sat down on the bed, heard a car engine start up in the street, and began to cry.

# 28

'DULCE ET DECORUM EST PRO PATRIA MORI – you were wrong, Horace,' thought Archie, on day two in his nest. 'It's not glorious to die for your country if you only die on the inside. I'm a fucking zombie,' he thought. 'I'm walking about, but I'm rotting inside my own arms and legs. Are there any medals for that?' He pulled out his phone and stared at the screen. No one rang him these days. He scrolled through the messages he had ignored when it all kicked off months ago. They were mostly from his best friend, his best man. The box was full and he deleted it without reading them – not that anyone would ring now. The space he had made was pointless. His thumb danced between the Google and Twitter icons; 1.6 billion search engine enquiries every day. The number had stuck in his head, a fly buzzing at the window. He googled 'Why am I so fucked?' The search engine returned eight pages of sites. He laughed in surprise and scrolled down the 'So you think you're fucked-up quiz', the 'How fucked are you really?' comparison site, the 'Hug-a fellow-fuck-up-ee' meet-up, the fucked-up suicide attempt stories, and a Facebook page inviting him to 'embrace your inner fucked-up-ness'. He had not expected any answers. It was a whole other world. A year ago he would never have asked the question. It wouldn't have occurred to him. He would not have put it like that. The language was the key to the door. 'Are any of us asking the right questions?' he thought. Ol' Twitter Jack feeding on 'chirps from birds' and 'inconsequential information', except that it wasn't so inconsequential any more; if Rouhani and Obama were tweeting, then it was the temperature of the planet, the group psyche stretched bare, as if it were all spread out in God's mind, as if the things previously known only to a supreme being, if such a being existed, were now laid out for all to read. It was all being channelled into marketing ploys and political analysis and economic opportunities – a stream of universal public opinion that could be mined for gold. But the big questions were still unasked, remained unasked, unanswered and unanswerable. The big questions he had asked under fire from three or four firing points – the why am I here questions, the what-the-fuck moment of death at the sharp, pointy end of an AT4 rocket launcher questions, the Striker, Javelin and Stinger questions. Even death had a barcode. The guy with the scythe was redundant; men were doing his work for him. He probably had his feet up in front of the telly somewhere, or was on a training course with Orange James to prepare himself for the modern workplace and keep up with new technology. Yields were up. The grim reaper had hung up his scythe, taken a back seat, but the harvest was bigger. Archie pocketed his phone, pulled a stubby piece of charcoal from his ashes with a stick and drew Death with an RPG on his shoulder on the planks of his burrow.

Outside he could see the teenage couple from the previous night, dancing in school uniform. They were sharing iPhone ear-pieces, jumping in front of each other joined by a thin white wire, laughing, their arms and legs mirroring each other, their pelvises together, dancing to the music of their universe in the lull of the afternoon.

His arms and legs were stiff and cold by the time the man with the bike locked up the garden hut and waved goodbye to his volunteers. It was a daily ritual driven by the seasons. Greet, dig, drink tea, dig, have lunch, dig, harvest, plant, bed. Archie envied him his connectedness to the land. The land that had to be humoured and fed, for it to give. Archie remembered how there used to be a season to war. How it would start in the spring after planting and end when the fighters had to go home for the harvest. The threat of starvation had been the biggest tyrant. Time limited the killing. Now war was supermarket fed; rows of gleaming freezers and wheat mountains served the new 24/7 warriors, who tore open chemically heated ready meals and kept fighting, never sheathing their swords. Death was gorged on his own food bank.

*  *  *

With evening, a mist descended over Edinburgh, as if the grey sky were a blind pulled down on the window of the view. A fine drizzle covered the plants with small glass beads, larger on cabbages than on grass. Archie ate some more berries, splashed his face at the stand-pipe and set off for Mike's flat. He needed his bag of clothes, some food and to see a friendly face. There were a few people walking across the Meadows, their heads down behind umbrellas.

At Mike's flat Archie climbed onto a bin, up onto the flat roof of the extension and caught hold of Mike's kitchen window-sill. He pulled himself up, his arms trembling as they took his weight. Mike turned round as the window was pushed up, drawing back his arm to throw a glass at the intruder.

'Oh,' he said, as Archie levered himself over the sill. 'Hello, Romeo.'

Romeo, alpha, bravo, foxtrot … Archie dismissed the call signs – heard the crackle of the radio in his ears, or the back of his mind, or wherever that memory sat, in the space that was inside and outside at the same time. He tuned it out. 'Very funny,' he said. 'Shame you're no beauty.'

Mike put his glass in the sink. 'The police told me to phone 101 if you showed up,' he said.

'And are you going to?' asked Archie.

'I'm not a grass,' he said. 'I'm guessing you could use some food. You look like shit.' He reached into his eternal bag of unpacked shopping on the counter. 'Instant macaroni? Beans? Really push the boat out and have both?'

'Both, please,' said Archie. 'I'll pay you back. Do you mind if I go and get cleaned up?' he asked.

Mike nodded, pouring the pasta into a plastic dish and adding water from a mug to microwave it.

There was no hot water from the bath tap so Archie climbed into the shower. A plastic duck with an eye patch stared at him from the soap dish as he washed. He towelled himself dry and wandered through to the alcove to get his SSRIs. There was no sign of them. 'Where are my pills?' he shouted, coming out into the kitchen.

'Can you try not to look so fucking scary?' asked Mike, and then pointed to his stomach. 'I thought I'd give them a whirl,' he said.

'Please tell me there are some left,' said Archie, his heart beating faster.

'Of course,' said Mike, pulling them out of a drawer stuffed with bills. 'I'm not the kind of kid that eats all Santa's chocolate on the first day. I could make an Easter egg last till the next new moon. I'm a past master of the art of eking out treats.'

Archie took one of the pills and pocketed the rest.

'So are you going to tell me what's going on?' asked Mike, as they sat down on the sofa in front of the telly. Archie had crammed his mouth full of pasta. He nodded. The newsreader was immaculate as her daily litany of disaster spooled from her lips. 'The Fitch indicator predicts that America is on the brink of defaulting on its debt repayments if Congress doesn't agree to raise the debt ceiling from sixteen trillion dollars. International markets could be plunged into chaos,' she said. Archie leaned forward. Mike snapped the telly off. 'I don't care about those clowns in Congress,' he said, 'and their stupid fucking tea parties. I suppose I really want to know why the police were at my door hunting for yours truly.'

'I don't know,' said Archie. 'Honest.'

'When people add the word "honest" to what they've just said, then a tiny alarm bell goes off in my ear. Do I say "blah, blah, blah, sincerely", or "blah, blah, blah, sadly"? If you're adding a commentary, then you're being bogus.'

'Okay,' said Archie putting down the plate. 'A woman I walked home has disappeared. A woman I happen to like – from the hospital.'

'And you're the local nut-job?' said Mike.

'Looks like it,' he replied.

'And is she chained to a rock somewhere about to become lunch for a passing dragon?'

'What do you think? How would I know?' said Archie.

'How do they know she's missing anyway?'

'There is a fucking poster stuck to a tree for her. She's the reliable type who turns up when she says she will, doesn't throw sickies, loves her patients, her friends, her family. When women like that go AWOL, then something has happened.'

'Like what?' asked Mike. 'Aren't you overreacting?'

'I went back to her flat. She wasn't there.' Archie pulled the Cupid Calling number from his pocket and passed it over. 'Some randy bastard? A lone wolf?'

'Looking for his Red Riding Hood?' Mike took the number with his free hand. He had a thin roll-up in his right, which he waved. 'A Saughton fag,' he said. 'I've just been shown how to do it. You roll them thin to make the baccy last. What you don't learn on the street ... Ring-fencing resources in the university of life. So why aren't you going to the police with this?' he asked.

'PTSD, a restraining order, my prints all over her flat. Take your pick. I'm number one suspect if she cops it, and the prick that took her never shows up. I mean, who keeps a track of those numbers in the paper? I mean, really? She's a gorgeous girl, Mike.'

'Smitten?' asked Mike, blowing out a puff of smoke.

'No,' said Archie, 'but I could be.'

Mike's mobile rang. 'Yeah,' he said. 'See you in five.' He stood up. 'Sorry, pal. I've got to go. Stay here tonight. I doubt the police will be back.'

'Thanks,' said Archie. 'Could you do me a favour?'

'What?'

'Get a girl you know to ring that number and set up a meeting? Eight pm?'

'And you'll be there in shining armour to see who turns up?'

'Yes.'

'No.'

'Please, Mike,' he said. 'I don't know what else to do.'

'Take another of your pills and go to bed. Ever heard of an early night? It might do you the world of good.'

'I'm begging you,' said Archie.

Mike sighed and looked at the time on his phone. 'Okay,' he said, 'but only because you look so undignified begging. I'll ask Jackie. I'm late for her as it is. She's an old mate. That's the good news. She's thinking of moving in here. That's the bad news. Sorry. I didn't know how long you'd be gone. I had to rent that room. You can have it till Saturday. I'm assuming you're not coming back permanently?'

Archie nodded. The SSRIs must have been kicking in because it didn't feel like a disaster.

Once Mike had gone, Archie fired up the computer. He hovered his mouse over Facebook and then googled car tracker devices. They were cheaper than he thought. He caught sight of himself in the mirror. His cheeks were hollow and he looked cold. His buzz cut was a bad idea. He had cut himself shaving and the blood showed as a red dot under the tissue he had stuck over it. The blood was fresh and bright – not dried black by a road side, or brown and stiff on a uniform in fifty-five degrees of heat. He selected a mini car-spy with cellular vehicle tracking for urban use. Three in stock. He reckoned there was no need to pay extra for GPS, have satellites triangulate a position for an extra twenty quid when any wireless provider could do it straight to his mobile. He noted down the address of the nearest store and logged off. He went to bed and dreamt of the toys Santa wouldn't buy boys for Christmas and then woke up in a sweat. It was five in the morning. There was a note by the kettle. 'Jackie made the call,' it said. 'Your date is at the Jupiter Bar, Saturday, 8 pm. He's called Calum Ben. Forty, bald as a coot apparently, blue suit. Borrow my bike if it helps. PS. You are fucking insane.'

*   *   *

Early on Friday, he lay in bed listening to the radio. America had pulled back from the brink and agreed to raise its debt ceiling to seventeen trillion dollars. He thought of their spending in Afghanistan, wondered if they regretted their Afghanistan shopping list: the Apache attack helicopters, the RPGs, the SUVs, the briefcases of cash for goodwill. John Reid had thought he could leave in a year without firing a shot, but it had been an expensive trip for him too in more ways than one. They had gate-crashed the party to find all the guests had left, searched mountains and caves for Bin Laden and come back empty-handed. Now they were propping up Karzai's government, and who knew what would happen when they drew down Operation Herrick. ISAF was melting away, leaving the Afghan National Army to stand up alone.

# 29

IT WAS RAINING when he met Brenda the next day, and they started running in silence. He wondered how he could face lying down in his den again, alone and outside. The thought of his face near the mud he saw squelching beneath his feet chilled him. He wouldn't be able to sleep out for much longer. 'You seem a bit subdued,' said Brenda. 'No inspirational thought for the day?'

He shook his head.

'Have you looked at my chart?' she asked.

'Let's leave it for a bit,' he said. 'We can't do it day by day. You can't measure progress like that.'

'I found a quote,' she said, '"To fail to plan is to plan to fail." What you really need, Archie,' she said, 'is a good e-marketing plan. It's not customer acquisition that counts but customer conversion and retention. You need a concrete product – an app, or a T-shirt. Print it up with your extracts from the Psalms. I've got it,' she said. '"When you want to dip into the fridge, dip into the Bible"; "Fill your soul, not your belly".'

'Let's increase the pace,' he said. 'Get out of this rain.'

'Did you hear me?' she said. 'You want the best return on your investment. A hyper-personalisation of your product. I think you've got that,' she said, 'with the charts. That's where the apps would come in too. You want to inspire and enlighten.'

'I can't really get my head round this at the moment, Brenda,' he said.

'It's crucial to have a digital strategy,' she went on. 'Some synergy between the social media divides – Facebook and email. I'm trying to help you here.'

He stopped running. 'I'm not taking the business further at the moment,' he said. 'I've got some stuff on.'

'What stuff?' she asked.

He didn't reply.

'Archie. You need to focus. I can't help noticing that you've been wearing pretty much the same gear since I started.'

'It's not the outside that counts,' he said.

'I know,' said Brenda. 'It's the inside. The inside becomes the outside, Archie. Isn't that your message?' And he wondered where that left him with his shredded heart and his bomb-blast brain.

She looked at her watch. 'I'll get off now,' she said. 'I'm in Dubai next week, but I'll see you the one after that.' She ran off without giving him his money.

'Brenda,' he shouted. 'The money.'

She ran back. 'Sorry,' she said, jogging on the spot. 'You're such a cheap date that I completely forgot.'

*　*　*

He looked like any other punter in a waterproof with his hood up when he picked up the tracker on the way back to Leith. The rain lent anonymity to the people on the street. Everyone was dressed in blue or black. Everyone was cold. Nicola Sturgeon was on a bank of TVs in the store window, '349 days, 15 hours and 30 minutes' to the independence referendum ticking down on a clock behind her. Big, digital numbers flick-flacking on a board.

As he walked past the gardens of some flats on his way to Leith, he reached up into an elderflower tree hanging over the wall and grabbed a handful of elderberries. A magpie in the tree chattered at him as he stopped to pull the berries from their stalks with his teeth. They tasted bitter. The bird, in his feathered uniform of black, white and brilliant green, was staring at him. Where did this eternally perfect magpie come from? Where were all the old magpies, the sick magpies, the magpies down on their luck?

As he neared the funeral home where his grandpa had been laid out, an old warrior in a cardboard coffin, a hearse pulled out of the drive. It was gleaming grey. He stopped to let it pass and bowed his head. The driver waved a hand at him in thanks. The face at the window was pasty as if he had spent too much time with the dead.

There were no flowers on the casket. Archie wondered who would mourn this soul. The expensive coffin with its brass handles must have been a last gift from the person to themself, chosen from a catalogue in the old folks' home with a social worker kneeling at their feet, turning the pages. For a moment, Archie wished he had died in combat rather than face his internal battle alone – a battle in which, for some reason, he was now cast as a misfit, ashamed of his own inability to maintain a social front. This failure had cost him everything. It wouldn't have mattered, he thought, if he could have contained the damage inside, fought the odd skirmish with his thoughts. It was his traitor eyes that made him a target, and the fire they returned at him was social fear. He was the warrior who could not contain his own power, fit the acts permitted by international rules of engagement back into his daily life. 'Permission to fire, sir? I have a clear line of sight.' The social act of death.

# 30

WHEN PETAL WOKE UP, a tray of breakfast and a dustpan and brush had been put into the room. There was a carrier bag of charity-shop clothes – a pair of trousers, a jumper and a dress.

'No hard feelings but I thought we might have made more progress by now,' said a note. 'Let's try again tonight.'

Petal ate the food and went back to bed. She had to think of a way out of this situation, but her mind was empty. She lifted one of the chairs onto the bed, balanced on it and looked out of the grille. There was a small cavity and then a thick panel of frosted glass fixed over the opening to ground level. It was a street. She could hear muffled traffic, see footsteps passing over the glass, between her and the light. A child's shadow stopped and jumped up and down on the barrier. 'Help,' Petal shouted. 'Help.' She banged on the grille, dislodging dust and powdered moss. She was so close to life, and yet had never been further away. Calum's will stood between her and everything she had expected would happen to her in the days ahead: her weekends; her holiday; the larger events of courtship, marriage and children. She looked at the future she had anticipated through the smelted puncture marks of the grille and cloudy glass, each blank circle a lost opportunity. 'If I ever get out of here,' she promised herself. 'I will never complain about anything ever again. I'll book that trip to Machu Picchu, shout my gratitude from the top of the mountain. I'll walk the labyrinths in the Nazca desert, and sing. Perhaps Calum would see reason,' she thought. He was the key to the door.

That night he seemed distracted, less focused. She had tidied up the room and put on the charity shop dress, determined that looking as normal as possible might move them back towards discussion and away from confrontation. 'To be honest,' he said over a dish of tagliatelle and clams. 'I'm not enjoying your company as much as I thought I would. I thought you might be a little friendlier, so I'm going to meet someone else tomorrow night.' He raised his glass and drank half.

She didn't reply.

'My point about you, exactly. No conversation – or perhaps you are a teeny, tiny bit jealous?'

'Don't flatter yourself,' she said. 'Look, it's not too late to let me go. Then you can start again.'

'That might be a little awkward,' he replied, 'for obvious reasons.'

The muscles in her jaw tightened and she shivered.

'Look,' he said. 'Let's see how it goes.' He stood up. 'I think I'll call it a night. You're not as much fun as you were on our first date.'

'Are you surprised?' she said. 'Look at this place.'

'That's not very nice, Petal,' he said. He walked towards the door. 'I've made a big effort for you.'

She got up and threw her arms round him. 'Let me go,' she sobbed, 'I'm begging you.'

He unpicked her fingers from his shirt. 'Don't be so undignified.'

She grabbed his ankle and bowed her head down onto the floor. 'I said let go.'

She looked up at him. 'Please. Please, Calum. I can't stand it.'

'That's too bad,' he said. 'What kind of girl answers an ad in a paper anyway?'

She looked up. 'It's not a crime to be lonely.'

He pushed down on her hand with his free foot. 'No, but it might cost you.'

She let go and lay on the floor. 'Get back on the bed, Petal. I don't want any trouble when I open this door.'

# 31

IT WAS 19.45 ON SATURDAY according to his phone. Archie stood in a shop doorway opposite the Jupiter Bar, pressed into the shadows, as far back as he could go. Fifteen minutes later, a small, grey car parked on the opposite side of the road. It was quiet. Laughter and conversation burst onto the street as the man opened the door to the bistro. He was bald and wearing a navy-blue suit. Archie pulled the tracker from his jacket pocket and strolled across the street. He tried to look as if he might be toddling out for a beer, or going to pick up a takeaway. Single bloke on a Saturday stuff. He crouched down as he reached the car, pretending to tie a shoe lace, and slipped the tracker under the rear bumper. There was a clunk as the magnet bit onto the metal. He walked back across the street. Through the window, he could see the man standing at the bar, holding out a twenty-pound note to attract the attention of the barman. He pointed at a bottle of wine on the back wall and moved towards a table in the far corner. Big, shiny, plastic stars hung from the ceiling, and planets were projected round the walls, travelling in a celestial loop over the diners' heads. Without dragon lights, no one would see him in the dark beyond the circle of light; without dragon lights they hadn't seen the Taliban beyond the perimeter. The rocket had slammed into the store.

Archie walked back to his doorway on shaking legs and sat down on his haunches to wait. He had to focus. He didn't want the police to get a GPS fix on his phone, so he would put it on twenty minutes after the guy left. That should give him a position if he stayed in town, but the man seemed in no hurry to leave. Archie pulled his knees up to his chest. The microscopic world of the pavement spread out before him: bits of chewing gum stuck to the concrete slabs, a sweet wrapper, a can rattling along, blown by an intermittent breeze. In the camp, they had rehearsed sorties with cans of food to stand as forward operating bases, jackets dropped as crumpled mountain ranges, socks as compounds. He remembered the desert stars, the thin mountain air, and he wondered at his stagnation in an Edinburgh gutter, questioned his hunch that this man could be connected to Petal. She was probably tucked up in some warm family home, her mum bringing her hot cups of tea, and ice packs for her ankle. The poster was most likely a premature alarm call posted by an over-anxious Joy via her fag-fetcher on a shop run – a case of too much time on her hands and a TV diet of *Crimewatch*. He resolved to leave. He pushed his hands into his pockets and pulled out Petal's elf. 'This is so fucking ridiculous,' he said to himself and laughed, an out-loud laugh. He looked up. The bald man was staring at him from the doorway of the Jupiter. Archie reached for the beer can at his feet and raised it. 'Cheers,' he shouted, hoping he sounded drunk.

The guy turned away and beeped his car. There was a short burst of orange light running over the wet street and the sound of a door banging. Archie saw him framed in the window as he passed, his mobile phone to his ear. Archie crouched down, his back against the wall, and watched the car take a left at the end of the street.

Operational silence. The long hours of waiting on base, till boarding the Chinooks, till contact. Waiting. Waiting till the picture changed, and a larger picture was understood. He remembered landing at Camp Bastion at three in the morning and going straight into an orientation session. 'Life here can get a bit sporty,' said the second-in-command who was briefing them. 'Our principal difficulty is resupplying the forward operating bases. They're mostly in old police stations but since the locals abandoned the villages, the TB are getting in a bit of target practice on us. Most of you will remain on base, but if there are any volunteers I can guarantee you a piece of the action. Twenty-five thousand Soviets couldn't subdue this place but, hey, we have four thousand six hundred British troops. And how do we maintain morale? We dig deep. We remember why we're here.'

Why are we here, sir?' shouted a voice from the back.

It was ignored. 'Remember to keep your helmets on at all times,' he continued, 'so that those of you with brains,' he looked towards the back of the room with a wolfish smile, 'keep them.'

Archie stood up and switched on his phone. If the guy wasn't local then he would be going out of range in thirty minutes, leaving the city. It would be back to the drawing board. He would have to invest in a GPS system. He had ten minutes to kill before there was any point in accessing the app. The newsfeed on his screen was all about the NSA tapping the German chancellor's phone. If Angela Merkel wasn't immune, then no one was. Her spokesman, Jan Albrecht of the European Committee of Civil Liberties, had travelled to Washington to tell Obama that snooping wasn't a nice thing to do to friends. Now he was asking David Cameron to explain the fibre-glass listening station on top of the British Embassy in Berlin, asking questions about his Five Eyes eavesdropping coalition with the US, Canada, Australia and New Zealand. Was it news that there were spies and monitoring, Archie wondered. Was Edward Snowden in his Russian refuge wise to have told the world what it already suspected, but didn't want to hear – that they were all suspects, and international bonhomie wasn't much more than the froth on a social media promise of coffee. Now everyone was tweeting in a confessional frenzy of squeaky clean while the real terrorists hid as avatars in virtual worlds.

Archie looked along the street and wondered if the police had other suspects in Petal's disappearance. And then it occurred to him, had their visit been about something else? Perhaps something had happened to his wife or son? He hadn't thought of it before. A tight feeling grew in his chest. His neck constricted and a pulse began to beat a 'Hey, Stupid' tattoo in his forehead. He stood up, swung his arms and stretched them above his head. He rolled his shoulders. They were stiff and cold. He couldn't catch his breath. He began to cough, fighting for air on his hands and knees, his eyes watering. Is this how it would end? Choking on anxiety in a derelict shop doorway? The coughing fit subsided, his throat gulping. He sat back on his heels and tapped the tracking app on his phone. The tracker highlighted a spot on the map not ten minutes away. He should have accessed it sooner. Archie turned up his collar and set off. The dot was static and he switched off his phone to avoid being located. He would turn it back on when he got to the location if the car wasn't in sight. Then he would check on Hannah and Daniel.

\* \* \*

The street was dark. The tenements had given way to high metal gates and long walls with hoardings advertising building companies and hauliers. He came to a wire fence and stopped. He switched the phone back on. The car was here, but not on the street. There was an unlocked gate to his right. He pushed it open. In the glow from a light in a portacabin, he saw rows and rows of cars. 'Daily hire at mates rates,' proclaimed a banner. There was no sign of life. A car engine ticked as it cooled in the night air. He walked over and laid his hand flat on the bonnet. There was almost no heat left in it. He bent down and retrieved his tracker from the bumper, glancing round to check that he wasn't being watched. He wished he had night-vision goggles and a pistol in his belt, a Sig Sauer. He was a sitting duck. There was a slither of gravel nearby and he threw himself flat. He held his breath. The sound grew closer and he risked a glance under the car, turning his head millimetre by millimetre. An urban fox stopped in mid-track, turned his amber eyes on him, their mirrored surface flashing an unearthly silver in the light from the hut, and trotted off. Archie rested his head on his folded arms. The parking lot was quiet, the man he was hunting either long gone or laughing at him from the shadows.

He got to his feet, brushed the gravel from his front. On impulse he shouted, 'If you're still here, I just want to talk. I'm looking for a woman called Petal.' His voice carried a long way in the night air. There was no reply. He looked round a last time and began to walk towards his old home. 'They'll be alright,' he said to himself, over and over again, pushing the images from his mind of families lying dead in their homes covered with their furnishings; curtains and spreads of flowery fabric, sewn on happy days, now shrouds.

As he walked along the back alleys and side streets, he imagined he could put his key in the door and shout, 'Hello, darling. I'm home.' He imagined the food on the table, his son wrapped in a towel after bath-time, smelling of shampoo and baby oil. He imagined sitting him on his knee as he ate his meal, enjoying the soft weight of him, seeing his luminous eyes as the lids fell and he dropped into sleep to wake with a startle. He missed the shared warmth of two people sitting together, holding each other, those precious moments of loving touch. What had anything else been about. Really? He paused to catch his breath, holding onto a rusty railing.

The houses in his old street were growing quiet as he passed along the back lane, rolling his foot down on each step, heel to toe, a cat's tread. He depressed the new handle on the back gate. It didn't give. He put his hands on the wall and heaved himself up onto the top. His wife was sitting at the kitchen table with her mother, Frances. They were talking over a bottle of wine that stood beside the baby alarm. There was the faint glow of a night light from Daniel's room. He dropped down onto the ground and a flood-light flashed on, triggered by the movement. Margaret must have spotted him on his last visit. Security had increased. His wife looked towards the wall, and froze. Her mother picked up her phone and dialled a number. He climbed back up onto the wall and dropped into the lane, running, the alley close about him, a smell of household rubbish and cat pee. He tripped over a bin and its metal lid crashed to the ground before he could catch it. The noise stunned him. He stopped and covered his ears, then walked towards the road. Three streets later, a police car passed him, and slowed. He opened the nearest garden gate and strolled up the path, reaching into his pocket as if he was looking for a key, as if he lived there. The police car picked up speed and turned right at the end of the road towards his old home. He turned on his heel and walked back to the gate. A lone poppy, the last of the season, drooped over the path. He remembered walking through the poppy fields with his unit; their camouflage was yellow in the sea of pink, their weapons black like the centre of the flowers. At the end of the summer, he had slashed at the small, green grenades of their seed pods. Their gossamer flowers had been nothing like the wreaths laid for the fallen, those boys from yesterday and a hundred years ago – clay men cast in bronze on war memorials, eternal and indestructible. Was he one of them, the glorious dead, although still walking? He twisted off the poppy's head and crushed it under foot. One less. Stepping over the gate, he headed for Mike's flat, his head down.

He went in by the front door without scanning the street, too tired to care about anything; made an outcast by the flood-light at his old home, as if he was the enemy, to be identified and then eliminated. He called Mike's name as he went in but there was no reply. He walked into his box room. It was strung with fairy lights, and a faux-fur bedspread from a pound shop safari had been added to the bed. Women's clothes were strewn over it, the strange fronds of legs of worn tights trailing onto the floor. He reached under the bed and found his sleeping bag stuffed behind his rucksack, then he stepped over hair tongs on the floor and walked into the kitchen. The bags of food had all been unpacked into the cupboards, there was a bottle of bleach by the sink and a different microwave on the counter. Mike's friend must have moved in. Archie was an intruder now. He put the keys on the counter with two pounds and took a loaf of bread and a packet of raisins from the cupboard. He plugged in his phone to charge and logged onto the computer in the hall to bring up his Facebook page. 'Take a week off to consolidate your own practice, girls,' he typed. 'Follow the routine I have shown you, and use the verse from James 1:4 as your motivation. "Let patience have her perfect work that ye may be perfect and entire, wanting for nothing." I'll review your progress next week.' He shut down the computer and set off for his den.

# 32

CALUM LOOKED TIRED when he came into Petal's room with some tea and toast. 'How was your date, you slimy bastard?' she asked.

He looked up sharply and put the tray on the table with a sigh. 'I've warned you about your manners before,' he said.

She moved away from the wall on which she had been leaning to the edge of the bed. Her ankle still hurt but the pain was less now. 'I'm sorry,' she said, 'I've been too hungry to sleep. You've been gone a long time.' She was determined to keep him on side. 'How was your date?'

'Sarcasm won't get you anywhere,' he replied.

'I wasn't being sarcy,' she said.

'Okay. The evening wasn't what I expected.'

'No?'

'No. Let's just say that when one arranges to meet a beautiful woman, one doesn't expect some hairy male bastard to turn up. One who has two homes but lives in a wood pile. The interesting fruits of shadowing someone.'

'You're not making any sense.'

'No,' he agreed. 'I'm working on it.' He passed her a cup of tea. 'Milk, no sugar. You see, we're getting to know each other.' He took a sip of his own. 'Would anyone be looking for you?'

'Apart from the police, you dickhead?' she said.

'Language, Petal. Your behaviour really is most challenging sometimes. Believe me when I say, the loser I saw was no cop. Let's just say, he pinged my radar. I have a feeling for these things. It's a gift.'

'Why would you have a gift like that?'

'We all have it, Pet. Our primitive instincts. We can feel if someone is watching us. Have you never looked up at a window on the street and seen someone looking straight at you? How did you lock onto them when there were hundreds of places you could have looked, other windows? Your inner cavewoman, your Paleo-pal, deep inside, told you they were there. It's your animal instinct and it talks to you all the time. We just forget about it, tune it out, in this world of computers and 4G. The primitive world is all around you, Petal. It never went away, only nowadays the hunters are watching their prey from the ether, hiding in the Cloud. They're waiting to pounce when you break cover.'

'Calum,' she said, 'I'm too tired and hungry to listen to this.'

'Hell's empty and the devils are all here.'

He smiled and picked up the plate of toast, picked up a piece and held it to her lips. 'Bite this, Petal,' he said.

She leaned back. 'No, thanks.'

'Just one bite to keep me happy, then you can eat the rest yourself.'

'You're making me uncomfortable,' she said.

'One bite. Here comes the plane.'

She opened her mouth. He pulled the toast away as she bit down. 'Why would I feed someone like you?' he shouted. 'Why should I even be interested? Eh? You tell me that? Why should I bother talking to you when you can't be bothered to listen?' He walked out of the room and banged the door shut.

Petal put her head in her hands and looked at the plate of cold toast before her. She picked it up and began to chew the pulpy flour. 'He will not beat me,' she said. 'He is mentally ill, and I am a skilled mental health practitioner. I will not jump into his traps. I am Francine the Brave. I am Francine the Survivor. He just needs a good felt workshop.' She laughed out loud at the thought. 'I am positive-talking myself. I am positive-talking myself because I am so deeply in the shit.' She swallowed the last piece of toast and began to tap her head, eye sockets, chin, collar bone, chest and fingers. 'I will get out of this,' she said. 'I am a professional mental health practitioner. Emotional Freedom Technique is my friend. EFT and tapping will help me control my thoughts. I will survive.' She tapped the message into her body. Morse code. 'I will survive.' Tap, tap, tap. 'I will survive.'

## 33

Archie's sleeping bag was warm and he slept till mid-morning. Sunday had disappeared in a blur of tins of beer drunk on an empty stomach. Through the branches of his home, he could see the volunteers gathering round the portacabin at the start of the week. The main man, the gardener, opened the shed full of spades and hoes. There was a bucket of gloves, fingers poking out over the edge, others reaching up into the air. He remembered the hand he had recovered after the IED went off under the Snatch Land Rover in front of him on the road to Now Zad. It had seemed fake, a Halloween prop, and he had put it into the Bergen with other body parts from the road. It was a child's game, gathering pieces of an action doll with pop-on, pop-off limbs. The torso bulged under a tarpaulin in the back of the Land Rover and in his worst nightmares, it crawled along the road, wailing through the gaping lips of its severed neck. Archie picked up his can of water to take a sip but spilt it down his front. He rolled onto his side, pulling the wet fabric away from his chest. The air was cold, although the sun was breaking through the sea mist from the estuary. There was the clang of gates opening at the end of the drive, and three powerful black cars rolled up to the hut. A number of men and women got out laughing, then pulled on Hunter wellies and put waxed jackets over their suits. Their leader shook hands with the head gardener. There was more laughter as the group plunged their hands into the bucket of gloves and shared them out.

'Gather round everybody,' said their leader. 'As you know, the bank likes to give you the opportunity to actively promote team-building while giving something back to the community. David here,' he waved at the head gardener, who smiled, 'has kindly organised a team challenge. The first team to fill six buckets with windfall apples from the orchard will be served a vegetarian lunch by the losing team. Although it goes without saying that everyone who has turned up today is a winner. As the Governor of the Bank of England, Mark Carney, said of the miraculous growth in our economy, the glass is half full.'

There was a cheer. David stepped forward. 'I'd like to welcome you all to the therapeutic community garden in Edinburgh's oldest surviving orchard. The hospital here was founded by Andrew Duncan after the poet Robert Fergusson died aged twenty-three in chains in Bedlam. Duncan was so shocked by what he saw that, like Philippe Pinel, who smashed the chains of inmates at the notorious Salpêtrière in Paris, he wanted to establish a humane and therapeutic environment for those suffering from mental distress. The orchard here was part of that programme. Nature is nurture. It connects us all to a fruitful world outside our own immediate concerns.'

A mobile phone went off, and one of the group turned away, pressing it to his ear as he strolled towards the wall. David continued, 'Nature places us as fellow creatures in a true relationship to all the other eco-, macro- and micro-systems around us. It is not a place for ego, but simply a place to be. Harmonious co-existence is essential to our survival and the larger environment. As the economist Schumacher said in 1973, "Small is beautiful." I commend his book to you. We need to move away from the all-consuming systems of industry and downsize, literally return to our roots – please excuse the pun. If the world consumed at the same rate as Britain then we'd need three planets worth of resources to support the human race. You do the sums. I hope that today's experience will give you a sense of proportionality.'

'Do you mind if I light up, David?' asked the lead banker. 'Sorry to interrupt. You were saying?'

'I'd finished,' said David.

'Great,' said the banker and started a short round of applause, banging his gloved hand on one thigh.

Archie rolled onto his back and sighed. He could hear the group walking along the gravel path to the orchard and heard their laughter and the thump of apples as they hit the bottom of the tubs. He looked out again, wondering if he could slip out from his hiding place and stretch his legs. There was a man he hadn't noticed before sitting in the shadow of one of the shrubs in the circle of chairs. Archie was sure he hadn't got out of one of the cars. He was looking towards Archie's log-pile house. He was about the height and weight of the guy he had tried to follow on Saturday night. The man pulled a packet of cigarettes out of his pocket and put one between his lips, then, still staring at Archie's hiding place, he pulled a lighter from his pocket. He held it up in the air and clicked it several times. A small yellow flame appeared. He lit up, and then, putting the lighter in his pocket, walked over to the shed. A can of petrol was lying at the door, ready to fill the mower. The paths were overgrown with grass. The man picked up the can of fuel and swung it to gauge how much was left in it. It was heavy. He looked back towards Archie's den. He smiled and patted his lighter pocket. Archie wanted to bomb-blast out of his shelter and crash into him, crush him to the ground and grind his nose into his skull with his bunched fist. He held himself rigid. He began to count to ten, then twenty. He tried to breathe into his abdomen. A groan escaped from deep in his chest. 'He is not a target,' he said to himself. 'I am not a target.' He wished he had a gun. He could sort this fucker out. Watch his head pop and his brains flower red under the boiled egg-shell of his skull. He took another breath. Thirty. Thirty. Count to a hundred. Thirty-one, thirty-two, and he was back on a rocky road, driving up into the hills behind the Snatch, thirty-three, closer to the target area … thirty-four. Stop counting. Stop counting. Archie threw open the door of his hiding place and ran towards the shed. The man was gone. The shed was deserted, everything stored neatly in its place: rows of spades, forks and rakes hanging above the petrol can. He looked right and left, nothing. He stopped and turned round, fast-walking away from the inhabited part of the garden towards the deep cover of the shrubs along the wall.

He crouched there watching as the bankers returned with their buckets of apples; watched as they sat in a circle chatting and eating plates of vegetable stew with bottles of wine on the table. Archie's stomach rumbled. He closed his eyes. He must have dozed off. When he woke it was growing dark. The gate clanged shut and the cars drove off, changing up through the gears as they pulled away. His limbs were stiff and he hobbled back to his hole and pulled out his sleeping bag and phone. He picked up a few sticks thinking he might cook some potatoes when the beam of a torch illuminated the path from the hospital. Was it the dick with the lighter? Two policemen swung into sight. He could hear their walkie-talkies. The beam of the torch swung left and right scanning the area. He ran back to the shelter of the shrubs and threw himself flat. If he didn't move, they wouldn't be able to pick him out. He froze to the ground, averting his gaze. He heard their feet crack on the rough surface as they walked round the huge pile of wood and debris. He risked a look and saw them pull back the door to his cave. 'Someone's been here alright,' said a voice. 'Welcome to the Ritz.'

'Could be a rough sleeper,' replied the other. 'Do you want to hang around and see if they come back? There's water in his mini-bar and fresh fruit.'

'Knowing our luck we'll wait all night. Log it, will you. We can look back later.'

There was the green glow of a screen and the tapping of a plastic stylus; the words of a report snaking across the surface in a black, continuous line – the thin line of his misery that stood between him and his old life, the brilliant place he had thought dull.

When they left he shouldered his rucksack and walked in the direction of the Commonwealth Pool to find shelter. He pulled up his hoodie as he reached the steps of the public building and slipped in with the crowd of office workers heading for the gym after work. He strolled over to the desk, trying not to look for security cameras. 'I wonder if anyone handed in a pair of trunks last week?' he asked.

The receptionist pulled a basket out from under the desk. 'Take your pick,' she said.

He selected a pair of Hawaiian shorts from the bottom, reasoning that they had been there the longest, unclaimed.

'I'm surprised you're prepared to admit to those,' she laughed.

He smiled without looking up, hiding his eyes that were memorable for all the wrong reasons. 'There goes my better half,' he said, waving towards a young mother walking away from the self-service till towards the changing room with her child. He hoped the receptionist would assume she had paid for him too.

Downstairs, he slipped his feet into blue, plastic shoes and strode to the nearest cubicle. The trunks weren't a bad fit, but then almost anything would have done. He had lost a lot of weight. He showered, letting the trickle of warm water run down over his head, washing the grime and the cold out of his body. He lathered up with soap from the dispenser, rubbing pink gel that smelled of carbolic and poverty all over his body and hair. He hoped that no one would notice the puddle of water at his feet, gritty with earth. It was a long way from the sandalwood body scrub of his spa membership.

He wandered out into the lit arena of the pool, dived into the fast lane and set off in a crawl. One, two, three, breathe. His strokes were still powerful, but on his third length a man came up behind him and overtook him on the opposite side. 'You might want to try the slower lane, mate,' he said at the end, before pushing off from the side.

Archie watched as the red latex cap of his head dipped into the water, disappeared and reappeared, effortless, athletic, and his own limbs grew heavy as if they could pull him down, leave him weighted on the tiled bottom, a sightless corpse, drowned in his comedy Hawaiian-paradise shorts. He ducked under the plastic discs of the lane divider, and swam on his back, back-stroking with slow strokes up and down the middle lane. His muscles warmed to the cold water. In a small adjacent pool women were pushing floats through the water to 1980s disco music. A pregnant woman floated in the crescent of a yellow foam woggle at the back of the class. Her protruding belly-button on top of her bump pushed through her costume, the strange distortion of swelling as the child grew inside her, displacing her, as Daniel had displaced Hannah. He looked back at the ceiling, kicked his legs faster and completed the length in under a minute thirty. Not as good as his old time but not bad, he thought. The women were applauding their teacher, who had sketched out the underwater movements in a slow-motion dance on the poolside. Archie recognised the heavy movements as his own, the exaggerated awareness of a mimed normality in the wrong element. He moved through the water of memory in the thin air of the present. It was all laborious, disjointed. He swam to the metal steps and pulled himself out, soaping down in the shower with more red jelly, revelling in the warmth of the water, the relaxation in his muscles. He didn't care if the police caught him. He wondered if he could ask the receptionist to phone them for him. They would take him to the womb of the cell, and ring Dr Clark. He got dressed, comforted by the thought that he could end it, and put his blue plastic shoes in the bin by the door, disposing of the forensic evidence of his solitary visit.

Upstairs in the café, there was a half-eaten baked potato and cheese on a tray on the clearing station. With a glance over his shoulder, he took it across to a table overlooking the pool and sat down. It was still warm. He ate the uneaten half first and then the skin of the scooped-out second half, washed down with a glass of water from the cooler. There was a copy of the local paper on the table. The news was playing on a continuous feed on the telly behind the counter. BAE systems had shut down operations in Portsmouth but kept orders for the Clyde. 'This is a cynical manoeuvre to keep Scotland on-side before the referendum,' a Southern docker was shouting. 'There have been five hundred years of shipbuilding at Portsmouth. We've been sacrificed,' he said. The screen switched to men streaming out of the Govan yard, shaking their heads: eight hundred and fifty jobs were to go there too.

'Archie Forbes,' said a voice behind him, enunciating every syllable in his name at half speed. 'How on earth are you doing?'

He looked up and the speaker came into focus. 'Stephen,' he said, without warmth.

'It's all going to kick off,' said Stephen, waving at the screen, 'because no one told the silly buggers the real orders have gone to Korea. We've had peace between Scotland and England for three hundred years and now they're at each other's throats before they've even had the referendum. It'll start as a war of rhetoric and end as a trade war, you mark my words. They thought the malt tax was bad; you watch how tough a game of hard ball England will play if we split. That Govan contract will be the first to go.' Stephen caught sight of the Hawaiian shorts drying on the top of Archie's rucksack. 'Not your usual style,' he said.

'No,' Archie agreed, pushing them back into his rucksack, and standing up. 'How's tricks?' he asked, looking towards the door.

'Not bad,' said Stephen. 'Lots to tell. Sit tight and I'll get you a coffee. You don't need to rush off, do you?'

'Actually –' Archie said, conjuring the word from his previous life.

'Nonsense,' interrupted Stephen. 'I insist. You need to get back in the loop. There's more than one of us thinks you were badly treated by Forbes, Stock and Wilson.'

'Shafted is the word you're looking for,' said Archie, 'by the kangaroo court they call the shareholders. I got my twenty-eight days' notice of the vote, but the ordinary resolution was passed as I knew it would be.'

'Still, they'd give you a nice settlement,' said Stephen, rubbing his fingers together.

'No, they got me for personal liability on the contract with Fitzroy Ltd when it went into insolvent liquidation. I was only a shadow director, but you know the rest.'

'The civil action against you.'

'So you heard,' said Archie. 'I'm bankrupt, but at least the house was in Hannah's name.'

Stephen nodded. 'I'll get those coffees,' he said.

He returned with a tray. 'Flat white Americano, okay?' he asked. 'I got you a large. Looks like you could do with it.'

'Thanks,' said Archie. 'I thought you swam at the Calton Hill Club?'

'Still do, but I have the grand-sprogs staying.' He waved a hand in the direction of the soft-play area. Tiny people were screaming in the nets and crashing into the ball pool. Archie waited for an intrusive thought, but nothing came. He looked back at Stephen, who held his gaze. 'How's the wife and kid?' he asked.

'Long story,' said Archie.

'And the long story short would be?'

'Another time,' said Archie.

'Look, Archie,' said Stephen, leaning forward. 'You look like shit. I'd better tell you that it's common knowledge that you've been having some difficulties. I can help you. Get you back across the Rubicon, so to speak. I've made a nice killing on the Lloyds and Post Office flotations, although you know they pegged the PO back to seven hundred pounds worth of shares per applicant. Purely political to keep the man in the street happy, of course, but there are some nice things coming up in Twitter and some derivatives. Here's the thing: I know of a good deal coming up in Stan. It's a bloody gold mine, and if Karzai can sort out a deal with the Taliban, get a bit of stability, well, I don't need to finish the sentence. Open market. Chaos breeds opportunity, especially when there are nice, juicy assets.'

Archie got to his feet. 'I need to go,' he said.

'I'm not impugning your efforts,' he said. 'You and the boys.'

'Right,' said Archie. He could feel something flexing its muscles inside him. Was it rage?

'Keep in touch,' said Stephen, sliding his card across the table to him. 'Seriously.'

Archie nodded, but left the card on the table. He dropped the shorts on the desk as he passed. 'Sorry,' he said. 'They weren't mine after all.'

*   *   *

Unable to decide where to go, he walked towards his den and found himself back on Warrender Park Terrace. The lights were still off in Petal's flat but he rang the bell anyway. There was no reply. As he reached the pavement, a student was coming out of the main door of the block. 'Hold the door,' Archie called, with a cheery wave. He could check one last time whether there was some clue as to her whereabouts that he had overlooked. It was a risk but worth it. He was running out of ideas.

The back garden was as before and Petal's rear windows were still dark. He could hear the hens clucking in their nest box. He put down some more feed for them, pushed open the bathroom window and climbed in. He walked into the kitchen and closed the blind before turning on a lamp. There was an unopened carton of almond milk standing on the counter and he drank it, before sitting at the table with its pots of wilting herbs and burnt-down candles. He lit one and looked into its flame. He was tired. The light danced in a corona before his eyes. The edges of the room grew misty and dissolved in trailing colours. He lay his head on his arms, folded on the table. His forehead was pressed into the crook of his elbow and the warmth from his body was comforting. It was a quiet corner in this noisy city where he wandered in a state of vigilance. He drifted off, aware of the warmth of the candle and a distant rumble of Petal's central heating boiler starting up. As it ignited, Calum puffed up in his blank mind, popcorn light, and took form. He was without boundaries, blasted from a hard kernel on a withered stalk. He was the transformative being who could not be, who should not walk but did, and he reached out through Archie's eyes and ears to find a new existence in a world between now and never. His voice was melodic and deep. It rumbled in Archie's head, and oppressed the captive woman trapped out of sight. Archie heard him, but could not challenge him – his volume, his purpose, his threat of rage hidden like a cudgel behind his back. Archie knew he was there, and wanted to pacify him, soothe his anger, his unpredictability, but the popcorn man, the horror, walked from his imagination and lived; unchallenged because of all he might do, could do, does.

Archie lifted his head from the table and looked round panicking. He wasn't sure what was inside and what was out. It played in his head like a radio that hits the channel before being turned down. There was static. He stood up, knocking the chair over, and tried to out-walk the image and the sound, wandering from room to room. He trailed his fingers over the perfect, polished wood of the sideboard. He drew circles along the grain of walnut veneers, tracing the torsos of men trapped in the wood, encasing sherry glasses and playing cards. He felt close to her here, certain she would come back somehow, and he viewed the movie of her in his mind, saw her captivity unfold towards crisis and knew that she would escape. He knew it, willed it, so that she could come back to him, and the police wouldn't think that he had abducted her because at that moment, this moment, he couldn't make sense of her absence, her missingness. She was/wasn't the girl on the poster on the tree. He was/wasn't dreaming her. All would be well. If Archie patrolled, he would spot the crack she had slipped through. He knew it was there somewhere – perhaps in the wallpaper in the hall, tucked in behind a wrinkle in the pattern, or between the joins where the long strips didn't meet but should. It was in those special places that only the owner of a house saw: the crack in the floorboards that has been filled but is working loose; the hole where the radiator pipe disappears into the dark where hair gathers. Those were the places he would find Petal, but he had to be quiet, surprise her captor – the voice/man in his head who was holding her.

He marched in slow time along the hall to calm down, stopped at the front door and turned back, placing each foot heel first in a choreographed march, swinging his arms as he passed the empty archways of the doors to unlit rooms. It was here in this hallway that he would find the portal, reach in and seize Calum by the throat and strangle him, silence his voice. 'Petal is here. Petal-is-here. Petalishere,' he whispered. He turned at the end of the hall, turned and returned, slow march. He looked down and noticed the hole worn in the rug. This could be it. He knelt down and pressed his eye to the floor. Calum's voice was louder here. He saw him talking to Petal beneath the boards. He had him. Calum was right here beneath his feet and he was talking to Petal, gesticulating. The words became clearer, he saw her fear but he knew she was brave. He jumped to his feet and pulled at the rug.

There was a knocking sound, at the kitchen window, a staccato spray of bullets. Archie threw himself flat and covered his head. 'Is that you, Petal?' asked a voice. 'It's Mrs Robb. I was just checking the hens. Petal? I see they've been fed, so I'm assuming you're back. Perhaps you've had an early night. Give me a ring when you have a minute then, dear. Bye, now.' Archie heard the back door to the communal stair close, and the sound of feet passing along the passageway. A door banged upstairs. He stood up, staring at the planks of wood under his feet. The floor looked ordinary. The woodworm voices were silent; the rug crumpled on one side. He straightened it, and walked into the kitchen to blow out the candle. Calum's voice was gone. Archie tipped his head from one side to the other, like a swimmer with water trapped in his ears, but there was nothing. He filled a glass at the tap and as he drank, scanning the room, he noticed that there was a phone on the wall and written on a faded sticker above a line of numbers were the words, 'My mobile.' He added it to his contacts and called the number. It rang. He drew a deep breath. He could solve the mystery. There was a click and then the operator's voice, 'Please leave a message.' He ended the call and looked round the empty room. He wiped round the surfaces he had touched with a dish-towel from the sink and rinsed it out in the basin. He couldn't stay here, compound the picture of his guilt by association. He pushed up the bathroom window and climbed back out into the night.

* * *

Archie paused as he neared his den in the hospital grounds. That comedian with the lighter was creeping him out, and the police might come back. He needed time to think; to think how to mesh his worlds into one. He walked back to Canaan Lane and over to Braid Road past the spot where Edinburgh's last two highwaymen were hung. He walked past rows of bungalows to the crest of the hill at Fairmilehead and left the city. The buildings stopped at the boundary of the by-pass, a new city wall. There were fields beyond. He dodged the cars exiting the dual carriageway, and walked up the country road towards the ski centre. Turning off the path, he climbed up through the trees to the brow of the hill, then dropped down over the ridge onto a sheep track. He followed it until he came to a ruined shepherd's cottage that he remembered from summer picnics with his wife. Had they really fed each other strawberries here? Kissed until they grew dizzy on wine and each other? He threw his bag into a corner and sat with his back against the wall opposite the empty doorway, looking straight out over the estuary and the city. Orange lights twinkled under a full moon. An aeroplane approached over the cone of Berwick Law, its landing lights flashing as it lost height, the wind pushing its belly playfully back up. He thought of the passengers fastening their seat belts, the reunions they looked forward to, the kisses of welcome on the concourse, the context of lives over which they still had control.

He looked up at the sky sparkling with stars. Was there someone up there on another planet as unhappy as him? Had they sailed in front of the Kepler telescope – a blip in a star's brilliance; their misery no more than a mote floating in the eye's black jelly of a distant observer, ungrasped, indefinable. Somewhere among the four hundred billion stars of the galaxy, there would be someone like him, trapped on a planet in the Goldilocks zone, neither too hot nor cold for life. The question was, what sustained them when the vacuum was inside? Where were the planets that could sustain love – constant, free-flowing – not frozen solid, or boiled dry by too much want and desire; by politicians waving their troops on; by businesses hungry for profit; by jealous lovers and armed men? His limbs sank around his empty stomach and his head dropped onto the bed of leaves. He remembered Daniel's baby fist closing round his proffered finger. The love in his eyes. He curled his body against the contours of the hollow in which he lay, and he gazed at the stars and his distant, fellow beings, empty and sore.

Hours later, he surfaced to the first diamonds of frost strewn by dawn across his green carpet, her face a pitiless yellow, smiling on the horizon. His choices would fall with the mercury. He couldn't live outdoors much longer, and he couldn't return without knowing Petal was safe. Petal's disappearance would be laid at his door. He was sure of that. His staring eyes would look great in the *Crimewatch* mug shot. He was watershed man now.

# 34

PETAL LAY ON HER BED IN THE DARK. She had lost track of the days. The light from the street fell in a chess-board pattern on the floor of the basement: black and white dots on the bare concrete, stark and unyielding. She was out of condition, her hip bones were curved blades under her clothes as her hands traced their contours. Her injured ankle felt shrivelled, like a trailing plant cutting itself off from its roots, drying its stem until it narrowed and separated from the parent. She would leave her foot in this bed as it dropped from her withered ankle under the pressure from the sheets. The basement was a plain in a dark land in which she was stranded. She had thought that in tough times she would inhabit her mind, feed her dry life with a nectar of memories from summer holidays – long days on picnics, in rowing boats, lying in the heather on high mountains, laughing with friends at the exertion, the relief of having reached the top on legs that trembled. Now there was nothing. The uncertainty of not knowing how Calum Ben would behave was paralysing. He stood between her and all that had gone before – everything she was, everything she knew. She thought of Queen Mary's Bothwell going mad in his Danish cell, his bottle dungeon. She was trapped in the bottle dungeon of her mind by fear. This was no light place of inner resources, of mental treasures, and she wished she had paid more attention to all the good things in her life – revisited each one at the end of each day she had survived in health and freedom; catalogued them in memory and stored them away on the shelves of her inner being. On days like these, days of captivity, filled only with long hours of pain, denial and deprivation, those jewels were the only light. How could she have been so rich and so unaware? Now the shapeless figure of Calum peered down into her captivity from the bottleneck above, searched her face through narrowed eyes, and everything she was, or had ever been, was his. He stood between her and her life: anonymous and immovable.

She got up and walked over to the bathroom, put on the light and splashed her face in the sink. The water escaped down the drain in its perfect helix, swirling clockwise. She put her hand over the hole. The running water filled up the basin, covering her fingers. She took off her socks and stuffed them in the overflow and put in the plug. She pushed her jumper down the toilet and pushed the flush. The bowl filled up. She did it again and then, taking off the lid, jammed her shoe over the ballcock to keep it down and the cistern filling. The basin was overflowing now, the rushing sound a gurgling brook, a free-running stream. She turned the taps on full and paddled across the floor to her room. She leaned against the wall behind the door, so that she would be hidden when it opened. The water spread. It covered the chess-board shadows from the grille, an unearthly checker-board in a new Atlantis. 'Come on, you bastard,' she thought. 'Come and play my game,' and she laughed. The water was cold as it passed over her feet and under the door. There was silence from the rest of the house. The sound of the cascade from the basin filled her ears. 'Help,' she shouted. 'Calum, help.' But there was only silence. It was colder than ever. She waded over to her bed and lay on the island of her mattress, watching the water creep up the walls. It must have been seeping away through porous bricks because it never rose above her bed legs, and she lay on her raft in the black ocean and waited, wondering.

*   *   *

Daylight played on the pool of water when she woke. A bus ticket was floating on it and a cigarette butt from under the bed. She watched them lazily circling each other and then there was a shout of exclamation from outside. There was a slap of a tray hitting water and the door shook as it was unlocked. 'For fuck's sake, Petal,' Calum shouted as he ran in and splashed towards the bathroom. The door to the hall was open. Petal sprang from the bed and waded towards it. She tried to pull the door shut behind her, to lock him in his own horrible chamber, but he had already turned. His eyes were blazing. She ran. There was a short flight of stairs ahead with a threadbare carpet that had once been red with gold roses. She ran up them, her legs heavy, lop-sided as her ankle took her weight. Adrenaline roared through her blood as she reached the landing. There was another door and she closed her hand on the handle even as she saw the keyhole shining empty and bright. It was locked. She banged on the door, looking over her shoulder. She shouted 'Help', but her throat was dry. Calum wasn't running up the stairs behind her. He was standing at the foot, his arms folded across his chest. He wasn't laughing at her. He was silent. She sat down with her back against the wall and rested her head on her knees. She turned her head to look down at him: a Colossus in the dark water, the bus-ticket sailing ship sinking at his feet. The water depth fell, shrinking fibre by fibre against the water mark on his jeans.

The silence grew. Petal could hear bird-song beyond the door, feel a cool breeze from a window, burnt fresh with early frost. Somewhere in the garden a robin would be turning over an iced brown leaf, looking at the ground with its beady eye for food. She was trapped here with this un-man, her captor. 'I am not your prisoner,' she said. 'I am Arabella Dexter and I want you to let me go.'

'Petal,' he said.

'And I am not Petal; not to you.'

'But I'm all you've got,' he replied. 'Come back downstairs.' He held out his hand in invitation.

She shook her head.

'Come back downstairs and I'll see what I can do. I'm not a bad man. I don't want you to be unhappy.'

'I don't trust you,' she said.

'You have no choice,' he replied.

She walked down the stairs, trailing a hand on the cold plaster wall. 'Where am I anyway?' she asked.

'Do you really expect me to tell you?' he asked, and held out his hand.

She took it, her ankle painful, and they paddled to her bed. The water was less now, ankle deep. There was a smell of sewage and old drains. 'I can't stay here,' she said.

He nodded. 'Stay on the bed and I'll see what I can do. It's almost over now, Petal,' he said.

'What's almost over?' Her throat was tight.

'This,' he replied. 'This – is almost over.' He walked over to the door. 'I find it pays to time-limit my projects. If there isn't a return in an anticipated time frame then it's time to pull the plug.' He laughed, and waved a manicured hand at the chaos. 'Literally, in this case.'

'I thought you said you couldn't let me go?'

He sat down on one of the chairs and put his feet up on the other. 'We live in a curious world, Petal. Let me tell you how this will play out,' said Calum. 'You phone the police and you say a man you went on a blind date with locked you up and refused to let me go. They come round and knock on my door, if they can find it, and say, "Is this true? Did you hold this woman against her will?" And I say, "Why, Officer …" His voice was high, outraged, celluloid, "She's having you on. We've had a fight and she stormed off in a huff. I think I said she was past her sell-by date. I admit that was unkind but, you know. She's no spring chicken. It's a risk you take on blind dates. Not everyone tells the truth about their age.'

'You're sick,' said Petal.

He held up a hand. 'You're interrupting, Petal. I don't like that. And anyway, nothing happened, not really. You can't point a finger at me and say I ravished you like a Victorian villain, or a Greek God. There was no Leda and the swan. I treated you like a child, an honoured guest. You enjoyed my food.'

'They'll never believe you. I'll tell them the truth.'

'Well, you can tell them, but you'll have to prove your lies, your horrid lies, Petal, because really you're a bit of a hysteric, aren't you? We were casual lovers who fell out and you have a bit of a grudge against me, or maybe you're making it up to discredit me for some strange, warped reason of your own. I'd save yourself the trouble.'

'They will believe me. I'm a professional with a good job.'

'You're a crank in crank-ville. You're a bit left-of-centre, a bit "arty".' He made an inverted comma sign as he spoke the last word, pushing down his middle and index fingers as he held his hands level with his face. They framed his dark eyes. He was his own mythology.

'You're crazy,' she said. 'You are truly fucking nuts.'

'That's gratitude for you, and I went to some trouble to text your mum and friends at the top of your contacts list so they wouldn't worry,' he said. 'But never mind. It's your word against mine. If they find me.' He emphasised the word 'if'. 'My work is about to take me out of the country. So this is how it will go. You'll say I locked you up. I'll say I didn't. Corroboration is my get-out-of-jail-free card. They need proof to get me and you can't give it to them. There is no proof. No witness. If there is no corroboration, there is no crime. Who came up with that, eh? It's genius. It's a gift – to me. So why don't you just suck it up and get over yourself? It was all in your mind, Petal. That door was never locked. That's what I'll say.'

'I don't want to hear this,' said Petal. 'You are very, very sick.'

He stepped forward and breathed in her ear. 'Why don't you admit it?' he said. 'You fancied me. All that stuff in the bar. "I'd like kids one day",' he said, imitating her voice. 'But it's getting too late, isn't it, Petal? Tick-tock. I don't think you're thirty-five at all.'

She turned her face away. 'You have got it all so wrong.'

'Not so wrong,' he said, 'because I'll come out of this with what I wanted. It's all part of the game. It's my massive, multi-player, off-line, role-playing game, and you've got a starring role. It's real-time strategy in real life. I'm a hacker using Heartbleed, except I'm syphoning you into my world, meshing you into a new, multi-dimensional reality. Fun, but the best bit will be when they come after me. You'll play your role well. You'll be very convincing, very distressed, but I'll elude the hunt, because ultimately, where I'm going, they can't follow.'

# 35

ARCHIE WATCHED THE LONG LINES of cars on the by-pass grow like beads on an abacus; the worker bees going to the hive. He wished he was one of them, sitting in his car on the leather seats, his satnav at his fingertips, his wife's belly swelling with the new life he had planted there, his home built of solid stone minutes away.

He huddled in his sleeping bag and nibbled his bread ration from Mike's flat, and sipped water from his bottle filled at the stream nearby. He hadn't passed any dead animals lying in it, polluting the water. The clouds were pink over the Forth and they melted away until the sky became an icy, cornflower blue. He turned grey with cold and tried to sleep again to forget the chill creeping into his fingers.

A dog woke him. Noon. It was pulling the bag of bread from his rucksack. 'Leave it, Nelson,' shouted a woman's voice but the dog bounded over to her, trailing slices from the plastic bag. She grabbed the dog by the collar and threw the bag into the dying grass. 'Hey,' he shouted from his doorway and hopped into view in his sleeping bag, filling the doorway of the derelict cottage, larval and incongruous.

'Sorry,' the woman muttered, turning away and snapping the lead onto the dog's collar. 'I didn't know it was yours.'

'You stupid bitch,' he shouted after her. She walked faster. He pushed down his sleeping bag and untangled it from his boots. The landscape looked huge and there was no cover, but he forced himself outside to look for the bread. His heart was pumping as he stumbled over the grass. It had landed in a boggy patch and was soaking up brackish water like blotting paper. Archie ground it into the earth under his heel and returned to the cottage. As he paused in the doorway, he remembered entering the warehouse full of almonds near Kandahar, wading through them knee high on the floor, crackling and popping – the crepitus of bones. He had been surrounded by food there. Here there was nothing: a dying year; the imprint of his body in the wet grass. He was endlessly revisiting his life in snapshots, but unable to re-enter the picture of the part he treasured. The difficult memories were his most regular guests now. He sat with his back to the wall and watched the plain. He was on stag – the patrol would relieve him soon. He had to keep his eyes open. He had to make a plan. The sound of male voices and the bleep of a radio brought him to his feet – the tango-charlie-foxtrot trash of radio static. Creeping forward on his belly, he risked a look round the door-frame and saw two police officers making their way towards him, their dog straining at the leash. He threw his rucksack out the back window and climbed through it. Keeping low, he ran as fast as he could towards a coppice of trees. The officers would crest the hill in about five minutes. If they were looking for him, they would check the cottage first. Too late he remembered his sleeping bag. The dog would have his scent, the promise of a reward firing it up. It would bay and gambol, slip its leash. He tried to run but he was stumbling, the tussocks of grass catching his feet. The dog gave an excited bark behind him, still not in view but it wouldn't be long. He reached the trees, forced his way between the springy pine branches and hobbled down towards the stream gurgling at the foot of the slope. Late autumn leaves spun on the surface of the water above rocks speckled brown like trout. Jew's ear fungus curled on the bark of elder trees, listening for pursuit. He knew not to linger here – knew from his training that the water would concentrate his scent for the dog, its radar nose seeking him out. He was the prey. He pulled himself up the far bank, sliding on the mud, which clung to autumn leaves in this gully, unfingered by frost. The field ahead would be better. If he could make it to the far wall before the dog sighted him, it would have to cast around to pick up his trail, gaining him time. The officers' voices behind him were encouraging the dog on. 'Seek. Seek,' the voice on the wind shouted, 'Seek. Seek.'

He skirted the newly ploughed field, white gulls drifting ahead of him, the sticky, black earth clogging his boots. He clambered over the gate at the far end and ran across the country road, dodging a car. Rounding a cottage on the far side, he reached the road to Easter Bush. The university's bio-science research centres stretched out in a new estate near the Roslin Institute. A double-decker bus wobbled along between the hedges, tourists and students sitting upstairs. He threw himself flat in a ditch and wormed his way under a fence into a field planted with experimental crops, small green shoots in beds with white labels on sticks at the end. A student was hoeing nearby, his head nodding to music on his headphones, the occasional word escaping from his lips, a staccato chain of nonsense fragmenting in the air. Archie ran along the hedge-line, keeping low, willing the man not to turn round. There was a spade resting at the gate and Archie put it over his shoulder. It was perfect camouflage, changed him from a fugitive to a worker, and gave his presence in the landscape a rationale that would be acceptable to the casual observer. It meant he would go unnoticed. He walked along the edge of the road. To his left, the steel frame of a new building sketched its skeleton in the air – a blueprint for a lab.

The bus moved off ahead of him, a couple of tourists stranded on the back seat. The students had reached the buildings among the trees. He came to a beech wood, dried leaves crackling under his feet and green, plastic tubes popping up from the ground like shell casings, protecting new saplings from deer and rabbits. He sat down with his back to a tree to catch his breath. He was hungry. He could see students in the cafeteria thirty metres away, filling coffee cups at a coffee machine and carrying trays to tables. Their lives were lit by strip lighting; blue and silver lives at plastic tables; laughter and friendship as they cut and pasted living plants together to make new species – pest and drought-resistant; sought to guarantee the human race food in an inhospitable world; aimed to conquer the inhospitable places, the bad lands, to green the desert. 'What if the bad lands were inside?' he thought. What if the fighting never stopped? What if the real problem was other human beings and not the planet? He saw Adam biting into the apple with strong, white teeth. Which had come first? Apple or desire? The long fall from grace.

There was the wail of a siren, and he saw the student with the headphones walk over to a police car and point in the direction in which he had gone. Blue lights flashed across the field – a disco pursuit of an escaped lunatic. He crawled towards the ditch at the edge of the adjacent field, pushing his rucksack ahead of him, and rolled into the crack in the earth. Sheep looked down at him, chewing, their razor teeth no longer shaving the grass short in small, even strokes. The officers would guess he was here if they read the animals, but as he peered out, the car moved on. The chase was ahead of him. He rolled onto his back and looked at the sky. It was clouding over. The sun was low on its autumnal arc, handing itself from branch to branch among the trees. There was a portacabin nearby and a luminous, orange jacket had been left hanging on a post. The men were at the building site digging a hole with a yellow digger that roared. He put the jacket on, shouldered his spade and walked back onto the road. He was Orange James going to work. The YouTube fanfare sounded in his head. It was blowing a last post for him. He reached the main road and sat in a bus shelter on the edge of a settlement of oatmeal-harled houses. When the light began to fade, he wandered over to the huge metal expanse of an out-of-town supermarket. As he thought, the jumbo bins at the back were being filled with out-of-date stock. He could eat tonight.

'I wonder if I could have some of that, pal?' he asked a teenager.

'No,' he said. 'Piss off.'

'Please. I'm desperate,' he said.

The young guy pulled one earphone out of his ear, looked at Archie's muddy legs and wet shoes. 'Come back later,' he said, 'but don't say I told you.'

# 36

PETAL WAS SHIVERING when Calum came back with a glass of hot chocolate, carried in on a tray, held up shoulder-high. He was a waiter in a Viennese café, a high priest. 'Madam,' he said, presenting it to her with a bow. She took it in both hands, warming them on the glass. His eyes were bright again as he looked at her. 'Drink up,' he said.

She looked at the brown, frothy liquid.

'You want to get out of here, don't you?'

She nodded.

'Then drink it.'

'Is it poisoned?' she asked.

'This isn't a fairy tale,' he replied.

She thought of her life stored behind him, wondered if he was a barrier she could pass through, a neutrino flying unnoticed through the mesh of his being.

'You have to get through me to get out of here, Petal,' he said.

She raised the glass to her lips, too tired to care. 'I would rather die playing your stupid games because I choose to, than spend one more minute here, because you choose to keep me.'

'You're being very melodramatic,' he said.

She waved a hand at the flooded room in the half light, and then raising the glass in a mock toast drank the first sip.

'Good?' he asked.

'Fucking marvellous,' she replied.

He gestured to her to drink the rest, moving closer. 'It's Madagascan chocolate, hand ground …'

'… from the finest cocoa beans,' she finished.

'By me. I'm a connoisseur of the good things in life.'

She looked at him. He seemed to be shrinking. He was watching her, his dark chocolate eyes, cavities in the mask of his face. Their blankness drank her in, drip by drip, drop by drop. Her limbs grew heavy and he stepped forward and lifted her up. 'Close your eyes, Petal,' he said, and he carried her up the stairs, one at a time, each jolt taking her closer to the light. And then there were more stairs to another floor, and she glimpsed a front door behind her, from the corner of her eye that was oh, so heavy, the lid powering down to rest on the rim of her sight.

The water in the bath was warm and scented as he held her head in the crook of his arm and rubbed her body with his free hand, slick with soap. His hand was gentle, rolling over the line of her breast, across her belly and between her thighs. There was glorious light and her mind and her body floated there, willing nothing to be other than it was. It was a strange eternity. He lifted her out, dried her with her silk evening dress and pulled it over her head as if she were a child. He brushed her hair with his fingers, pulling gently at the resistance in her curls. He propped her up against his chest and arranged her shawl around her shoulders.

'What are you doing?' she mumbled.

'Sending you home,' he replied. 'You're not suited to my world after all, and the real thrill, as I say, is eluding the chase. You were merely the appetiser.'

His voice was growing more distant. 'Anyway, this was all I really wanted from you,' he said, kissing the fingers of his left hand, which he bunched to his lips, a diner praising the food, 'to taste your nectar.'

\* \* \*

At the front door, he pulled her arm over his shoulder and guided her out onto the street. It was deserted and they walked, stumbling, along a quiet road, two drunks, two lovers on a date, holding each other up, unremarkable in the city. As they neared the junction with a busy road, he hailed a taxi. 'Get this one home, will you mate?' he said to the driver. 'Here's twenty pounds and her driving licence from her purse. I found her a bit the worse for wear on the street. Don't want anything to happen to the little lady.'

The driver nodded and glanced at the licence. 'Alright,' he said, 'but she'll have to get herself to her front door. I'm not allowed to touch her.'

Petal heard the thud of the cab door and felt herself gliding along the road back to her old life. Home. It was all so remote, so simple. She was the passive player in events framed by others. She would be home soon. She was going home. The cab's tyres jolted over the cobbles on her street. Like a sleep-walker, she saw the dead heads of the sunflowers on her path, her red front door, the key in her hand. She pushed it into the lock, heard the teeth lift, admitting her to her old life, and stumbled into the hall.

# 37

ARCHIE WAITED FOR THE SHOP ASSISTANT to go back into the
store, swiping a card round his neck on the security sensor to
open the door. He had a quick look round and lifted the lid on the
huge bin. There was less in it than he had expected. Raw chickens
gleamed at the bottom, their plucked skin pressing against plastic
wrapping on trays, date-marked and priced. Rotting satsumas
and soft vegetables lay in a midden heap in the corner and near
the top, just within reach, were squashed, premature Christmas
mince pies, still boxed. He put two packets in his rucksack and
closed the dumpster lid. It was beginning to rain, like Nad-e Ali
in winter, cold and muddy. He opened his mouth to catch the first
drops of water and let them trickle down the back of his throat.
He swallowed and saw himself from the outside, a man by a bin
drinking rainwater from the sky. It had been a long fall. He shook
himself and walked round to the front of the store, straightening
his back as he marched in past the barriers to go and fill his water
bottle from the sink in the gents. He hoped the security cameras
would be scanning the aisles and not the front door. The security
guard was leaning on the customer service desk, chatting up a
young assistant as she pulled size tags from empty coat hangers.

A jet of air-freshener released into the air as it sensed him
come into the toilet, filling the air with a citrus scent that sick-
ened his empty stomach. It was the hiss of soldiers spraying cans
of air-freshener at Camp Bastion to cover the smell of the latrines.
It was the fake lemon of his desert home. His hand shook as he
reached out for the tap. He stood his water bottle on the back of
the sink and looked at his reflection in the mirror. A derelict stared
back at him, mud on his jaw-line and grass stains on his sweatshirt.
He only ever saw his face in tiled, public spaces these days. He

had lost the intimacy of his connection to himself, those private moments trying to glimpse the man in the mirror that other people saw: trying to tilt his head to the best angle that might catch that elusive expression that had made him attractive to others. It was the mystery of self, experienced only from the inside, and never seen objectively, and now this nightmarish synchronicity between inside and outside that he couldn't hide, as the shattered, inner man overpowered the outer, and looked at the world without dissembling – with a frankness that terrified, and a knowledge of death that had no place here. His was the land of the human abattoir and he walked it as a butcher with sharpened knives.

The air-freshener sighed behind him as the door opened. An old man came in and walked over to the urinals. Archie leaned over the sink and splashed his face, cleaning the mud off his sleeves with a damp paper towel. He swished his mouth out with water from the tap. 'You don't want to do that, son,' said the old man.

Archie looked into his rheumy eyes.

'You don't know what you might catch,' he added.

Archie nodded, and shouldered his bag. As he left the store, the sky was dark grey, a theatre back-drop behind the fields. The rain had stopped. Traffic was running south along the main road out of the city. A car transporter carrying damaged cars splashed him. He had left the spade by the bin, but still had the orange jacket. He picked up his pace and swung along the road to Roslin, hoping he looked like a man on his way home after a long shift.

Bungalows and pubs lined the street of the village. Old poppy wreaths lay at the foot of the war memorial, and he turned down the lane to Rosslyn Chapel. Beyond the hedge, on green velvet, the chapel was a jewel box of pink and yellow sandstone studded with carvings of gargoyles and angels. He skirted the new visitor centre, plastic knights gazing from the window, and climbed over the back wall into the grounds. The side door was open and he slipped inside. There was a last knot of tourists at the altar with a guide. He beckoned to Archie to join them but Archie shook his head, genuflected to the altar and sat in a pew at the back as if in devout contemplation. He wondered how the nuns were doing, feeding their flock at St Phil's. He reached into his rucksack and popped one of the mince pies into his mouth. The raisins were cinnamon-sweet and sugary, and a tide of saliva washed to the back of his throat. Even now, raisins were drying in their huts in the Green Zone, small houses of dried fruit with slits cut into the walls to let in the warm autumn air. The air there smelled of Christmas pudding and cordite. He sat back and focused on the ceiling of the chapel. It was covered in carved daisies, lilies, marigolds and five-pointed stars. A single crescent moon clung to the sandstone. 'You can see the face of the donor, Sir William St Clair, carved to the left of the gentleman seated at the back,' said the voice of the guide. 'And if you stand beneath Sir William's portrait you can see the face of Christ hidden among the stars.'

Archie looked up – a bearded face peered over the lintel into the world below with a hand raised in blessing. The guide's voice continued, 'To the right, in the far corner above the door, you can see the face of the master mason and, to the left, that of his apprentice. As you are no doubt aware, the master was absent for a considerable time during the work on the columns. On his return he discovered that his apprentice had carved this elaborate column by the altar. It didn't match its companion on this side, which the master had completed before his departure. Enraged, the master mason raised his mallet and struck the apprentice a fatal blow to his forehead.'

There was silence. The tourists looked from one column to the other and back to their guide. Archie's eyes ran over the ribbons and curlicues of the apprentice's column, thinking of each hammer blow carrying the young man nearer to his death. The carved animals of his destruction chased each other in an eternal circle round the base. 'The master was hung,' said the guide, 'and his portrait head doomed in perpetuity to gaze at his apprentice's work.'

Archie looked up at the blank eyes of the master's face in stone, and back to the asymmetry of the columns flanking the altar. All of the other columns lining the chapel were plain, holding up the heavy canopy of stone flowers. The building smelled damp with centuries of rain. The guide highlighted the carvings of shells worn by pilgrims to Santiago with the luminous green dot of his laser pen, and the tracer light danced over Archie's head to a single teardrop carved on the wall. 'Beneath our feet,' said the guide, 'lie the bodies of the earls of Rosslyn in a tomb sealed over two hundred and fifty years ago – some say it is three layers deep. Within the catafalque, it is rumoured, lie not only the true Stone of Destiny, but the testament of Mary Magdalene.'

The tourists gazed down at the ground as if they could catch a glimpse of the lost treasures. Archie walked along the transept and down into the crypt below the altar. He stood by the tomb of a sleeping knight. He crouched down and traced the words, 'Knight Templar of the Thirteenth Century'. A cherub balanced on a ball on the next carved tombstone, the grim reaper behind him, pointing at a praying man. Archie looked at Death's bony finger, remembered the duck shoot of taking down leakers from the high ground as they tried to escape the killing zone. He heard the banter of the marines shouting 'hoofing' as each man fell, targets on a coconut shy. Death wasn't a harvest, it was a sport.

'The chapel's closing,' called the guide's voice from the top of the stairs. Archie jumped. 'Sorry to cut short your visit,' he added. 'We're closing, but you are very welcome to return to our Garden of Eden, Monday to Saturday.'

'What?' said Archie.

'The flowers and animals,' said the guide. 'The carvings. A Garden of Eden cast in stone. We're pretty much open every day except Christmas and New Year.'

Archie looked round the vault. There was nowhere to hide. Nowhere to stay warm among these old knights, these sleepers who still dreamt of wars, buried with prayers and their families' tears. He envied them sleeping secure in their beliefs. Archie climbed the stone stairs, waved to the guide as he passed along the edge of the chapel to the side door and slipped out. It was almost dark. The light faded as he followed a winding path down towards Rosslyn Castle away from the village. He kept to the raised green grass in the middle of the track in case of IEDs and then forced himself to walk in the earthy rut, breathing in time to the swing of the metal detector of the soldier ahead of him, a transparent companion who walked in his waking memory, comforting, his desert camouflage bright against the tree trunks and the dark spaces between. The path ended in a bridge over a gorge. Its parapets were only knee-high, and on the other side he could see an old house sheltering in the ruined walls of a much bigger castle. A dog was barking on the drive. A chain was stretched across the road like one of the Mujahideen's on the Kandahar Road after the Soviets left. He looked at the canine toll-keeper. Some kind of lurcher. It ran towards him and he knelt down to greet it, murmuring, 'Good boy.' It skidded to a halt against his knee, and licked his face. 'You're not much of a sentry,' he said, turning its face up to rub its ears. Its eyes were mismatched – one blue, the other brown. After a hopeful sniff at his bag, it turned and bounded back to the house.

Archie slithered down the steep, leafy slope to the foot of the gully and walked towards a small doorway he had glimpsed from the bridge. It was an abandoned ice-house. There was an iron grille just inside the doorway. He pushed against it, but it was secure. The dog barked at him from the parapet, looking down, its head on one side – its blue eye staring, and then its brown. Turning his back on the dog, he picked up a rock and crashed it against the padlock. The dog barked as the stone grated on the metal. He wished he had a charge to blow a way in. He brought the rock crashing down again, and the gate swung open. He switched on the torch on his phone and looked round the walls before jumping down into the pit. The curved dome of a beehive-roof rose above him, crowned with the face of a green man, a vine sprouting from his mouth. He sat down and, opening his bag, raised a mince pie to him in mock salute. 'Bon appetit, my stony friend,' he said and his voice echoed in the chamber with a dull boom. 'My friend,' said the echo, 'My friend.'

He pulled bracken from the slopes outside into his ice-house to make a bed and then lay down, pulling the vegetation over him to keep warm. He couldn't feel the wind blowing here, but heard it whooshing under the bridge, turning over the dried leaves on the floor of the gorge. He put on his phone and dialled Mike's number. The phone beeped on low battery, the handset signal flashing as it tried to connect. 'Hello,' said Mike's voice.

'Hey, it's Archie. Just wanted to hear a friendly voice.'

'This isn't a great time, mate,' said Mike. 'I need to keep the line open for business. No rest for the polyamorous.'

'Sure,' said Archie. 'Sorry.'

'You okay?'

Archie swallowed. 'Yes.'

'What's that echo?' asked Mike.

'It's my new place,' said Archie.

'Sounds big.'

'More bijou,' said Archie. 'It's near Roslin.' He gave a laugh that echoed. The dog barked outside.

'Look, do you mind if I phone you back another time?'

'No,' said Archie. 'That's fine.'

'Glad to hear you've got a place.'

'Yes,' said Archie. 'Bye.'

'Cheers,' said Mike.

The line went dead. Archie tried Petal's number again but there was no reply. He put the phone in his pocket, forgetting to switch it off to save the battery. He was thirsty and longed for a forbidden desert beer to wash the dust from his throat. He closed his eyes and heard the guide from the chapel describing another William St Clair carrying Robert the Bruce's heart to Jerusalem, carrying the excommunicated Scottish king's heart encased in lead, sweating on its journey, to the Church of the Holy Sepulchre. He thought of the Scottish knight dying on the end of a curved sword, the crescent slicing through his flesh, the lead heart baking on the Spanish earth where it fell among the hooves of the Moorish cavalry. So many disputed lands, so many challenged thrones.

Archie looked out at the sky, a narrow strip at the top of the gorge. A star jumped in the oasis between the urban clouds puffed orange by the city lights beyond. He gazed at the star and felt nothing. One star. One star when there had been thousands above him in Afghanistan, the Milky Way a smudge in an extravagant sky. Why care about one when there were so many? He was no more than an ice crystal, a frozen man, a temporary shape, and these chemicals and hormones that made him were polluted with fear. It would all melt away one day. He was no more than a puddle of water to be absorbed into the grass of his grave. Why did any of it matter? How long could he live a horror that replayed in his head on a loop? A loop-the-loop of internal anguish; of unanswerable questions; of the trick the politicians had played on him, to make him a pawn of empire in a tussle across the silk routes of Afghanistan, a shadow in the orange groves. There was supposed to be no empire now. He was an ant on the parapets of Alexander the Great's ruined forts. He was the bogeyman running through the mouse-holes blown in the walls of the compounds of sleeping children and screaming mothers. He still stood in their nightmares. He still stood in his own nightmare. Those jirga meetings with the elders to capture their hearts and minds never made him feel he had a right to be there, to travel on the road the Mujahideen had denied the Soviets. They had seen camel trains and steel travel along it from India to Persia, and Pakistan to Iran, for generations. Only names changed. He rolled onto his side and sat up. Tears he couldn't shed were pounding in his forehead. His throat was tight and he couldn't breathe. He stumbled outside and pulled at his jacket. Someone was shouting and groaning. He fell onto his knees and curled into a ball, jack-knifing and curling as if he could give birth to a new man. 'Hey,' shouted a voice from the bridge. 'If you don't clear off, I'm going to call the police.'

Archie went quiet, buried his face in the earth and held every muscle still. If he didn't move they wouldn't see him. The torch beam swept over him and back towards the ice-house. He crawled under the bridge. 'I know you're down there,' said the voice. 'I'm serious – any more noise and I'm calling the police. Can't you find some other place to jack up? I'm more than sick of this.'

Archie rolled onto his back. 'Man down,' he whispered. 'Man down.' He heard footsteps crunch on the gravel of the drive and then a door bang. He imagined the key turning in the lock.

A door opened in his mind and he was walking in the poppy fields, slashing at their heads; he was heaving sacks of wheat seed out of the backs of trucks; he was building a better world. In a week, or a month, or a year the Chinook would come and he would spin away, a seed blown on a hot wind; a samsara rotating against the sky, one of thousands. He had landed here in this green gully. The temperature was falling, and he crawled back towards the ice-house. He was shaking, his teeth chattering. The earth packed itself in under his nails as he crawled up the slope, grasping tufts of grass and loose handfuls of leaves to pull himself up towards the gate to his den. He reached it and tumbled in. He crammed a mince pie into his mouth to ward off hypothermia and curled into a ball under the jacket, his head inside his rucksack. He was his own prisoner. There was no other truth he could confess. Warmth returned to his fingers, making the bones ache. His nails were on fire.

*　*　*

He remembered Hannah curled round behind him, spooning in bed, imagined her warm arm thrown over him, light as feather, resting on his ribs. Downstairs Daniel was crying and his mother-in-law, Frances, was singing a song, turning tears to laughter as the kettle boiled: 'Nobody loves me, everybody hates me. I think I'll go and eat worms.' He remembered the mattress levelling as Hannah got out of bed, her footsteps on the stairs, the bright 'good morning' of the women greeting each other with a kiss. He joined them an hour later, pausing to tie his dressing-gown belt in the doorway before going into the kitchen. He heard her mother say, 'You mustn't mention this to anyone. They'll take the baby away. You're just over-tired.'

'I'm scared,' she said. 'I can't make the thoughts go away.'

'You won't hurt him.'

Archie walked in and they stopped talking. Frances stood up. 'Oh, I never heard you come down,' she said.

'What were you talking about?' he asked.

'Nothing.'

'It didn't sound like nothing.'

'Women's troubles,' she replied, and he saw a glance pass between them. Hannah left the room.

He turned to follow her. 'It's fine,' Frances said, moving to the door and putting her arm across the opening.

'What's fine?'

'Everything.'

'Everything's not fine when people are whispering in kitchens.'

'We weren't whispering.'

'You were,' he shouted. 'About something that affects me.'

'Don't shout. You're scaring the baby. You've been a bit touchy recently.'

Archie picked Daniel up and carried him to the window to distract him.

He looked back at Frances. 'When I got back from work last Friday, I found Hannah at the top of the stairs. She had climbed over the banister and was walking along the outside of the railings on the ledge, like we used to do as kids. There's no carpet in the hall. She'd have been hurt if she'd fallen onto the stone tiles. Don't you think that is a bit weird?'

'Not really,' replied Frances, picking up her mobile phone. 'No messages,' she said.

'Please, Frances,' said Archie. 'Talk to me.'

'Lots of people revisit their childhood games once they've had a baby.'

'She was naked,' said Archie.

'What did you do?' asked Frances.

'I put her in her dressing gown.'

'There you are, then.'

'She couldn't stop crying.'

'It's just the baby blues.'

'It's more than that.'

'No, Archie, it's not. I'm here and it's nothing I can't handle.' She took Daniel from his arms. 'You'll see. Time for this young man's change.'

He watched her walk out of the room. It was the door of the

ice-house. He woke. He felt sick and dehydrated. His limbs were stiff, and he wiggled his fingers and toes to get the circulation going. He crawled out. A watery sun was skimming the treetops. Midday. An old man was sitting there. He was wearing a tweed jacket and tie. 'Your pal ran off,' he said.

Archie tried to focus on the speaker before him. He was sitting on a rock with the lurcher at his feet.

'I don't have a pal,' said Archie, straightening up and brushing the dust from his clothes.

'Well, he was sitting over there, looking this way. I thought he was with you.'

'What did he look like?' asked Archie.

'Average,' said the man. 'Shall we say follicularly challenged? Look, I'll be frank with you. I don't want your type using this place for whatever it is you do. I'm going to fit a steel door, so you can all clear off.'

'I won't be back,' said Archie.

'Sure,' said the man. 'Until the next time. I'm trying to be reasonable here. The police do bugger all, but I will call them again and make a complaint.'

'I won't be back. I'm just a bit down on my luck.'

'It's not about luck,' said the man. 'Life is what you make it.'

'That's right,' said Archie, turning to pick up his bag. 'I was born like this.'

'Is that a private school accent?' asked the man.

Archie was silent.

'I'll take that as a yes, then,' he said.

'And what's a private school boy doing sleeping in an ice-house?' asked the man.

'So you want to talk now?' asked Archie.

'Look, son,' said the man. 'I don't know what your story is, but I can help you.'

'No one can help me,' said Archie.

The old man's eyes ran over him. 'I'm guessing ex-army. You look pretty fit.'

'Something like that,' said Archie.

'Come up to the house and I'll phone the police for you, or social services. The barracks are just up the road. Help for Heroes?'

'Thanks, but no thanks,' said Archie. 'There's something I have to sort out.'

'And that would be?'

'It's a long story.'

'Well, you know where I am if you change your mind.' He pointed up to the house. 'It's a strange place to live, I can tell you. Attracts all sorts, and its fair share of ghosts.'

'I have my own ghosts,' said Archie.

The old man stepped closer and touched his arm. 'You take care,' he said. He looked into Archie's eyes. 'I had my own troubles.' He held out a twenty-pound note. 'I want you to take this to tide you over.'

Archie nodded. 'Thanks,' he said, taking it, and looking down.

'The defence industry's worth twenty-two billion. That's all I'm saying. They owe you. Anyway, with these drones, you'll all be redundant soon. You were the last of the guys with the guns. They'll be outsourcing to teenagers in bedrooms next, geeks on computers miles from the conflict. Geeks who won't sue for bodily harm.'

A little, red Google map balloon popped like a blood corpuscle in Archie's mind.

'We were the last of the battlefield warriors,' said the man. He saluted Archie. 'I'm not saying it was good, but at least we were there. We remember the guys we took down. That's a kind of immortality, isn't it? For them.'

'Is it?' said Archie. 'What if there was control Z? What if it could all be undone?'

'There's no going back, son,' said the man. 'We've come this far.'

'I'm not sure I ever got out,' said Archie. 'It's still in here.' He touched his forehead as if it were tender.

'Let go,' said the man. 'You can't change it, but you can change what happens next. That's the good news, but don't expect too much. Life is hell with a little bit of heaven, or heaven with a little bit of hell. It's never entirely one thing or the other.' He released

Archie's sleeve and turned away, leaning on his stick as he walked. The dog leapt ahead along the path through the gorge.

Archie watched until he turned a corner and disappeared from view. There was no sign of the watcher he had mentioned, and Archie heaved himself up to the path back to Roslin. Hunger was making him dizzy. He'd heard the Syrians trapped in Homs were eating stones to kill the pain in their stomachs, give the acid something to bite into. He picked up a pebble and threw it against the trunk of a tree. It bounced off, and dropped into the desiccating autumn leaves. There was a crack of a stick breaking behind him, a slither of gravel rolling on the path. He crouched down and turned. He couldn't see anyone. 'Show yourself,' he shouted, standing up.

There was no movement. 'I know you're there,' he said. 'Show yourself.' He grabbed a fallen branch and, bracing it under his foot, snapped off a short staff. He swished it in the air in front of him. 'Come out,' he shouted. He waded into the bracken and climbed up a short slope through the trees. There was no one there. The chapel still stood in its field. A groundsman was raking up leaves, his head nodding to music on his iPhone. Archie turned and leaned against a tree, scanning the scene. The path was quiet. Nothing. He walked round the chapel wall to the main road, his eyes darting from side to side. Every few paces he stopped and turned round. Up ahead, a doggy day-care van pulled into the car park and a young woman jumped out. There was no one else in sight. He stuffed the jacket into a bush and pulled up his sweatshirt hood to change his appearance. At the junction, he bent to re-tie his shoe lace and scanned the road. A bus was coming and he stayed crouching, peering round behind to check no one was creeping up on him. An old lady walked past with her shopper. 'Good morning,' she said, with old-world charm.

He nodded and stood up, moving up the main road towards the supermarket. There was a furniture store next to it that offered half-price cooked breakfasts and he marched in with a couple of mothers with toddlers. The revolving door kept stopping as one of the toddlers reached out to touch the glass. 'Why does that man smell, mummy?' asked a piping voice behind him.

There was no answer, and he didn't turn round. Someone laughed. The door began to move again, and they moved with it, automatons, stop-starting in a glass jar. Upstairs in the café, he selected an all-day breakfast, pointing at the greasy bacon and yellow suns of fried egg in silver trays. He filled a cup with coffee at the self-service machine and sat down in a corner near the stairs. There was no sign of his tail. All around him people were chatting about their plans. A man behind him was trying to reach his wife on the phone about the length of the Roman blind she wanted. 'Yes, you gave me the measurements, but is that for the inside or the outside of the window frame? I know, darling.' There was a pause. 'The assistant here said you need to make an allowance to match the pattern when you are joining two pieces of fabric together, otherwise it looks funny. No, it doesn't work.' Another pause. 'About forty centimetres. It's quite simple. You have to match the pattern to get a good result.'

Archie filled in a loyalty card application form on the table with a false name and address so that he could get a second breakfast half price. He thought of his derelict cottage, imagined it with bright floral blinds but no glass. He laughed out loud. The security guard, who had been leaning against the far wall, stood up and clocked him. Ex-services by the look of him, going out of his mind with boredom. Archie raised a hand, an emigrant from the same world. The guard nodded, an almost imperceptible dip of the chin, then jerked his head towards the door. Archie stood up to leave. The toddlers were charging each other in the play pen as he passed, waving pieces of foam, throwing plastic balls at each other, the colourful spheres filling the air. Fairy lights hung from the ceiling, strings of stars. One of the kids started to scream. 'For fuck's sake,' he shouted, covering his ears.

A mother jumped to her feet and scooped up the child. He heard quick, heavy footsteps behind him and the guard had him by the elbow and was marching him downstairs towards the exit. 'Think you're a big man, do you? Scaring kids,' he said.

'No,' said Archie. 'I'm a bit strung out. Sorry.'

'Go and be strung out somewhere else,' he said. He pulled the loyalty card out of his hands. 'You won't be needing this.' The guard waited until he had completed the revolving door shuffle, and disappeared back upstairs.

# 38

Archie bypassed the car park, each car sitting in its place, orderly, logical, part of the seamless dance of the ants' nest. He crossed at the lights on the main road, but didn't take the turning to the research centre. It was too long and too busy. He was tired. He wanted to get back to the cottage, to sit on the hillside above the city and think it all over. He cut across the straggling scrubland parallel to the city bypass and put his fingers in his ears to shut out the noise of the diggers scraping away the earth for new family homes. 'Quality Living,' proclaimed a sign, 'for Happy Families.' Ahead of him, the Pentlands stretched in a long line. Nine peaks, three like the pyramids from his honeymoon at Giza. He reached the cottage and lay down, a pharaoh waiting for the starlight to strike his face, waiting for the gods to find him and take him home, to lift him up to hang from Orion's belt, or pass through its holes into an ether where it was light and everything made sense. He was cold. Through the doorway, he could see the day unfolding in a concertina of snapshots: the traffic building up on the bypass, old couples returning from a shopping trip to fill the day, the school run, the first of the workers to escape their call centres and battery-farm offices. The Forth was battleship-grey and hazy. The clouds flirted with the land and then soared above the sea, pink in the sinking sun. The icy blue of the far distance, which looked flat but was limitless, waved a finger at him in admonition: 'Don't stay out, brother, night is coming.'

He didn't care. If he lay here long enough without water he could die. Dry out the pain that flowed, juicy with regret through his mind, and slip away. 'No one ever left a life worth living?' Had David Hume written that? Was his a life worth living? Petal seemed remote, a figure in a story he had stumbled into. The girl in the garden. His cell phone buzzed in his pocket. 'You have one voicemail message,' it said, in a mechanised female voice, as he pressed it to his ear. It was Bitchin' Betty; it was the unexpected item in bagging area; it was the cinema help-line that didn't recognise human speech. 'Press one to retrieve your message. You were called today at 16.45.' The voice slowed over the numbers.

'Where the fuck have you been?' said Brenda's voice, angry, demanding, real. 'I have a good mind not to …' Her voice was cut off.

'Contact operator services free on 212,' said Bitchin' Betty. The low battery symbol flashed.

He dropped the phone into the grass beside him. 'I love you, Brenda,' he said. 'I fucking love you.'

'Anyone I know?' asked a voice.

Archie looked up, startled.

'A friend for the road on the epic journey of a broken man? The hop-a-long kid? Dead man walking?' Calum Ben was standing there, the man from the bar, the shadow by the bonfire. He was wearing an overcoat over a sharp-cut suit. A pair of binoculars hung round his neck. 'I enjoyed our sleep-out, and our little shopping trip this morning,' he said. 'Most amusing.'

Archie tried to scramble to his feet but stumbled on a tuft of grass. He steadied himself against the wall.

'It's polite to knock when you enter someone's house,' he said.

'Forgive me,' said Calum. 'Knock, knock.' He smiled. 'Not looking too hot,' he added, 'after your night in the ice-house. Very touching bromance with that old geezer. Looked like a very animated conversation. Shame you won't be having another one.'

'What do you mean?'

'That's for me to know and you to find out.'

'Who the hell are you?' shouted Archie, but his voice was hoarse. 'And what the fuck have you done with Petal?'

'She's at home, Archie. Where she always was.'

'You're a liar,' he shouted, but his voice was no more than a croak.

'Pardon,' said Calum, putting a hand to his ear. 'I can't hear you.'

'If you've hurt her, I'll get you,' said Archie. 'I'll make sure you pay.'

'I don't think you'll find me, Archie,' said Calum, and suddenly his voice was cut-glass southern English and then Scouse. 'You can try. That would be fun.' It was French, then American, and then Spanish, and, as he spoke, it kept changing. 'You can search the world but you'll never find me. I'm a peeled man,' and his bald head gleamed. 'An independent nation of one.' Calum rubbed his hands over the stubble that was just beginning to break through the surface.

'You bastard,' roared Archie and launched himself at him, but Calum side-stepped and tripped him up. Archie put his hands out as he fell.

'You're not as quick as you used to be. Not quite the big man you were. Where's your power now? You can't even live with yourself, can you? Is that why you're here in this ruin, all alone?' His voice had slowed to the patronising pout of an adult talking to a child. 'Eeyore in his thistle patch?'

Archie closed his fingers over a rock as he climbed to his feet. 'Put it down, Archie,' said Calum. There was a movement over his hand and something protruded from his coat sleeve before sliding out, a dark length of pipe. Calum braced its end against his chest. His finger on the curve of a trigger. Archie saw he had a pipe gun made from an old ball thrower for a dog and a length of steel tubing.

'Good, eh?' said Calum. 'Up-cycling is so à la mode. Home-made and untraceable.'

'You don't scare me,' said Archie.

'Not as much as you scare you. I'm guessing again, of course. I'm guessing you scare yourself more.'

Archie's face looked more murderous.

'Look in the mirror, Archie. We're the same – you and me. Animal men. We got here by different routes, that's all; but the answer is really simple. Embrace it. I love that counsellor speak, don't you?' His voice was American now, a New York drawl. 'Embrace your inner animal. Don't fight it. It's the new world that can't accommodate it, not you. And if he gets an outing in a war, let out of his cage and used by the state as a trick circus animal in their game of Realpolitik, then why should you be surprised? Why should any of us be surprised if he doesn't want to be locked up again? Let's face it, it's fun being out. He's too big for his old world – his office, his living room, the evening bath, his children's nursery, his bar stool.'

'There's more to me than that,' said Archie. 'There's more to me than teeth and sinew and hate.'

'I have to say, I'm not seeing it just now,' laughed Calum, and his voice was holy, self-righteous. 'I mean, have you seen your eyes recently, Archie? They're not a pretty sight; not for the faint-hearted.'

'You don't know me,' said Archie.

'I don't need to,' said Calum. 'I can read it all plain as day in your face. It's there for everyone to see, but believe me, it's not a story they want to read. There are some chapters of human history no one wants to read. They don't want to be reminded of it by the illustration of your face. It's not a pretty picture. You're the page everyone wants to turn over.'

Archie slumped back against the wall. Calum stepped closer, his gun pointing straight at him. Archie knew he could bat it out of the way, get in under his guard, and live, but there was something hypnotic about the depth, the dark depth of Calum's eyes. Death looked like a restful place, a soft, velvet vortex in which he could float. Death was a friend to the friendless, a final refuge. He could lodge with the innkeeper of silence. There were no noisy neighbours, no voices shouting in the night.

'You can't cheat Death, Archie. It's coming. You can deal it, but can you take it?'

Archie closed his eyes, felt the small circle of the end of the gun rest on his forehead. He was peaceful. Here was the full stop, the solution to the puzzle – the end point and the beginning – peace.

'Shoot,' he said.

The pressure eased off his head. He opened his eyes. Calum was walking away. He paused in the doorway and turned back to face Archie. 'Death is the soft option for you, Archie,' he said. 'You'll have more fun here.' He laughed. 'You've got one huge fucking puzzle to solve. I'm leaving you in the labyrinth with your monster. He's hungry, Archie.'

'Who the hell are you?' shouted Archie.

Calum turned. 'I'm a game master,' he said, 'and the game's over. Perhaps you could tell Petal I'll dispose of her phone. Your number's on it, in case you're wondering. Good of you to call. You're on her new tracker app. Top of the list. I call it locate a loser.'

# 39

WHEN HIS LEGS STOPPED TREMBLING, Archie began to walk. He didn't know if Calum was lying in a depression in the earth with the gun pointing at his back. He felt the prickle of a gun-sight between his shoulder blades, a caress on his skull. 'Pop,' he said out loud, but nothing happened. The sense of waiting in him grew, a long elastic of expectation stretched tight. It stretched from the cottage towards his old life, pulled as he walked until it snapped, and, snaking towards him through the air in great loops, it laced itself round his mind. It set up a pressure in his skull, coiled behind his eyes, which he felt must burst. If only he could cry. He thumped his forehead with his fist.

He walked down to the main road, stood into the side to let a 4x4 pass as it performed a three-point turn in the road-mouth to the ski centre, and drove off – its two red lights receding into the dark. Eyes travelling backwards. He was so hungry; his stomach had shrunk onto the inside of his ribs where it stuck like a limpet to the rocks. He ignored the pain and walked to Petal's on feet of lead. The world was as he remembered it: bright shops selling chocolates; tables outside bars for smokers; a poster trapped under wire on a newspaper board – 'Marine on trial for insurgent shooting'; joggers on the Meadows; the glow of lights from jewel-case living rooms with open curtains.

Petal's flat was dark. He rang the bell. No more windows. No more tricks. There was no answer. He rang again and was about to turn away when he heard the slow shuffle of feet across bare boards.

'Who is it?' her voice called through the door. It became a whisper. 'Who's there?'

'It's me, Archie,' he replied.

'I'm not feeling well,' she said.

He rested his hand on the door handle. 'Petal,' he said. 'Thank God, you're back. Can you please open the door?' He looked down. The elves were clinging to the stems of the sunflowers as they drooped towards the frosty ground. The moss on the pots gleamed green and silver.

There was silence. 'One of these elves is going to get it if you don't open up. Just for a minute,' he said. 'Please.'

A bolt slid back and the door opened. She was leaning against the door-post, ethereal, ashen-faced, as if she had returned from a long journey.

'What's happened?' he said.

Tears poured down her cheeks, and he put his arm around her, pressing the light switch by the door with his free hand. Light flooded into the hall and they blinked, surfacing into a new domestic reality. He guided her into the living room and helped her to lie down on the creaking chaise in the window. 'I'll get you a hot drink,' he said. Was it always like this, that times of homecoming and crisis were punctured with small actions of no import?

There was tea in the kitchen cupboard, soft apples in the fruit bowl on the counter. He bit into one, piercing the wrinkled skin with his teeth. The sweetness filled his mouth even as the texture gave way. In another cupboard, he found a bottle of whisky and downed a glass with two of his pills. He filled the kettle. The familiar click of the switch connected him to his old world – a sound and muscle-memory so familiar to his daily routine it had gone unnoticed. It heralded a return to a place he wanted to be. A simple, non-elemental place away from nature that had inspired and terrified him, holding him down with cold fingers that could crush him under the beauty of her night sky. It was safer here. If he could sort out his two halves, mesh his inner selves, inner worlds, into one tiny whole, even if it was of a density packed with energy that might not hold but, equally, which might exist safely within, if his will was strong enough; if he could find enough words to speak and an ear to listen to relieve the pressure; if he could stop feeding his own black hole with fear – then it might recede, become a quiet and distant object in his universe. It was, and would eternally be, a place that might suck him in if he flew too close, but one that might also be distantly observed, a place he had once thought a bright and heroic star before it imploded and collapsed, his dream of his own heroism, the great adventure when he never knew he was so tiny a man and thought life and death were forces he could control.

He carried two cups of tea laced with whisky through to Petal. She had fallen asleep and he covered her with a rug and then lay down on the sofa in the quiet room. The tea warmed his stomach, and he closed his eyes and drifted off.

Was it a day later that he woke? Petal was sitting in an armchair with her feet propped up on the sofa. The warmth of her feet against his calves comforted him. 'Archie,' she said. 'You've slept a long time. I need to speak to you.' Her eyes were huge, shocked. 'I need you to phone the police for me.'

'Now?' His head was a heavy reminder not to mix medication and booze. He sat up and drank a glass of water from the table.

'Yes. I was on a date and he took me to his house and wouldn't let me go when I wanted to come home. He locked me in a basement. Does that sound ridiculous?'

"No,' said Archie. 'I was trying to find you.'

'I rang my mum just now,' said Petal, 'She couldn't believe what I was telling her. She said she had a text from me saying I was taking annual leave to mend my sore ankle and could she ring work for me to let them know, and I'd see her soon. She's really shocked. She's on her way now. You know, that creep kept my mobile. He could be sending all sorts of rubbish to my friends.' She rubbed her forehead. 'All the time I was in that horrible room, I thought the police would be looking for me, but everyone thought I was fine. No one was looking.'

'I was,' said Archie.

'How could you know I'd gone?'

'I broke in,' said Archie, 'at the back. Well, I climbed in the bathroom window. It wasn't locked. There was a poster nailed to a tree on the Meadows saying you were missing. I was worried the police might come looking for you and they might think you'd gone because of me. I was the last one here before you disappeared. My prints would have been all over the flat.'

'Why would that matter?'

'I don't have a good record around women. My wife has a restraining order out on me.'

'Combat stress?' asked Petal.

'No,' said Archie, 'not entirely – not the whole story.'

Her chin sank onto her chest.

'Keep breathing,' he said.

She looked up. 'He kept me in a basement room with a chain on the door and when I thought he was going to kill me, he let me go. He washed me, so there would be no trace of him or his stinking place, but I can still smell the damp on my skin.' She breathed out onto the skin of her forearm with an open mouth and then breathed in. 'I can smell I was somewhere else.'

'Where was it?'

'I don't know. I think he drugged me before he let me go. It was like sleep walking.'

'What did he look like?'

She shuddered. 'Average – average height, average build – completely hairless.'

'I saw him too,' said Archie.

Petal jumped up. 'Then phone the police now. You're a witness.'

'Not exactly,' said Archie. 'They were hunting me – are hunting me. I've been holed up in the Pentlands. I had a sprint through the Roslin Glen to shake them off.'

'When did life get so fucking weird?' she asked.

Archie tried to sip a last drop of water from the glass, but it was empty.

'Eh?' she said. 'Tell me when.'

'I don't know,' said Archie. 'Maybe it's still normal for some people. People who shop in department stores and don't go too far from home.'

Petal threw the crocheted blanket off her knees and ran to the bathroom. He heard her throwing up, and walking into the bathroom, held her hair back for her as she leaned over the sink. There was nothing in her stomach but green bile. Nothing. She was retching nothing. He passed her a warm facecloth. 'If you were in his house,' said Archie, 'there must be DNA all over you.'

'Not since that weird fucking bath,' said Petal. 'He washed me and put me back in my evening dress and shawl. He'd washed those too. It's as if I was never away. It almost seems like a bad dream.'

'Except I saw him too,' said Archie.

'Who did you see, Archie?'

'The same as you.'

'So you saw no one. Average is not a description. He was so average they'll never find him. God, if he slapped a wig on that slap-head of his it wouldn't even look like him. I mean, for Christ's sake, was he even clinically bald?'

Archie remembered the small dots of stubble on the white skull. 'I bet that bastard disappears,' he said.

'He might come back,' said Petal.

'Not likely. He's had his fun here. He has a whole world to play in and an internet world within that. It's a Chinese ivory ball of worlds within worlds. We all flirt with it, live out our fantasies. Reinvent ourselves. They'll never find him.'

'My life is still real,' she replied.

'Said the gamer with elves on her doorstep.' He took her hand. 'You're not even in this world half the time, Petal. You live inside the head of some comic-book genius who has you jumping around his picture-book fantasy world online, thinking you're living when, really, you're trapped, sitting in your living room in an armchair – and out there,' he pointed at the window, 'governments are playing real games with real people's lives while a whole generation of active individuals, who could make a difference, think they're elves. They're not even pieces on the chess-board, Petal. The revolution isn't being televised, it's real. It's your life that's on screen, and it's an illusion.'

She remembered the chequered lights drifting under the water.

'It was a nightmare,' she said. 'I need to call the police. Feel like there could be justice. Stop him hurting someone else.'

Archie nodded. He had nothing left to say. Silence fell in the room. Outside a car engine started up, a bin lid shut, a young person passed, talking in a phone monologue of pauses and sudden laughter. 'You should know,' said Archie, 'that I didn't want to hurt my wife. I was saving my son.'

'I thought you punched her or something,' said Petal. 'Staff were warned that you had a restraining order for domestic violence.'

He picked up his phone, which he had left to charge on the coffee table, pinched the picture of Daniel on the homepage to expand it, and surfed his finger across the dune of his cheek. His baby eyes were huge pools in the landscape of his face. Archie sank into them. He was back in his old house, hanging his coat on the peg in the hall, standing his briefcase on the hall table. He looked up and saw his wife on the landing again, lifting his son up in the air, her arms outstretched, saw her turn to face the banister, and walk towards it, Daniel held out before her, like an animal that had soiled itself, like a creature that couldn't be held close. He remembered calling her name, her glazed eyes as she looked down at him. He remembered how fast he ran up the stairs, the blow he struck her, so that she fell. He took the child from her arms as she crumpled; took his Daniel, so tiny, swaddled in a shawl, and pulled him to his chest and held him close, breathing in the powdered, caramel scent of him. He looked down and saw his wife's cheek was split and bleeding. She was unconscious on the rug, still in her pyjamas, and as he returned from laying Daniel in his cot to lift her up, he saw a spider-web of cracks appear in the ice he walked on and he slipped under.

He was an Eskimo on the shoreline beneath the slabs of ice left when the tide went out, a mussel hunter. The soft molluscs were everything he had hidden from himself. They were the fragments of flesh, the misplaced footsteps on the path, a wrong turn, the sniper's fire; they were the commands, the rules of engagement, the finger on the trigger; they were the call-signs and Apaches; they were the spit, spit, spit of death, the sighs and the groans, the screams of the injured; they were the morphine shots and the death knocks; they were the amputees and the regrets, the men limping in the street and the drink, the failed marriages; they were the rough sleepers, the help-line call numbers, the silence on the end of the phone. They were all these things. He was trapped here with them in the half light and he could hear the tide flowing back. Its seaweed ropes would catch his ankles if he wasn't quick, couldn't climb out. The icy water would lift the blocks over his head and fit them seamlessly back together above him in an ice pack that would trap him here below. He would drown beneath an ice-blue ceiling, corniced and perfect.

He sat down beside his wife, cradled her head and cried into her hair, which smelled sour.

'Don't tell anyone,' she had begged him as she came round. 'They'll take Daniel away from me, Archie. I couldn't live without him. Please, Archie, don't tell.'

'I have to,' he replied. 'You're not safe. Daniel's not safe. We can fix this, but we need help.' He pushed her off, loosened her hands from his shirt. She fought him for the phone as he dialled the doctor's surgery, but he batted her away and she fell against the wall. She lay there propped up, glaring at him, the blood running down her cheek. He gave their address. Daniel was crying, a small, reedy cry muffled by the door to his room.

She got up to go to the baby. 'Stay right there,' he shouted. He heard the receptionist on the end of the phone say that someone would be there right away.

'Can you stay on the line until doctor comes?' she asked. He hung up.

The bell rang and he answered the door, his arm gripped round his wife's sleeve. Daniel's cries were louder and more piercing now. There were the blue lights of a police car outside, the figure of an officer behind the duty doctor.

'Mr Forbes,' said the doctor. It was the one from the local surgery who had offered him antidepressants after his previous tour, but he had refused. 'I believe you called us. Do you mind if we come in?'

'My wife's not well,' he said.

'Well, let's all get inside and we can sort this out. Hello, Mrs Forbes?' He took her arm from Archie and steered her towards the living room, 'Are you alright? Let's get that cut seen to and then we can sit down and talk. Perhaps you could put the kettle on, Mr Forbes?' It was an order.

Archie nodded and walked through to the kitchen. His wife had copied the furnishings straight from a department store catalogue: the French dresser, the gingham blind, the hand-thrown pottery tea caddy. It was picture perfect. His wife was bleeding next door and his son lay crying upstairs; his voice was the mewling of a kitten.

'I'll get the child,' he heard the officer call. There was the thud of feet on the carpet. When Archie came back through to the living room, Daniel was in his wife's arms. He put the tea tray down on the coffee table and handed her a cup. The glass compartments of the table were filled with souvenirs from their wedding day and shells from their holidays. 'We'd like to talk to you both separately,' said the doctor, 'and see if we can establish what's happened.'

Archie nodded and followed the officer back through to the kitchen. 'Nice place you have here,' said the officer.

'What?'

'Nice place,' she repeated.

'Yes.'

'Your wife says you're ex-forces?'

'A lieutenant in the Reserves,' said Archie, 'Afghanistan.' His voice trembled.

'That must have been tough.'

'Yes.'

'Difficult to adjust to being back?'

'No,' said Archie. 'Until today.'

There was silence.

'I was glad to be home.'

'But you must have been affected?' said the officer.

'Not as much as you might think,' said Archie. 'I got used to it.'

'What?'

'Death. If I didn't know the guy who got it, or he was the enemy, then it was just tough shit. Chance. He fired at me. I fired back. I could still eat and sleep. Still laugh with the boys.' There seemed to be an abyss opening up at his feet. His legs were shaking.

She sat down at the table and pulled out a small black handset and stylus. The screen glowed green. She tapped it. 'Do you mind if I take a short statement?' she asked.

He sat down.

'Where did you spend the day?'

'At work – Forbes, Stock and Wilson in the city centre.'

'And what time did you return home?'

'Eighteen hundred hours.'

'And your wife was here with the child?'

'Yes.'

'Alone?'

'Yes.'

'And then what happened?'

'I saw her on the landing with the baby. I thought she was going to throw him over the banister.'

'And then what happened?'

'I ran up the stairs and punched her to the ground. I knocked her out.' He flexed his fist remembering the impact. 'And I got Daniel and put him in his cot and phoned the doctor.'

'And what time was that?'

'I don't know, about eighteen-fifteen?'

'So you believed your wife might have been about to harm the child?'

'Daniel.'

'Did you have grounds to suspect that she might have been capable of this?'

He didn't answer. He remembered her taking her hands off the buggy at a busy crossing when they were shopping. He remembered the pram rolling towards the traffic. He remembered catching the handle and turning to her as she said, 'Sorry. My hand slipped.' And he remembered seeing that something was not right. 'I'm tired,' she had added. 'Completely knackered.'

He looked at the officer. 'I don't think she was coping after the birth.'

'So she was depressed?'

'Not exactly,' he said. 'I don't know what it was. She didn't want to pick him up. She often asked me to do it, said she was a bad mother.'

'And was she?'

'No. I didn't think so, but then I'd never done this before either. First-time parents.'

'And you were just back from the Front? And it was hard to adjust?'

'No, not really, as I said. I was glad to be back. To lie in a real bed, have a bath, eat fresh food, go out for a drink.'

'So did you have any other reasons to suspect your wife was unwell?'

'No,' said Archie. 'Nothing concrete. I heard her mother say to her when I walked in on them talking once, that she shouldn't say anything or they would take the baby away.'

'What do you think she meant?'

'I don't know. I didn't think about it very long. I was very busy at work – trouble-shooting, catching up. There was a big deal going down.'

She read his statement back to him. 'You returned to the house at eighteen hundred hours to see your wife at the banister upstairs with your baby, Daniel. You believed she might be about to throw him into the hall below and punched her to the floor to stop this happening. You then phoned the doctor. You have recently returned from active combat in Afghanistan to your job with Forbes, Stock and Wilson. Sign here please.'

'What about the bit about her strange behaviour?' asked Archie.

'That testimony would have to be given under oath to be used in evidence.'

'Evidence?' said Archie. 'What do you mean?'

'If you could just sign the statement please, sir, and wait here while I speak to your wife, and the doctor next door.'

He had finished his second whisky, standing at the back door looking down the garden when the officer returned. The gate was flapping. 'I'm sorry to say, Mr Forbes, that your statement doesn't tally with what your wife has told me and the doctor. She says you arrived home in an excitable state, took issue with the fact that she was still in her pyjamas and attacked her. Her injuries corroborate her account.'

'It's not true,' said Archie, jumping to his feet. 'That's not what happened.'

'Please control yourself, Mr Forbes. I need to tell you that the doctor will speak to you himself, before we draw any conclusions, but it seems likely your wife will press charges.'

'Ask her mother,' said Archie, 'ask Frances. She'll tell you she wasn't well.' Even as he said it he knew that Frances would back her daughter. It was a kitchen-table conspiracy of silence; it was a dangerous, middle-class game of happy families, of make-believe. 'I was told it was a difficult birth,' said Archie. 'A really long labour.'

'But she was discharged okay?' said the officer.

'Yes. She got out after three days. I wasn't here.'

'So there was additional stress?'

'Yes,' said Archie.

'For both of you?'

The words cornered him. The doctor had come through and was standing at the door. 'Don't stereotype me,' Archie said. Walls were crumbling inside him. He had to save his son. Guns on the other side of the embankment were sending sizzling-hot bullets to bite into his skull. He was firing back. The picture was breaking down. The worlds were getting mixed up. It had been right, but now it was going wrong. He was the good guy. It was simple – goodies and baddies playing at war in a poppy field. Pop. Pop. Pop.

He poured another whisky. 'She's lying,' said Archie. 'It's a ruse. She's afraid you'll take the baby away.'

'We wouldn't do that,' the doctor answered, sitting down and screwing the lid back on the whisky bottle. 'There are specialist mother and baby units. Not as many as we would like, of course. Anyway, she seems fine.'

'She's not fine.'

'She's the one who was beaten. You don't deny that.'

'I didn't beat her,' he said. 'I had to get Daniel. She was going to drop him.'

'She says she was taking him to bed.'

'Yes. She says she was taking him to bed.'

'I'm sorry, Mr Forbes, but you can see this is a very confused picture. As a precaution, I wonder if you could stay somewhere else tonight? At a friend's? A relation's?'

'She's not safe,' said Archie. 'Daniel's not safe.'

'Her mother has agreed to come over and stay.'

'She's in on it too,' said Archie.

'In on what?'

'The cover-up.'

'Mr Forbes, I don't want you to distress yourself further. I really think it would be better if you left the house tonight. I can call you a taxi, if that would help.'

'I can manage,' said Archie.

'I can assure you, we won't leave until her mother arrives.'

'It's a missed opportunity,' said Archie.

'What is?' asked the doctor.

'To get her help.'

'I think we've been over this,' said the doctor. 'If you could pack up what you need for the next couple of days, we'll take it from there.'

'Can I at least say goodbye to my family?'

'It might be better if you just go,' said the doctor, standing up.

'I hate you,' shouted Archie, 'and people like you. You think you can see what is going on but you can't because you don't really listen. You want everything to be alright, because you know then that you won't have to spend any of your money trying to put it right. But you leave people like me out in the cold, and you leave people like my wife and my son in danger.' He smashed his fist into the table. 'She's not coping.'

The officer reappeared with her hand on her radio. 'I think it's time for you to go, Mr Forbes,' she said. 'We can revisit this in the morning, okay?'

Archie grabbed a jacket from the coat stand and opened the back door and walked out. 'You're fucking insane,' he shouted. 'I'm not the one that's dangerous.'

* * *

He realised that Petal had stood up and come to sit beside him. She took his hand. 'I don't know what's going on, Archie, but we need to phone Dr Clark. The police can wait. You look like shit.'

He nodded. 'I've felt better,' he said. 'I thought I'd found all the answers out there. Looking up at the sky I thought I'd worked it out. Everything here is just the politics of the ants' nest. It doesn't even feature in the scheme of things. Everything that's going on up there in the sky is so much bigger than us.'

'But it matters to us, Archie.'

'I worked out that if I am just a soldier ant then I'm not really to blame, am I?'

'For what?'

'For killing other ants.'

'Except we're not ants, Archie.'

He smiled. 'No, but we are super-tiny. Could you cut me some slack here? I'm trying to work something out. Something that will let me go on living.'

She took his hand.

'I worked out,' he said, 'that Hawking was right. If the whole universe can be reduced to what he called a singularity, then, when it exploded in the Big Bang, and became many things, the things were still part of the single, original whole. I think that's it.' He was talking very fast. 'So I'm not uniquely responsible for what I am. I'm part of a bigger whole, although it's fragmented, and that whole thing is all of us. We are all responsible for the way things are. The brokenness.'

'That's illogical, Captain,' said Petal.

'Don't *Star Trek* me. I'm serious.'

'You are responsible for your actions.'

'Yes, but not the context and if my actions make sense in the context, then I'm not responsible for the whole thing, am I?'

'So who is, if not you?'

'Let's say God,' said Archie. 'If he exists and, if he doesn't, then all of us are responsible in this mad place we call the Universe. We're all hurtling through space and everything is fragmented, or imploding, or unravelling, or being born, or dying, and no one can control it, or put it back together again. It's one massive Chinese puzzle that's gathering more pieces as it goes on. It's a nightmare.' He clutched his head and stood up.

'You've got to hold it together, Archie. Think of Daniel. He needs you.'

'I'm trying,' he said, 'but it's getting more difficult. You know, Emperor Qin Shi Huang, who unified China, built a subterranean terracotta army to keep the ghosts of his enemies at bay in the afterlife. He was so damn scared of facing them on his own that he spent thirty-seven years of his life making pottery men with real weapons. Did he really think that was going to work: that he could ride his bronze chariot through his own guilty conscience, all the pain he had caused? He couldn't admit that each of those figures didn't represent the warriors who would defend him, they represented the lives he had taken. They were all his angry ghosts, and they were at his back. I don't know how to face it all down, Petal. It's too big.'

'Start small,' she said. 'Start with yourself. See Dr Clark and then look out for your son. Maybe that's enough. Maybe it's all that anyone can do.' She stood up. 'I'm going to call him now, okay? And once you've gone, I'm going to phone the police.'

He put down the jacket he had just picked up, and nodded. Surrender was a release after all.

# 40

A WEEK LATER, Petal was sitting by Archie's bed on the ward when he came back from lunch. 'Are you going to see Dr Clark?' she asked.

'Yes,' he replied, 'but I expect the bastard will still be trying to make me count to a hundred.'

'One, two, miss a few, ninety-nine, a hundred.'

'Exactly,' he said.

'You'll get there. I'm going to see him myself.'

'Why's that?'

'The police haven't got much hope of a result. I told them a man locked me in a room and made me eat toast. The more I told them the more it sounded like the deluded ramblings of someone with a high fever. They said they couldn't take a prosecution without proving a crime had taken place, without corroboration. It's my word against his. There was no evidence of physical harm, but I can tell you it's made me paranoid. I don't feel safe. I don't feel I can trust anyone.'

'I could testify for you,' he said.

Petal waved her hand at the ward. 'Look where you are, Archie. They say the texts received by my friends and family contradict my complaint. They said they have to keep an open mind. They can't rule out the possibility that I have another agenda, or it's a lovers' tiff, or I was at home all along.'

'I know you weren't.'

'I know you do. I've squared it away by saying that at least I got out and nothing happened. Nothing awful. You hear about those women who disappear for years. How can that happen, Archie? It's really freaky.'

He thought of his wife's own disappearing act in full view.

'People aren't very observant,' he said. 'They don't always see what's really going on.'

'You never said a truer word. Dr Clark has got in touch with Hannah too. I tipped him off. It'll be alright. It will take time, but it will be alright.'

He tried to smile. 'There's more news,' said Petal. 'The Slim for Jesus Fan Club went viral.'

'I've got a fan base?'

'You've got about a million hits. Apparently Sooze filmed your antics on her camera phone. Hundreds are testifying to your brilliance. You've changed their lives. There's talk of a T-shirt. The Slim for Jesus Fan Club. Men of Clay.'

'It's all bollocks,' said Archie.

'Who cares – if it works? Maybe it's the hand of God, after all.'

'If he exists,' said Archie. 'And if he exists, I'd like a word.'

'Well, you'll have advertising revenue to help you get there – build that rocket.'

He laughed.

'You look nice when you smile,' she said.

He looked down at the bedspread. 'Don't give me any cheese,' he said. 'Keep it real.'

'I mean it,' she replied. 'I care about you, Archie.'

He blushed.

Petal cleared her throat. 'I mean professionally,' she said. 'I mean I care for you professionally.'

'Why are you crying?' he asked.

'I'm not,' she said.

'I never meant to upset you.'

'You haven't. I was already upset. I'm upset that the one time I try to meet a man, try to stop staying in night after night, wondering how old I look, I end up meeting a psycho.'

Dr Clark came into the room. 'Hello, stranger,' he said.

Archie felt vulnerable. Small in the bed, or too big for it. He sat up straight, and swung his legs over the side. Dr Clark was looking at Petal. 'You okay?'

'More or less. I'll leave you to it,' said Petal. 'Save some chocolates for me.' She waved at the wrapped box she had laid on his bedside table.

'I'll catch you later,' Dr Clark said to her. 'Hold it together for me.'

She nodded, and a huge sympathy welled up in Archie for her. Dr Clark was the rat catcher. He hid his net well, but he would scoop up all those thoughts that came out to feed in the night, before they could scuttle back to their dark corners; lay them out for examination – articles for his medical journals, scalps on his belt, trophies that shouted of his prowess; his uncovering of the dark, sticky places.

He turned to Archie with a bright smile. 'Well, soldier,' he said. 'We've caught you at last.'

'You're scaring me, Doc,' he said.

'You're a voluntary admission,' said Dr Clark.

'Affirmative, Captain,' said Archie, sitting up and sliding his feet into his shoes, as if being dressed would somehow make escape easier.

Dr Clark flipped through his chart. 'You're on an increased dose of the SSRIs to stabilise you.'

'Yes.'

'Feeling better?'

'I suppose so. It's a bit like a sea wall. I know the storm is crashing on the other side, but I can still go to the chip shop.'

'So, you admit there's a storm,' he said. 'Shall we go to my office? Or take a walk along the corridor. I know you're an active sort of person. Would you like to walk in the grounds?'

'I don't want to go out,' said Archie. 'I've only just got back. I lived out there for a while, near the orchard.'

'I know,' said Dr Clark. 'You were spotted. David, the head gardener, called the police. They were primed to bring you here.'

'Oh,' said Archie.

'You'd broken your restraining order, and after your tour of the cells, well, let's just say they were keeping an eye on you. I think it's important that we talk. The NHS can give you two more sessions with me and then you'll be passed to a community psychiatric nurse. You'll have to go private after that, or go through the ex-services support network. You were lucky to get a bed.'

'I could always drown my sorrows,' said Archie.

Dr Clark made a note in his notebook, his fingers tapping on the keys. 'You're cyberising me, Doc,' Archie said. 'Is that site even secure?'

'The data is encrypted,' said Dr Clark. 'Your notes are confidential, and you can have access to them at any time.'

'To read what a nut-job I've become? I already know the story. I wrote it.'

'Or maybe it was written for you, Archie?'

'By the powers that be, or a mighty Hand?'

'Perhaps. It depends how you view it.'

'How do you view it, doc?'

'I think you're the only one who can unravel it. As I say, you need to talk. Put the whole thing to bed and get on with your life.'

'You only get one life, eh? You only live once. YOLO.' He remembered the teenagers dancing.

'Shall we get started?' Dr Clark held out his hand to indicate the direction to his office. 'It's the first step on a long journey.'

'Or maybe it's the gang plank. Spare me the psycho-babble,' he said.

* * *

The room was as he remembered it. The television was still playing outside in the lounge. He waved at Joy, who was sitting there, but she didn't acknowledge him. Dr Clark noticed his gesture. 'Don't expect too much,' he said.

A woman reporter on screen was saying peace talks between the Pakistani government and the Taliban had fallen through.

Archie lay back on the couch in Dr Clark's office. His life was becoming horizontal. He was a salamander in his own dark place. He was a creature on all fours. He was a turtle on its back. He sniffed his jumper. It still smelled of leaves and rain-soaked turf.

'Before we start,' said Dr Clark, 'Remind me of your role in Afghanistan.'

'Stan,' said Archie. 'Life in the Great Afghan Fuck All.'

Dr Clark was silent. Archie's abdomen rose up and down as he drew in deep breaths to counter the tension building under his clavicles, the tightness under his ribs. 'I know you're waiting for me to fill the silence, Doc,' he said. 'What do you call it – reflective listening? Empathetic silence? Create a vacuum and something will fill it.'

Dr Clark remained silent. Archie sat up and walked over to a plastic chair in the corner. He rested his arms on his knees and leaned forward. 'I was assigned as one of six bodyguards to a certain chief of staff,' he said. 'We travelled all over – he headed up one of ISAF's provincial reconstruction teams. We were trying to get the locals to plant wheat instead of poppies. Cut that industry down to size, and stop it funding the Taliban. Only problem was, ISAF never thought to put roads in to get the new crops to market. All that grain, and fruit and veg, went to waste. They couldn't shift it. The schools we built were abandoned. The Kajaki dam was almost indefensible, five hundred million US dollars and counting. The infrastructure programme was … misguided.' He paused. 'I can't tell you how beautiful the place was. Snowy-white mountains, green ribbons of crops, incredible skies. We were running around like ants, stirring up the dust.'

'And you saw fighting?'

'I saw death.'

'Archie, I want you to close your eyes now and we'll start counting. You remember the routine?'

'Yes, it wasn't very helpful. No offence.'

'None taken. Nevertheless, I want you to try it now.'

Archie closed his eyes. Dr Clark's voice started counting. 'One, two …'

Archie opened his eyes.

'Shut your eyes,' said Dr Clark.

Archie was spinning towards a black hole. Time was stretching and he was pulled thin across the miles of darkness. Debris was flying out at him, as the vortex unravelled; the meaty scraps of battle; the glint of light from a drone hanging in the sky; a child's remote-controlled toy; the distant hum of a motor. Dust filled his eyes and his nose. It suffocated him in clouds of grey particles. It was hard to breathe; harder to breathe as he fell into the vortex; spinning, spinning away into that day when his wife held Daniel over the landing's banister, and there was nothing below his son but air. He groaned.

Dr Clark had reached seventy. Seventy-one.

He was running up the stairs. Seventy-two, seventy-three. His legs were moving in slow motion, too slow to stop her. There wasn't enough time. He was screaming her name. She was turning to look at him with the blankness of a sleepwalker. His fist was connecting with her jaw and she was falling as he pulled the child from her arms. His Daniel. His Daniel. And the policewoman was talking and it wasn't making sense, and his colleagues were turning away as he was walking into the board-room to hear the judgement on his performance – the deal that went pear-shaped, the wife-beating, the civil action against him, bankruptcy. Ground zero.

'Begin to come out of the memory,' Dr Clark's voice said, from a great distance.

Archie couldn't find the door. His eyes were screwed tight shut. The stock-market shares were falling in red light. His wife's knees were buckling. It was taking him down to a place where he was flat-lining.

'A hundred, Archie,' said Dr Clark. 'Archie,' said Dr Clark again. 'Can you open your eyes?'

Archie sat behind his lids in a closed room. His stomach tightened and he leaned forward and spewed onto the floor. There was nothing in his stomach but tea. It lay in a brown, acid pool at his feet. He looked at it from a great height. Snapshot. Dr Clark was kneeling on the floor mopping it up with a wad of paper towels. Snapshot. He passed a handkerchief to Archie. Snap. Shot.

'Don't worry,' he said. 'It happens. Cathartic. Very natural after a period of emotional stress. Can you make it over to the couch?'

Archie got to his feet and, leaning on Dr Clark's arm, walked across the room. 'Don't ask me any questions,' he said.

'I won't.' said Dr Clark, 'but I think we've got there.'

Archie nodded. 'I should have been there for Daniel,' he said. 'For Hannah.' The silence filled the room. 'It was a difficult birth. Life and death got all mixed up.'

'That must have been hard,' said Dr Clark.

'I don't need your sympathy,' said Archie. 'I'm trying to tell you something.'

'What are you trying to tell me?' asked Dr Clark.

'She was postnatally depressed and no one knew. No one except me, and her mum.'

'Did she get help?'

'No. It was a secret. Her mum told her not to say. It's like combat stress, except it's called depression, like it's a kind of failure.'

'Depression isn't a failure.'

'It is in the pull-yourself-together school of medicine.'

'No, Archie. It's not.'

'Well, it is out there. They think you're weak. Mums are meant to be happy, aren't they? Grateful.'

'It doesn't always work out like that.'

'And soldiers are meant to be brave, and war will put things right.'

'I think we know life isn't like that,' said Dr Clark.

'But you think it will be,' said Archie. 'You think it will be simple, the way you expect it to be, and when it's not, it's a shock.'

'Yes,' agreed Dr Clark.

'Life and death get mixed up, and when you're on the front line, or pushing your sprog out, and no one ever mentioned you could die, it's a shock.'

'Yes, it is.'

'It doesn't fit with the happy picture. The warrior and the mother.'

Dr Clark looked out the window. Archie followed his gaze. The seagulls were floating on the wind from the west, calling to each other in a throaty, unearthly cry.

'We'll get your wife help,' said Dr Clark.

'You're too late,' said Archie. 'I think her mum got her through it. She moved in after I was barred.'

'How do you know?'

'I used to watch them from the end of the garden. Surveillance. Easy. Hannah loves that boy. I do too. They look fine together now. He's sleeping through the night by the looks of it.'

'So what's the problem?' said Dr Clark.

'You don't get it, do you?' said Archie. 'Everyone is someone's child. That's the problem. That's my problem. I didn't get it until I became a dad and my wife broke the rules. The rules of engagement.' He looked back at the room. 'I can't live with myself. I'm afraid I'll hurt someone. I know how to do it. Take their son. I've killed someone.' He drew a finger across his neck. 'It's quick,' he said, 'but the replay's in slow motion.'

'You won't do it, Archie,' he said. 'You won't do it because you are aware of your problem. Your conscious mind is monitoring your thoughts. You'll make the right choices.'

'But when people look at me they can see what I'm thinking. What I know.'

'Well, maybe they can. Maybe they can't. We can work on that. The key thing is to be at peace with yourself and that will come with time.'

'And pills.'

'Again, maybe. Maybe not. The key thing is, do you want to get well?'

'Yes,' said Archie. 'I want to get back to my real life.'

'This is your real life, Archie.'

'And that's the best you can come up with?'

'It's all anyone's got.' Dr Clark leaned back in his chair. 'I'm not a miracle worker,' he said. 'I leave that to the man upstairs.'

In the next room, Joy laughed. 'What's she got to laugh about?' asked Archie.

'You'd be surprised,' said Dr Clark.

'I'm forever blowing bubbles,' sang Joy. Her voice was reedy, it pierced his head.

Archie strode over to the door. It was locked. He banged his fist on the wood. 'Shut the fuck up,' he shouted through it. A shadow passed in front of the keyhole. He bent down and Joy's eye stared back at him. It was blue, a summer ocean. 'Hello, my lover,' she said, holding his gaze.

# 41

ARCHIE STRETCHED OUT in his bed, held his arms up above his head and flexed his fingers. He was still young. He could come back from this. Rolling over onto his side, he picked up his phone and accessed the YouTube video of the Slim for Jesus Fan Club. Sooze had been busy while she waited for Louise. He was doing squat thrusts at Louise's feet; they were wandering along a path under the trees like Pooh bear and Piglet; he was inexplicably running ahead of her; he was eating egg rolls and shouting 'Hooah' and 'Hallelujah'. Granny and the killer mutt tutted from a nearby bench as Archie performed a star jump in the last frame. It zoomed in on his sunglasses and the screen went blank.

He laughed and was filled with a new optimism. Dr Clark had said he could make a call to his wife in the presence of a member of staff. The call had been arranged for 16.00 hours, so as not to coincide with Daniel's tea-time and bath. Perhaps he could rebuild the bridge between them, cross its dizzying fall to his home, however ruined, and rebuild the walls of his castle, brick himself back into his place of safety. Hannah knew the truth and would forgive him. They had both survived unimaginable stress. They had that in common: a bond of knowledge not commonly shared, in the anticipation of parenthood or battle. Aftermath. He knew now what the knowing had been, written on the faces of teenagers in the trenches of France – grainy films on hand-wound cameras – the *Boy's Own* adventure of war. It was the same stillness visible on the face of the birth-mother: the knowledge of the abyss, narrowly missed, but there for another day, and every other day, for someone to fall into. They had leapt the smooth, mossy walls, the drop, the stream gurgling over rocks at the bottom, its unimaginable depth. Urban runners. Free-runners.

Archie wandered along the corridor to find the nurse. The pink and silver lino lay flat under his feet, didn't leap up to torture him. He paused and looked down at it. It was dull, ordinary. He was coming home. He had reached his Cyprus, his staging post, and was waiting for the flight to Brize Norton. He heard the patter of small feet on lino and looked up. A woman was walking along the corridor with a small boy holding onto her hand. He waved. She smiled and pushed open the door of the women's ward. It wasn't Hannah. He found the nurses' station and sat down. The nurse took his phone from his hand, scrolled down to his home number and passed the phone back. 'Put it on speaker phone,' he said, 'so we all know where we stand.'

Archie nodded. The ring tone was a pulse in his head. He counted the rings. It would be eight until the answer phone kicked in. He swallowed. It was a long time since he had made a call to his old world. There was a hiss of static on the line. 'Please leave a message after the tone.'

Archie was silent. He held out the phone to the nurse who shook his head. 'Archie, you speak,' he instructed.

Archie hung up and sat looking at the screen.

'It happens all the time,' said the nurse. 'We'll try again later, okay?'

'She doesn't want to speak to me,' said Archie.

'You don't know that,' said the nurse.

'Want a bet?' asked Archie as he tried to smile.

# 42

His bubble of happiness receded as the clock on the ward ticked towards evening and there was no message from Hannah. When the nurse came to see him with his tablets, he lay on the raft of his bed pretending to be asleep. The ice blocks of his memories bumped against its foot. Time mattered less here. It became the squeak of the tea trolley, and the sticky peel and release of the rubber soles of the nurses' shoes as they walked along the corridors. They were anonymous in flowery surgical scrubs or white coats, and only ran when there was a beep on their call button, or a sudden scream. The screams came singly here, not a battle-field roar of men punctured by bullets or dismembered by mines. The wounded here were artists. Their cries were virtuoso solos of pain; they were opera singers performing to the crowd in an unknown language. The notes soared above Archie and became the crescendo of his own pain. The A Flat and C Minor carried across the water to his raft as he drifted.

In the morning, he let his hand fall over the side of his bed as if he could paddle to safety, a lonely survivor unsure of his direction. Dr Clark's office was a light on the shore; his disappointment about the failed call a headwind; his clothes a ragged sail. Now the adrenalin of Calum's manipulation had passed, and the police hunt – which had never been a hunt, but zookeepers rounding up a wounded animal – was over, he could look around and try to recapture the frankness of his reunion with Petal and the admission he had made to Dr Clark. There was a faint dawn. Hannah would find him. The truth was a beacon. He moved onto his bedside chair and sat looking out of the window.

'Archie,' said a voice from the doorway. It was his nurse. 'Your wife called. She's sorry about yesterday. Her mum had a fall and she couldn't make it. She'll reschedule, okay?'

Archie nodded, and looked down at his feet. He lay back on his bed and watched the day pass round the sundial pendant of the light in the centre of the ward until it grew dark. The nurse took away the tray of uneaten food from his bedside table, leaving the cup of cold tea and a menu card for the next day.

Becalmed in the night, his Grandpa came to him and stood at the end of his bed, a young navigator on the bridge of his doomed corvette. He had a black beard and sparkling, blue eyes and was wearing the slippers he had walked home in when the war ended. Burning his uniform in the back garden had not expunged his memories, put the bees of his rage to sleep in the curling smoke. He shared Archie's world, a world of thoughts that stung. Archie opened his lips and moaned, a small bubble of pain. It had no fixed shape but it had a sound, a huge sound. It was growing, filling his chest. It was powerful, it was erupting from him in great folds. It burst as he threw himself onto the floor. The squeaking feet came running. Strong arms caught him up and delivered a shot to his buttock. It restored silence to his world. It was beautiful.

\* \* \*

The next day, a nurse appointed as his key worker walked him to the garden past the mortuary and the greenhouses. He was on the inside now, not the outside looking in. Life was a two-way mirror. Dave was still orchestrating his volunteers. Archie's nurse stood smoking at the portacabin door. His log-pile house had been bull-dozed and a builder's yard established on the site behind a wire fence.

'What's happening?' he asked the nurse.

The nurse shrugged. 'New hospital. The garden has a year's grace, then they'll have to move it.'

'Where?'

'They've got a new site. Not as big.'

'Is my wife coming today?'

'No word yet.'

'Where's Petal?'

'Sorting out the studio. She's going to Spain with her mum.'

He watched the patients drill holes in the earth with muddy fingers and drop in seeds. A man was making his way towards them, skirting the beds and kneeling patients. Archie hoped it might be the takeaway he had ordered for lunch, but it was Mike.

'I got your text. What the fuck are you doing here?' Mike asked as he drew closer, and flopped onto one of the dining chairs someone had painted with butterflies. Mike sat very upright for a moment, and then moved onto an old deckchair and leaned forward.

'I handed myself in. Got tired of running,' said Archie.

'From the police?'

'No, from the shit circulating in my mashed brain.'

'You seemed okay to me. I thought you got a new place. It had an echo. Must have been pretty grand.'

'Far from it,' said Archie.

'Well, look on the bright side. Your current place is fucking huge. A real eighteenth-century pile.'

Archie laughed. 'It's good to see you,' he said. 'How are things?'

'You know,' said Mike, 'needs must.' He bit his lip. 'I'll get it sorted, Archie. It's taking a bit longer than I thought. Hard to get a break.'

'Still sober?'

'As a judge.'

'Good.'

'Yeah. So when are you coming out?'

'I don't know. I'm still under observation. This is my key worker.' He waved a hand at the nurse smoking by the portacabin and leaned forward and whispered to Mike. 'I can't remember his name.'

'Maybe he doesn't have one,' said Mike, 'maybe he's a robot.'

'You're insane,' said Archie, laughing. 'Compared to you, I really don't have any problems.'

'As long as you've got options, eh? That's the main thing. It doesn't matter if it's all temporarily shit; it's whether you can get out of it that counts. After all, as I say, life is not shit. Shit is shit.'

'I want to sort it,' said Archie, 'but I keep seeing things I don't want to see again in my mind and I don't know when they are going to start playing, or when I'll want to deck someone. There's no off button. That's the problem. It's tiring.'

'Problems are always tiring,' said Mike, 'that's why they're hard to fix.'

'Sometimes, I want to die,' whispered Archie.

'And that's the one thing you're not allowed to say. Jump around shouting you're John the Baptist, or a purple balloon. Be a bit creative. Be nuts, but be alive. That's what matters, Archie. It's all too short anyway. Even you and me will be old blokes on a park bench one day, and we'll be peeing into empty fabric conditioner bottles on long car journeys and wondering why no one finds us attractive any more.'

'That's the best you've got?'

'Yup. Apart from reminding you of your unique selling point.'

'What's that?'

'You're still a dad. There's work to do Archie boy.' He had raised his voice to the level of a sergeant major. 'You've still got some capital to realise.'

Archie looked up to see his key worker watching him. He wasn't sure when he'd started listening to their conversation.

'I'll get this soldier back to the ward now,' he said to Mike.

'I'm waiting for my takeaway,' said Archie.

'You're out of luck, I'm afraid,' said the key worker. 'They can't deliver here. Food hygiene rules among other things.'

'But they said they would,' said Archie

'That's what they always say to keep you sweet. If you didn't fill out your menu card this morning, then we'll go via the volunteers' café on the way back.'

It was full circle. More kindly ladies handing him cups of tea. 'It's still nineteen-fucking-eighteen,' he said. 'It's the end of the war all over again. Same war, different name. Same burnt bodies. Surgeons sticking on face transplants that don't stick. I saw it on telly. Boys looking out through holes cut in skin from their back and dying on the operating table because there are some things that can't be patched up.'

'Try not to get excited,' said the nurse.

'Or what?' said Archie. 'I'll be the next guy sprinting for the wall with you in hot pursuit.'

Mike reached out and touched his arm. Archie had forgotten he was there. 'Hold it together,' he said. 'This is important.'

Archie nodded. The nurse blew a last smoke ring into the air and they walked back to the sugar cube in a small procession.

Mike said goodbye at the door of the café. It smelled of baked potato. There was an honesty box for poppies on the counter. Archie ate from a polystyrene plate and drank a cup of tea, watched by the nurse. The Formica table-top was chipped. A television was playing a soap opera in the corner. An actress was pretending to cry, squeezing tears from her eyes. A woman was comforting her. He finished his roll and they took the lift upstairs. Hannah would come soon. The nurse popped into his station and left Archie to go back to the ward at the end of corridor but, with a glance over his shoulder, he took a quick left turn and wandered along to Petal's studio. She was carding wool and crying. She sniffed as she heard him come in and looked up, trying to smile. 'Thank God, it's only you, Archie. I had to hold it together for Joy and the new intake. It's a conveyor belt and half the time we release them just as we're beginning to make progress.'

'Sod's law,' said Archie. 'I heard you're going to Spain with your mum.'

'That's right.' She took his hand. 'They're going to get someone to stand in for me until I decide what I want to do. You can guess why. I can't forget what happened. I can't stay here wondering if that bastard is going to pop out of the woodwork.'

'The police will get him,' said Archie.

'Will they?' asked Petal. 'I'm not so sure. I'm going to look for work in Spain, but first I'm going to take some time out to get over what happened. I need to work out why I was such a fool.'

'You weren't a fool. It's not foolish to want love.'

'But when you can't find it, Archie, what then?'

'I don't know,' he said. 'Keep looking, I guess.'

'Keep looking. "The miserable have no other medicine but only hope." Shakespeare.' She put the coloured strands of wool into a plastic bag and tied it shut. 'I help other people to find answers all the time, but I can't find the answer for myself. How great is that?'

'Fan-diddly-astic,' he said, in a sudden memory of the teenagers' conversations outside his log-pile house.

She laughed. 'If you'd been single, Archie.'

'If I'd been single I might not still be around.'

'My point exactly,' she said. 'After a while, it gets hard to fill the days. To make them meaningful. I won't forget you, you know.' She held out her hand. 'I hope you make it.'

He nodded. 'I'll give it my best shot.'

'I know you will,' she said.

\* \* \*

On his way to breakfast the next day, the Rosslyn knights clanked past him in the corridor on their way to the Holy Land. They bowed, bending their stiff bulldog necks over their swords. When they looked up, their eyes were burning embers in the chimney of their helmets, their ostrich plumes nodding feather-light over their heads. He saluted as they passed on. He was a solitary figure standing to attention in the empty corridor. The ghosts of war. His mind was a larger maze than he had thought. The solution wasn't going to be simple. As he walked, Archie trailed his right hand along the wall, trying to find his way out. 'Always turn right to find your way back to the entrance,' he mumbled, but the start had been his fist connecting with his wife's face, the woman he loved. It was hard to slip past it and escape.

Dr Clark appeared, and steered him to his office. There was a man waiting who stood as Archie came in. His left forearm was missing. 'This is Brendan Fraser from Combat Stress Now,' said Dr Clark. 'It's a veterans' support organisation.'

'I don't need any more counselling,' said Archie. 'I need results.'

'I've arranged for Hannah to come and see you at the weekend. The missed call was a bit of a setback. You want to be as well as you can be for your reunion, don't you?'

Archie nodded, embarrassed in front of this stranger.

'Brendan is a veteran like you. I treated him a number of years ago.'

'It's been a long war,' said Archie.

Brendan nodded. 'I was in Iraq. I'm part of a peer-to-peer counselling programme,' he said.

'All boys together,' said Archie.

Brendan looked at Dr Clark. 'I don't know if he's ready.'

'Speak to me,' said Archie. The men looked at him: the man in the snow globe. He was banging on the glass. He could see them through the sticky finger-prints that handled his tiny world. His voice was muffled. 'Speak to me,' he said.

Brendan touched Archie's shoulder. 'Let's get a coffee,' he said. 'You can tell me about your last tour.' He steered him along the corridor.

'I could do with something stronger,' said Archie.

'Don't blame you,' said Brendan. 'We'll go down the pub when you get out of here. Deal?'

'Deal,' said Archie, pushing open the door to the café and wandering over to a seat in the far corner.

Brendan brought two polystyrene cups of coffee, balanced on a tray in his right hand, over to the table and slid it onto the surface.

'My wife would be here by now if she wanted me,' Archie said. 'I've nowhere to go.'

'We'll fix you up with temporary accommodation. Bed and breakfast.'

'Like I'm a tourist?'

'I wouldn't put it quite like that.'

'How would you put it?'

'Okay, just like that, but we've all been there. There are some good ones.'

'With buxom landladies who crush you to their bosom?'

'Sadly, no.'

'I'm not interested.'

'You can't sleep rough.'

'I did before.'

'Look out of the window, Archie.' The sky was black and heavy with rain. 'It's not an option.'

'And I'm short of options?'

Brendan tore open two packets of sugar with his teeth and poured them into his coffee.

'Let's talk about you,' said Archie.

'What do you want to know?'

'What tipped you over the edge?'

'Direct, aren't you?' Brendan looked straight at him. 'Do you really want to know?'

'I'm agog,' said Archie.

Brendan laughed. 'You're a comedian. I'll keep it brief. I was tasked to destroy an abandoned vehicle stuffed with electronic counter-measure equipment. Let's just say the drone wasn't on the coordinates I called in.'

'Send reinforcements, we're going to advance.'

'Send three and four pence, we're going to a dance.'

'It got lost in translation.'

'Or they're not that accurate.'

They fell silent.

'The problem is there's no front line any more,' said Brendan. 'It used to be a straight line. You knew where it was. It was finite. Now no one knows where it is. It could be anywhere and no one knows how big it is. It could be huge. It could be tiny. That's what creates the fear: the bad decisions. It's not knowing where the threat is located. They're not standing in a row on a particular day, at a particular place, at a particular time waiting for us. They could be anywhere; they could be next door having a special chat online.'

'You're making me paranoid. You're meant to be helping me.'

'I'm just saying.'

'I know.'

'Or they might all have shelved their plans.'

'True.'

'How would we know?'

The men lapsed into silence. 'I miss the guys,' said Brendan.

'Yes,' said Archie.

# 43

HE WAS DOZING IN BED when Hannah arrived, having sat by the window all morning looking for her. 'Hello, stranger,' she said.

He opened his eyes and smiled. 'Pud,' he replied. He tasted her old pet name in his mouth. Her betrayal was a bitter sauce. She read it in his smile.

'I'm sorry, Archie,' she said. 'Mum had a fall.'

'You didn't phone.'

'It was a bit crazy. I had to find someone for Daniel and...'

He cut her off. 'And?'

'And? Cut me some slack.' She waved a hand at the ward. 'I can't adjust just like that to all this.'

He didn't reply.

'Can I sit down?' she asked, pointing to the end of his bed.

He nodded, unexpectedly tearful. Her weight settled onto the mattress, depressing the end as if the corner might break off and she would float away on a piece of popping candy foam.

'I don't want to lose you,' he said, pushing himself up, so that he was leaning against the headboard. 'Come here.'

She slid along the bed, moving closer.

'No, here.' He patted the space beside him and stretched out his arms.

She slipped off her shoes and sat beside him. He put his arm across her shoulders. The familiar smell of her skin reached him. There was a faint scent of baby shampoo, and a new, floral perfume that smelled like their garden on a hot day.

'What's that scent?' he asked.

'Gentian violet,' she said.

'Gentian violet,' he repeated. The blue-purple of the flowers lay between them. It was a bower in the antiseptic of the ward.

Hannah sighed. No one else was around. 'It's funny to see things from your perspective,' she said, looking round.

'Hilarious,' he replied.

Joy passed the doorway with a tattered felt square in her hand, back-tracked, pointed two fingers at her eyes and then at him, and walked on.

'I'm a marked man,' he laughed, kissing Hannah's hair.

'Who was that?'

'Joy,' he said.

She looked up at him. 'Can you forgive me?' she asked. 'You know I thought they would take Daniel away.'

'We don't need to talk about this now.'

'Is there a better time?'

'Okay. You were ill. I should have seen it sooner. Done something.'

'What could you do? We were both falling apart.'

The silence returned. She reached across to the bedside table and offered him the plastic beaker of water.

'After you,' he said.

She drank. 'I let you down too,' she said, passing him the cup. 'Not at first when I was ill, but later, when you were crawling round the garden like some kind of beetle.'

'You saw me?'

'Of course.'

'It was surveillance.'

'It was crap. The gate squeaked every time you opened it. It wasn't rocket science.'

'You phoned the police.'

'Mum did. She was more scared than me. I knew what happened that time you hit me. She didn't. I knew it was to save Daniel, but I don't think I was going to drop him. I was testing myself to see if I could face down the fear that I was going to hurt him by holding him over the banister and not dropping him. Does that make any sense? It did to me at the time. I must have been really unwell. I see that now.' She pulled a tissue out of her pocket and wiped her eyes. 'Did you really have to punch so bloody hard?'

'Did you really have to lock me out?'

'This isn't the right time, is it?'

He shook his head.

She pushed herself to the edge of the bed. 'I can only say I'm sorry, Archie. I'm better now and you will be too.'

'So they keep saying.'

'These things aren't irreversible. They feel that way at the time but they aren't. I wrote an angry letter to the hospital about how long they let me labour on all their drips and induction fluid and it made me feel a bit better. It was a three-day spectacular. I let some of the anger out and that left a little bit of space to let some healing in. Anger can make you ill. Mum was great.'

'Not to me.'

'No.' Hannah took his hand. 'She's sorry too.'

'Thanks,' he said.

'Aren't you going to ask how she is?'

'How is she?'

'On the mend. Broken wrist.'

He lay down again. Hannah slipped off the bed, pulled up his covers and tucked him in. 'I'll sit for a bit,' she said. 'If that's alright? It took me an hour to get across town on the bus and, to be honest, you're better company than Daniel. You don't burp and dribble all over me or pull my hair.'

He smiled and sketched a halo above his head.

'I brought you some photos,' she said, 'of the bits you missed.' She passed him pictures of Daniel standing for the first time, his arms outstretched for balance, tiny lace-up sneakers on his feet. There was a close-up of his first baby teeth, a gummy dolphin smile. There was a picture of him sliding backwards down a chute in the park, laughing up at the sky.

'He's gorgeous,' said Archie.

'Or course,' she replied. 'Like his dad.'

He began to cry. 'I don't feel I have a right to be happy any more.'

She didn't reply.

'Say something.'

'I don't know what to say. I can see it hurts.'

'It does. It didn't at the time. In the heat of battle, but it does now.'

'You'll need to learn to live with it. We both will.'

'Yes.'

'It's going to be hard. We could talk about it. What happened out there.'

'No. I'm talking to a guy called Brendan. He saw service too. The things I saw don't go with home furnishings and babies. He said seven point six in a thousand get this.'

'So you're not a freak.'

He looked up.

'Or you could be the point six,' she said. 'Not totally shot to pieces, but nearly.' The silence fell again. 'Do you want to remember happier times?' She scrolled to her albums on her phone.

'You kept the pictures?' he said.

'Duh, you chump. We were happy, remember?' she held up the screen. It was a selfie of them laughing on the water bus on the way back from Granville Island.

He traced his fingers across her face. 'You're still cute and beautiful.'

She stroked his hand. 'We can trust again, Archie,' she said. 'Trust we'll be happy. Not cock it up. Go slowly. Talk.'

'Can I come home?' he asked.

'Soon,' she said.

'Soon isn't a date in anyone's diary.'

'When you've finished your treatment. I promise.'

'Will you bring Daniel to see me before then? When I'm released, I'll probably end up camping out at the City of Jasmine café with Karim and hiding from Brenda.'

'Who's Brenda?'

'It's a long story.'

'It's not to do with that ridiculous Facebook page, is it? It's made the local paper.'

'Thanks. I've got two hundred new followers. They're posting their success stories on my page. I'm on YouTube. I'm a guru.'

'I can think of a different word.'

'Don't say it.'

'I won't.' She stood up. 'I need to go now. Margaret's been holding the fort.' She looked into his eyes and bent to kiss him. 'I can see the old Archie,' she said. Her lips pressed onto his before he could reply. 'Don't say anything,' she said. 'I'll come back tomorrow.'

He listened to her footsteps receding along the corridor. The door at the end banged and to fill the silence he switched on the television and settled down. A photo from the space station showed a comet hurtling towards the sun, a sun so bright it shone red and black through the filter of the camera lens. It was the centre of a poppy. 'Magnitude measurements are being reported by the Minor Planet Centre and observers using binoculars. No one knows if comet ISON will emerge unscathed from behind the sun,' said the reporter. 'It will be December following its perihelion before we know, and scientists may well be relying on amateurs to pick up its trail. This sun-grazer is now thought to be a travelling debris field with no solid core, leaving only a trail of questions in its wake as it passes from the field of view.'

# NOTES TO THE TEXT

The history and events mentioned in this book span September 2013 to February 2014. To give a portrait of the time, they have been compressed to show the highly charged political atmosphere surrounding Archie at the end of his military service in September and October 2013.

# SOURCES

Chayes, Sarah. *The Punishment of Virtue*. Portobello Books, London, 2006.

Davidson, Donald. *Truth and Meaning*. First published in Journal *Synthese*, 17:304–23: Springer International, 1967 (for description of theory of truth-conditional semantics).

Du Plessis, Erik. *The Branded Mind*. Kogan Page, London, 2011.

Earl of Rosslyn. *Rosslyn Chapel*. Rosslyn Chapel Trust, 1997/2012.

Goleman, Daniel. *Ecological Intelligence: Knowing the Hidden Impacts of What We Buy*. Allen Lane, London, 2009.

Hogg, James. *The Private Memoirs and Confessions of a Justified Sinner*. Wordsworth Editions, Hertfordshire, 1997. (1824)

Hume, David. *On Suicide*. Essay, published posthumously c.1776.

Macy, Ed. *Hellfire*. Harper Press, London, 2010.

McNab, Andy. *Spoken from the Front*. Corgi, 2009/2010.

Shapiro, F. *Eye Movement Desensitization and Reprocessing: Basic Principles, Protocols, and Procedures*. Guildford Press, 2001.

Southby-Tailyour, Ewen. *3 Commando Brigade Helmand Assault*. Ebury Press, UK, 2010/2011.

# GLOSSARY AND NOTES

**Ace of Spades** A set of most-wanted Iraqi playing cards was compiled by the US military to help troops in the 2003 invasion of Iraq to identify coalition targets and their relative importance.

**Afghan bee** Incoming small arms fire that sounds like a bee.

**Al-Shabaab** In September 2013, Al-Shabaab were reported to have claimed responsibility for an attack on a shopping centre in Kenya. A bounty was subsequently placed on the head of Al-Shabaab's leader, Mohammed Ahmed Abdi, by the US.

**ANA** Afghan National Army.

**Anas al-Liby** Anas Al-Liby was reported to have been taken by American forces in Tripoli, Libya.

**Antabuse (disulfram)** Available since 1951, reduces craving for alcohol and makes drinker nauseous if alcohol consumed. Called 'anti-booze' colloquially.

**bam (ya)** Short for 'bampot', meaning fool or crazy person (Glaswegian slang).

**Bedroom Tax (Under-Occupancy Penalty)** Unpopular and controversial 2012 austerity measure imposed by the UK government to limit housing benefits for those deemed to have a 'spare' bedroom.

**benefits (acronyms)** WCA: Work Capability Assessment; DLA: Disability Living Allowance; JSA: Job Seeker's Allowance; Universal Credit, 2013 benefit with an upper ceiling designed both to streamline and cap benefits system.

**Bergen** Army rucksack; original models made at Bergen in Norway.

**Bitchin' Betty** Apache helicopter's automatic voice system said to sound like a nagging wife.

**Brize Norton** RAF station in Oxfordshire.

**Carney, Mark** Governor of the Bank of England – said of the economic recovery: 'the glass is half full' (reported in the *Financial Times*, 13.11.13).

**clarty** Disgusting (Scots).

**dickers** Army slang for look-outs during the troubles in Northern Ireland.

**dinnae dis' it** Don't show it any disrespect (slang).

**Dorsey, Jack** One of the founders of microblogging service Twitter. *Dulce et decorum est pro patria mori* 'It is sweet and seemly to die for your country'; Horace, *Odes*, Book 3, No. 2, 1:13.

**EFT (Emotional Freedom Technique)** Therapeutic treatment often used for stress, based on aspects of various complementary therapies.

**Fitch Indicator** A measure calculated by the Fitch global financial ratings agency (invoked here as a crisis was narrowly averted after President Obama and the Republican opposition in Congress clashed over debt levels in the US economy).

**Friends of the Meadows and Bruntsfield Links, Edinburgh** See www.fombl.org.uk.

**Google map balloon** Icon used on Google maps to show location.

**Hawking, Stephen** 'The Beginning of Time' lecture, found at: www.hawking.org.uk/the-beginning-of-time.html.

**'I'm forever blowing bubbles'** Song composed under the collective pseudonym of James Kenbrovin, which first appeared in 1918 in a Broadway musical.

**ISAF** International Security Assistance Force established at the Bonn Conference in December 2001 to help the Afghan Transitional Authority, and defend Kabul. ISAF's leadership was taken over by NATO in 2003 and its mission expanded across the country (see www.isaf.nato.int/history.html).

**jirga** A meeting of village elders in Afghanistan.

**Kajaki Dam Project** Article by Heidi Vogt (see www.huffing-tonpost.com, 23.3.14).

**Karzai, Hamid** President of Aghanistan during the period covered in this novel.

**Lady Justice Hale's ruling on duty of care/psychiatric stress** Ministry of Defence: 'Synopsis of Causation: Post-Traumatic Stress Disorder': '3.12. Employers generally have a "duty of care" to their employees, and in relation to PTSD this would demand that they provide a safe working environment for their employees, be alert to the possibility of them developing the condition, and treat them appropriately should the condition occur. Lady Justice Hale set out sixteen propositions relating to an employer's duty of care in her 2002 judgement on four cases of stress-related psychiatric injury.'

**leakers** Army slang for combatants escaping, or leaking, from a killing zone.

**Marine** Trial of Marine A, accused of shooting an insurgent in Afghanistan. Defence of combat stress was proposed.

**O'Brien, Cardinal Keith** Archbishop Emeritus of St Andrews and Edinburgh, left office in February 2013.

**Ochberg, Frank** MD on PTT (Post-Traumatic Therapy Work), The Counting Method; YouTube, posted 16.11.2012.

**on stag** British army slang for sentry duty.

**Operation Herrick** Codename for UK operations in Afghanistan.

**Prince Albert's 'Great International Exhibition of Science, Industry and Arts** Held on the Meadows in Edinburgh in the summer of 1886. Gate-posts were commissioned, and the whale-bone jaws of Jaw Bone Walk presented by the Zetland and Fair Isle Knitting Stand.

**'Red Ed'** In September 2013 Ed Miliband proposed a power price freeze policy, taking on the big energy companies.

**Rouhani, Hassan** President of Iran during the period of this novel. **samsara** As used here: denotes the helicopter-like seed of elm tree and other species.

**Saughton fag** Saughton is Edinburgh's prison and a Saughton fag is a thin roll-up made with minimal tobacco.

**Schiehallion** Mountain near Glen Lyon, in Perth and Kinross, Scotland, said to be enchanted.

**Schumacher, E. F.** Discussion re the economist E.F.Schumacher

(1911–77) and consumption: *Daily Politics Show*, BBC 2, 8.11.13. Schumacher wrote a collection of essays: *Small is Beautiful: A Study of Economics as if People Mattered*, Harper Perennial, 1989.

**Shapiro, Francine** American psychologist who developed EMDR (Eye Movement Desensitisation and Reprocessing), a form of psychotherapy that helps patients alleviate the symptoms of trauma and other disturbing events.

**Snowden, Edward** US intelligence insider who leaked classified documents in June 2013.

**SSRI** These antidepressant medicines are slow acting but may have a faster effect on some individuals. The story assumes they were faster acting on Archie but that he often failed to take his medication.

**'Stan'/'The Great Afghan Fuck All'** Troops' name for Afghanistan, and the desert/empty spaces of the country.

**TB** Abbreviation for the Taliban.

**'The miserable have no other medicine but only hope.'** Shakespeare: *Measure for Measure*.

**US Military Cadence Calls** Used in training. The manuscript quotes one called 'Superman'. See: Christopher Howell, YouTube, for examples.

**Warrior** Armoured vehicle.

**'You're my Judy'** LGBT term of endearment referencing Judy Garland.

# QUOTES OF INTEREST

'In an age of deceit, telling the truth is a revolutionary act.' George Orwell, quoted on BBC Radio 4, *Thought for the Day*, 20.2.14.

Comet ISON: www.earthsky.org. Deborah Byrd wrote, 'Comet ISON is now thought to be a traveling debris field with no solid nucleus or core.' Blogs/Human World/Space 6.12.13.

# ABOUT THE AUTHOR

Victoria's first novel, *A Capital Union*, was published in 2013 and shortlisted for the Historical Writers' Association Debut Crown, 2014. She is an Associate of the Museums Association and has a life-long love of history as a result of her work in museums and galleries. She has also volunteered for homeless charities and writing, therapeutic and community gardening projects. Victoria graduated from Nottingham University in Art History and German, and has an MSc in Creative Writing from Edinburgh University.